DRILLER

M. S. HOLM

Sentry Books

An imprint of Great West Publishing

For information about this title or to order other books and/or electronic media, contact the publisher:
www.sentrybooks.com
sales@sentrybooks.com
Library of Congress Control Number: 2015936053

Publisher's Cataloging-in-Publication
(Provided by Quality Books, Inc.)

Holm, M. S.
    Driller / by M.S. Holm.—First edition.
    pages cm
    LCCN 2015936053
    ISBN 978-0-9796199-8-4
    ISBN 978-0-9796199-7-7

    1. Whites—Mexico—Fiction. 2. Water well drilling—Fiction. 3. Wells—Sonoran Desert—Fiction.
4. Man-woman relationships—Fiction. 5. Sonoran Desert—Fiction. 6. Mexico—Fiction. I. Title.

PS3608.O4943245D75 2015   813'.6
                  QBI15-600076

ISBN: 978-0-9796199-8-4

Printed in the United States of America

Cover and Interior design: 1106 Design

For the Thirsted

Waiting for the Motor to Warm

At first light Driller stood by the wellrig, his gaze cast on the harvested cottonfields run to the land's edge. "What some men sow," he voiced without marvel to the Estacado silence. "Sow and reap. Sow and reap." The cotton stubble freshly snowdusted, white without cotton. The bloodspoor black. His cut hand dripped on his boots, these narrowfooted with polished silver buckles and embossed toe rands.

He knew not the farmer whose fields he surveyed. His name, this place, nothing to him. Driller knew only that someone, if not the farmer, was sure to visit the wellsite. Foreman, a hiredhand, someone come to drain the tanks before a hard freeze. This mess found.

Earlier he had drunk from the well, tasting the young driller Peterson whose body he had crammed into the newly sunk casing. Water flavored of denim dyed in Gujarat. Not his first taste of a deadman down a wellhole. The year before he had sipped the water of a villager fallen into a twenty-inch bore drilled for a date grower in the eastern Liwa of the Emirates. An old villager who smacked of gypsum, marl, and a woolen thwab.

Of what fell into waterwells, never a surprise passed Driller's lips. He had tasted errant riverhorses and unstrung rosary beads. Dropped candles. Fallen eyeglasses. A silk lungi stripped from a curious Bengali bent too close to whirling drillsteel. He had sipped the aspergillum sprinkles of priests and the salted taperings of a widow's tears. He had drunk the love men pour into the land, and their hate, the hate tasting better.

Driller waited for the rig motor to warm. To the east, grackles lifted from the harvested fields, hundreds of birds winged black on a pale sky. They swooped the machine, strafing with raucous sputters, their white eyes turned on him. He followed their motion with interest, having eaten grackle, spitted wing to wing and roasted over a sagewood fire.

He recalled Peterson's windburned face, the surprise come to it when he looked up from his drilling to find a newcomer arrived without apparent crossing of the Estacado, as though risen from the wellhole itself. Alarm in his blue eyes as he beheld Driller's unhinged grin, the large teeth, but he seemed to relax after a solid handshake, some genial palaver. Soon he was talking. Later he invited Driller to coffee.

Three hundred feet, Peterson reported when asked for the depth of his well. Red caprock, then sandstone. He claimed to have drilled the Ogallala before. For a young driller he knew his trade but not the deeper meaning of his labor. When asked what besides water he had come to drill in his life, what secrets he could share, Peterson looked perplexed. "Hell if I know!" he said. This exclamation his last.

Driller wiped his cut hand on his pantsleg. His blooded boots he swept on the snow. He was a big man built in the mold of a large quadruped privileged to walk upright. Eyes borrowed from nomadic tribes, their gaze sometimes sliding sideways, not quite right. His hair was permanently parted crossways from ear to ear where the scalp had scarred after a derrick tiedown whiplashed his crown to the bone, leaving his head imperfectly seamed. Strangeness enough for men to stare at, though most preferred to look away.

He watched the grackles wheel to the north, their squawking but a whisper to the land. At the wellsite his bloodtracks turned red on the daylighted snow. "Could hose 'em," he observed, speaking to where the remains of Peterson reposed. "But more will come. You know that. More and more."

Then he climbed into the cab and eased the wellrig across the stubbled rows.

La Noria y La Mujer

"THERE," RETCH SAID, pointing to the rooftin glint. Dig turned the Willys sharply off the rimland and accelerated onto the flat, lifting a gray dust no wind carried. They stopped before a mudbrick building cleared of thornscrub. The woman who watched from the doorway wore a sunfaded dress. At her feet cried a naked, red-haired boy.

"That can't be anything good," Dig said.

The boy's wail loud in the desert silence.

"Damn. He's got your hair."

Retch nodded. "Never met her," he replied.

Dig called to the woman. "Queremos agua y tortillas."

She lifted her chin toward a noria encircled with a laidstone apron. Then she took the boy and retreated into the doorway.

They got down and carried the jerrycans to the well.

No stench rose from the noria—a handdug hole rounded in an imperfect circle wide enough to swing a pickax. Retch tested the ixtle tied to the lardcan bailer before he returned to the Willys to fetch braitrope from the trailer. Brindled goats followed his movements, the females with deflated udders. Retch stared beyond them at ground grazed to dust. He saw trashmounds with liquor bottles, a washline strung with strips of dried meat, a stocktrough tipped on its side. At the noria he knotted the braitrope to the bail and lowered the lardcan into the well.

From a shed kitchen the woman watched the strangers fill their cans. "Ya, ya," she cooed to the wailing boy. "Ya se van." She cooked the tortillas on a barrel brazier, stacking them on the linoleum-topped table. Above the table hung a machete. She pointed to the tortillas when the redheaded gringo came to pay.

Retch wrapped them in his kerchief, leaving a five-peso coin on the table. "Gracias," he said. The woman silent. Her face pockmarked like cholla wood. Her cheek with a ribboned scar. When they drove away, the boy still cried.

An hour up the road, Dig stopped to refill his bule from the jerrycans. He drank, then gagged. "Damn her!"

Retch touched the gourdcanteen to his lips, the water salty. What you get for not tasting it, he thought.

Dig spat. "We're going back."

Retch shook his head, not wanting new trouble. Two weeks earlier, in Chihuahua's Lobero Range, west of Babanore, they had left for dead a mine watchman knocked senseless with a tapermouth spade swung by Dig. "Forget it," he said.

"Forget she tried to thirst us?"

"Yeah. Fill in La Fortuna." Retch knew that whatever reason the woman had for saying nothing about the water was not a reason Dig would understand.

"Fortuna?" Dig corked the bule. His jeweled watch a sunglint spectacle on the austere land. "Screw that." He turned them around and headed to the woman's ranch. Retch held to his hat as Dig floored the Willys.

At a trailer lot outside Modesto, they had purchased the silver Daxara. After hitching it to the Willys, they had driven to Jackson's Prospecting Supplies in Mariposa where they had loaded shovels, prybars, fuel cans, screens, a navvy barrow, a Primus stove, a power sluicebox, and a suction dredge—all paid for out of Digger's cash. When old man Jackson had asked if they were taking cordage, Dig said they were headed to where rope was made.

"And where's that?" old man Jackson inquired.

"Mexico, you fool."

They rode all night to San Ysidro where they crossed the border into Tijuana in the early morning hours. Dig gave the aduana officer fifty dollars to keep his hands out of the Daxara. They left the peninsular road at Vicente Guerrero, following a dry riverbed west into the mountains of San Pedro Mártir. In the arroyo of Santa Domingo downstream from San Antonio, they tested the equipment. Curious boys from the town came to watch. That night they drank solera brandy at the comisario's house. The constable asked how long they were staying in Mexico. Dig pointed to Retch and answered, "Until one of us dies or marries a local, God help him."

The constable laughed, not understanding.

A week later they took the ferry from Santa Rosalía to Heroica Guaymas, driving Highway 15 south to Ciudad Obregón. In the parkinglot of the Yuri Hotel, Dig laid a yellowed gridmap across the Willys hood. He traced a path past El Oviáchic, east of Palmarito and north of Potrero, into the cordillera cornerland of Chihuahua and the Hiak Vatwe basin. "Gonna spiral our asses," he declared.

From the coast they drove east under a cloudless sky, the land rising before them. The first night they slept in a Madrean woodland, their stomachs full with tequila and boiled beans, the babycries of onzas haunting their dreams. The next day Dig wound the Willys through gray granite hills, climbing the backbone roads into the jagged sierra. They traversed the rocky, ravine-cut slopes of eastern Sonora, halting on the third day to sluice in the streambed of a narrow arroyo. Dig ran the suction dredge, Retch the highbanker, each taking turns to screen the black-sand concentrate while the other panned for metallic flecks. They lifted camp after a week, following the water to a new site. Days later they moved again. So they prospected, the months passing, the panning all but luckless. "Pissant whorefetti," Dig called their sparse gleanings of gold, the pocket grams. He gave them to Retch, his gift, he said. "Payola, bud, for whatever hell comes next."

They resupplied in the ramshackle stores of the sierran ranchos, Digger a celebrity among the locals. El Topo Loco their name for the green-eyed, baldheaded gringo. Crazy—prospecting aside. He drank with the men, slept with the women, swore at the children, and bought and bartered for chickens, jerky, tortillas, liquor, fuel, good will, and safe passage. Retch, the silent, rusty-haired partner, watched his back.

Summer arrived, the dry mountain burn. Then rain, the arroyos running. They drifted from village to village like itinerant pilgrims devoted to a godless land devoid of hallowed places. Dig drank colanche and smoky-flavored lechuguilla sold in knotted plastic bags. In Urique he fistfought two Rarámuris drunk on tesgüino, disputing their claim that God drank cornbeer. They tussled and rolled in the street, two on one, Dig kicking them into submission. He emptied their liquor jugs in the dirt. Three weeks later in Tomochic, he was detained overnight by the Policía Rural after assaulting a tianguis trader for the sale of overpriced cigarettes.

Then came the incident in the Lobero Range.

They had driven to an abandoned silver mine west of Babanore, Dig taking the Willys over a sleeper road blasted for ore cars. At the mine they found timber buildings collapsed in dusty heaps of planks and splintered shingles. Railtrack, wheels, and the remains of defunct machines lay strewn like the artifacts of some ancient and precociously mechanical tribe. A brooding, dayheated silence hung about the place. Near the tunnel entrance stood a shanty built of incongruous gleanings—wood, tin, and plastic fitted together—a dwelling sprung of perverse promises known but to the builder. Dusty chickens pecked in the doorway.

The old man who emerged wore oversize coveralls and walked with a withered leg. His hair white, his chiseled face sunstarved. He carried a tapermouth spade over his shoulder. "Prohibido el paso, señores," he advised, blinking in the brightness.

Dig sipped from a wickerworked demijohn filled with silver sotol. "Ya pasamos," he replied.

The old man stood beside the Willys. He pointed to a faded logo on his coveralls. "Esta es propiedad de la Compañía Minas Alvarado de Parral."

Dig sipped. "Go to hell, you old fart."

"Soy el velador," said the watchman. He held up the shovel, his warrant.

Retch gazed at the rusted remains of machinery once comprising a prosperous mining concern. That its stewardship be left to an old man with a spade seemed absurdly appropriate.

Dig restarted the Willys. "Let's see how far we can drive in."

The watchman stepped in front of the Willys. Dig revved the engine. "He'll move," he said before he popped the clutch, the vehicle lurching forward, the old man not moving. He held to his spade as the Willys knocked him from sight.

A woman screamed. Dig braked. "The bastard didn't move!"

Retch looked to the shanty. The woman gray-haired, stooped. Her hands covered her face. She cried out again, "¡Lo mataste!"

"Damn!" said Dig, reversing the Willys. They saw the old man get to his feet. He held to the tapermouth shovel. "¡Malditos!" he wheezed. He careened toward them on his withered leg. He swung the spade, aiming for Dig, hitting the windshield instead. A starburst of cracks effloresced the glass.

"Sonofabitch!" Dig yelled. "You goddamn sonofabitch!" He jumped down and wrestled the shovel from the watchman's grasp, the old man not letting go until Dig kicked him in the groin.

The watchman grabbed himself, breath lost in a gurgled wheeze. Dig raised the spade and struck his head with the flat of the blade, knocking him to the ground.

The old woman shrieked from the shanty. The watchman quivered on his side, hands scratching the dirt. Then he lay motionless. Blood filled his ear and ran down his face, dripping off his chin.

Retch stared, mouth open. A dog barked somewhere, warning too late of strangers. When he closed his mouth, he smelled something cooking.

"We're out of here," Dig said, climbing into the Willys.

Retch looked back as they drove away. The old woman shuffled toward the watchman, followed by the dog. Chickens pecked at the blood-darkened dirt.

"Didn't kill him. Only knocked him into next week."

"Looked bad enough," Retch said.

"Look at this goddamn glass." Dig pointed to the broken windshield, ringed and rayed like his shattered mind. He lifted the demijohn and drank.

Retch stared ahead, thinking he would have to leave Digger. The time fast approaching.

They rode to Babanore where they hitched the Daxara. That night they left the Lobero Range, crossing the Chihuahuan border into Sonora and the Madrean rimland therein.

At the woman's ranch Dig ran down three goats before he braked in the clearing. "Make birria, bitch," he shouted.

The boy's wail loud in the dead engine silence. Retch wondered if the child had cried the entirety of their departed hours. The runover goats bled out in the dirt. "You're gonna have to pay for those," he said.

Dig sipped from a bottle of Moctezuma White. He reached behind his seat to find the gourdcanteen. "¡Mujer, ven pa'ca!" he called.

The woman did not appear.

"¡Mujer, te estoy hablando!" He stuck a finger in the bule, touched it to his lips. "Damn, that's salty."

Retch knew the time ordained for the woman to answer was soon to end. When he moved to get down, Dig grabbed his arm, pulling him into his seat. "Let her come to us."

Retch yanked himself free, surprised to hear his voice toughen. "Goddamn it, don't mess with them. They've got nothing."

Dig spat out the door. "Shove your pissmoaning, Retch."

The woman stood in the doorway. She held the child to her chest, the machete at her side. "¿Qué quieren?" she said, voice cut from stone.

Dig smiled. He beckoned with the gourdcanteen, inviting her to drink. The woman stared.

"¿No tienes sed?" Dig asked.

She stood silent.

Dig held out the bule, his words mocking the boy's cries. "Ándale, mujer . . . el niño tiene sed."

She held to the boy, her gaze impassive, unwavering. It said afflictions visited by men not new to her. Retch guessed her age to be twentysomething. In the daybrightness her scar a shiny keloid on a face borrowed from the heavy-lidded, lapidary masks of ancient tribes—aweless, inscrutable.

Dig let the bule spill. "The water is good," he joked. "Try it."

The woman spat. "Pruébela usted," she replied.

A maniacal laugh erupted from Dig. He reached under the seat. "A formal wench you are, mentirosa, hija de tu reputísima madre."

"Jesus," Retch said. "She's got a kid."

Dig removed the lug iron from under his seat. "Never too early for a boy to hear he's the son of a lying whoremother. Hell, I got the news when I was a lad." He gripped the lug iron by the pry and held it for the woman to see. His other hand raised the gourdcanteen. "¿Vienes o voy?" he asked.

The woman silent. The machete blade glinted.

"Pinche agua salada," Dig shouted. He told the woman she would drink the water from the bule or he would pour it down her throat and then he would make the boy drink.

The woman said nothing. She raised the machete. Her answer.

Before Dig could descend, Retch delivered a sharp, backhanded blow to the bule, knocking it into Dig's lap where it emptied on his pants.

"Goddamn you!"

Retch seized the lug iron from Dig's hand and he scrambled to get down. Dig collared his shirt, grabbed his hair, yanking his head toward the gearstick on the floor. The gearstick without a shiftknob. Retch saw the threaded tip of the lever and he saw the impending impalement of his eye as those who are shot through the oculus see the bullet's entry. He swung the iron above his head, striking Dig. The clutch of Dig's hands tightened in his hair as though to cling to the memory of it. Then his grip loosened. Dig's body slumped between the seats.

Retch raised himself and saw the gash opened on Digger's scalp, blood percolating. He dropped the iron and put his ear close to Digger's chest. Then he descended and pulled the body forward, sliding Dig sideways until he slouched across the seat. In the doorway the woman stood with the machete. The boy no longer cried.

"¿El agua buena?" Retch asked.

She lifted the machete and pointed past the kitchen to a free-standing structure of poles hung with a tattered tarpaulin. Retch found the bule on the floor. He emptied on Dig what was left inside.

The pole structure a rudimentary cactus still of the kind used by baysalt harvesters on desert coastlands to make freshwater from the condensed evaporation of succulents finely chopped. With his finger Retch tasted the contents of the still's collector pail, the water bitter but not salty. He dipped the bule into the collector.

At the truck he pulled pesos from his pocket. He held them out to her. "Por los animales," he said. When she didn't move, Retch returned to the still to leave the money under the pail. He asked for the name of the ranch.

She spat. "Anguamea."

"¿Rancho Anguamea?"

"Sí."

He started the motor and wheeled out of the clearing, maneuvering past the dead goats to retake the rutted road. Dig lay crumpled in the seat.

From the doorway she watched the yellow truck with its silver trailer crest the rimland. Even after it disappeared, she stood watching.

When the woman's father, Epifanio Anguamea, squatted the three hundred hectares of desert basinland, he was sixty years of age and fifteen months from the end of his life. In his left pantsleg bulged an incarcerated inguinal hernia that distended his scrotum into an elephantine appendage that many observers mistook for his penis. Mi maldición, he called it, and though it aggravated his bandylegged walk, he carried it proudly, refusing to seek medical remedy. True to his own virility and secretly fearing castration, he preferred to die from a strangulated bowel than to lose his testicles.

Thirty years he worked extracting blister copper at the La Caridad mine in Nacozari de García. His sputum turned pink from sulfuric mists. Two fingers lost priming boreholes with chesa-sticks. His right ulna fractured by a rockbolt hammer. The man a trampled but noxious weed. When he departed La Caridad for the last time, it was to return to La Fortuna to bury his commonlaw wife, a woman eighteen years his junior who had suffered from a longstanding illness that he had never understood and had mostly ignored.

He fueled his return on bottled Bacanora, his journey without hurry or shortcut. Five days the woman's remains lay buried in La Fortuna's caliche soil at the hour he arrived drunk on his doorstep. He sniffed the vacant rooms, her smell, before he departed for the cantinas. A week later, sobered by the domestic inconveniences of widowerhood, he returned to the house where he was met without welcome by his only blood relative, an unmarried daughter then twenty-six years old.

Her given name was Dolores Maria, christened after her mother, but the old miner called her Lola. Hard liquor inspired other sobriquets: Cabrona, Hija de la Chingada, and his favorite, Paloma Negra—this from a popular ranchera he sang when drunk, his voice graveled by quartz dust.

> Tengo una maldita suerte
> Paloma Negra
> Que me llevarás a la muerte

Eyes cut from coal, skin dark as coned piloncillo, Dolores hated the name almost as much as she hated the loud and quarrelsome miner whose black Indian blood blighted her own. Her loathing of him a long nurtured journey begun beyond his remembrance. From the day a child sees what a child shouldn't see of a man and thereafter sees but his dirted hollow, his bestial grime, so she saw him still. A crude and shameless caricature of an indecent self. The heartless miner of her mother's misery. A man who spat on the truth whenever he opened his mouth. Dolores smelled his liquor before he spoke, a stench that sickened her no less than the sight of him. What brutes begot in brutes grown apparent in the grotesque tuber that bulged inside his pantsleg. Who he was. True to his deformity.

Now her mother gone, abandonment complete. This man's lifelong work the same as how the blind passed the dead in the street. Dolores wept for her mother and she wept for what was left. Life with a snarling drunk. To breathe his foul air and cook his food. The quotidian chores. The grief-stricken nights. No one but him.

With pesos filched from his pants, she bought seeds from a local brujo. Toloache and coyotillo mashed with his dinner beans. Sicken him, her plan. Gut and flush him. Let his rotted liver do the rest. So he would be found, defunct in a urine-soaked bed, drink what took him, the house hers to keep.

He ate the beans with appetite. She served him seconds. He rose the next morning to a fresh helping plated for breakfast. That afternoon his bandylegged gait unswayed, the tequila started, only his curses louder. One week followed another, beans mashed at every meal, a rat sooner poisoned. After a month the old miner still kicked dogs in the street.

She waited, the days without end, the nights beyond measure. One evening she left him passed out in his room and she walked La Fortuna's streets, finding a stranger in a place where strangers gathered, returning in the early morning hours fornicated and semen choked, a twenty-peso bill pocketed. Soon other nights, the worst kind of men, learning fast the bad things taught. Her high and pointed breasts the kind that drew whistles on dark streetcorners. In the ensuing months her belly grew, a bump she hid under a huipil dress. Later the bulge concealed by how she stood before him, his drunken glower kept at her back in a choreograph of evasions to defer the dreaded day. When the old man finally sobered up enough to notice, he knocked her to the floor. "Puta," he shouted. "Sinvergüenza." He promised her hell.

Weary of townlife, its complications, he joined the communal expropriation of the Timmins Mining tracts, squatting the most distant and unwanted parcel of basinland—three hundred hectares of deedless dirt he could name. He cradled his hernia in a rigged cup and set about clearing a patch of thornscrub. He dug a shallow waterwell with sledge and chiselbar. He constructed two mudbrick rooms. He excavated a pit-latrine and built a stakewood corral. Then he sold the house in La Fortuna to buy buffelgrass seed, milkgoats, and a few head of bony-hipped criollo cattle. He kept nothing to remind him of his dead wife. The daughter memory enough.

"Stay, you starve. Come, you work." His offer spat outside an empty house.

She came, a choice without making. She kept to herself the promise to redress a life so given. Abide him until the child born—then what she did not know. Two months later under a canopy of indifferent stars, the baby boy arrived on the thirsted land with the old man drunk on dorada mescal. He lurched from the adobe rooms to escape her screams, cursing loudly, not reappearing again for a week.

Dolores birthed alone, begetting in the pain-nighted hours her twisted idea of requital, how most to spite the old man and embitter his last days. When he returned to the ranch, she welcomed him with the news that the bastard child with red hair had been given a name. His name. Little Epifanio.

"The hell he is," the miner growled. "I won't call him so." Then he slapped the woman senseless and spat on the child. Later he threatened to kill them both should she dare to take the rusty-haired boy to town.

. . .

Retch returned to the ranch in the hired truck of Rolando Arenas, a scrapmetal dealer in La Fortuna. The truck carried townwater in steel drums, a navvy barrow, two motored pumps, shovels, prybars, buckets, fuel cans, and a handbuilt ladder. Retch paid the scrapdealer two hundred pesos to drive him to the ranch. He promised to pay the same amount when the dealer returned for him in seven days—the time Retch calculated he would need to purge and deepen the woman's noria to rid it of the salt.

A grizzled man with ruststained hands and the paunch of a patrón, Rolando Arenas remembered the old miner who lived on Rancho Anguamea. He told Retch that two years earlier he had sold Don Epifanio twenty sheets of rooftin and a length of coldrolled rod to make a chiselbar. The scrapdealer said he knew little of the woman, his daughter, having last seen her as a girl on the streets of La Fortuna. He could not recall her name.

When Retch said he had seen no man on the ranch, only the woman and a toddler boy, Rolando replied that he had heard nothing of the old miner since the rooftin transaction.

At the ranch the woman watched their arrival from the doorway, time reclocked. She held to the machete. The boy cried at her leg.

The scrapdealer maneuvered his truck into the clearing, reversing over broken bottles and trash mounds. When he silenced the motor, the woman called out above the child's cry to ask what business they brought.

"¡Agua!" Retch replied. He saw fresh goatmeat drying on the washline.

Rolando observed the boy's red hair. "El niño es pelirrojo como usted."

Retch nodded. Dig had said the same.

They siphoned the water into drums set beside the building. Retch asked the dealer to refill the empties before his return in a week. For a rainy day, he quipped.

The woman held to the boy. She watched them work.

"Qué desmadre," Rolando muttered, shaking his head at the sight of the starving goats, the littered bottles. He called to the woman, asking after the health of her father, the old miner.

"Muerto," she said. She chinned at a dirt mound run over by the truck.

The men stared at the grave.

"Disculpe, señora," the dealer offered. "Que en paz descanse."

The woman said nothing. Rolando shrugged. He shook Retch's hand and promised to return in a week.

Retch carried the ice chest into the shed kitchen where he set it on the dirtfloor. Inside the chest storebought milk, canned softdrinks, cheese, and two kilos of skirtsteak packed in icechips. He returned for a sack of nixtamal and a box with drygoods unloaded from the truck. The box packed with green coffee, a carton of eggs, cans of powdered milk, a jug of cooking oil, plastic bags of potatoes, beans, rice, and sugar. A formula bottle. Shorts for the boy.

She watched. The boy cried at her leg. Retch opened the ice chest and pulled out the milk. "Dale leche," he said.

At the wellsite he topped off the pump's fuel tank before he attached a footvalve to one end of the suction hose. He lowered the hose into the noria until the valve rested on the bottom—a depth he calculated to be thirty feet. He filled the hose and fitted it to the pump's suction port. As he worked, he listened, not hearing the boy cry.

The pump's discharge hose he uncoiled until it stretched beyond the clearing. He added water to the volute chamber through a prime port before he yanked the engine pullcord. The Tecumseh caught on the first whirl, its roar taking him back to Madrean streambeds, to Dig loading the sluice. His maniacal laugh.

The hose swelled with pumped water emptying onto the adust land. Retch marked the time on his watch. He stood by the well, watching the water recede. He had yet to make sense of it, a woman living alone with a child in a place with no potable water except what dripped from a cactus still. *A goddamn disaster is what.*

An hour later the well emptied. He killed the motor and checked the time, clocking the minutes for the noria to recharge—the same minutes he would have to work in the well should it need chiseling. He peered into the hole. The basalt cleanly sculptured, the floor without sediment. On the bottom lay a flathead sledge with a broken handle.

When he looked up, the woman stood at the well. She held out a softdrink.

Retch took it. "¿El niño?" he asked.

The woman said the boy slept.

Retch drank. He asked if the boy was sick.

She shook her head. "Sed," she replied.

He pointed to the drummed water. "Thirst no more."

The woman observed his hands, the blisters, the jeweled watch. It made no sense to her that a man once gone returned with storebought milk and that he set about pumping a salt-ruined well. "¿Y el otro?" she asked.

"¿El otro?"

"El otro gringo," she said. "El mata borregos."

Retch looked to the rimland. A good name, he thought. Dig the goatkiller. "Se fue," he replied.

She spat. "Parecía loco."

He nodded. Crazy was what all men seemed. As much as they seemed sane. When he looked into the noria, the seepage had immersed the broken sledge.

He pointed to the watch. He told the woman he was waiting for the well to refill. He said he would pump it dry again, allow it to replenish, pump again, and so on until the salt was purged. If the taste remained, he would enter the well and deepen it until freshwater rose, an undertaking he would complete before the scrapdealer's return in one week.

Dolores stared into the well. She recalled last seeing the jeweled watch on the crazy gringo. "Hay comida," she said. Then she left him to his purpose.

The cántaro hung from a braided sisal rope. Retch dipped the drinking gourd, sipping townwater that tasted of the cántaro's clay. The same water he poured into an enamelware basin handed to him by the woman. He washed his hands without soap, tossing the dirty water outside.

The woman fried the skirtsteak and boiled beans. The tortillas she stacked in a grasswoven chiquihuite. On the dirtfloor the naked boy lay asleep. A ragged cloth covered his face.

Retch ate at a table set with a pinchbowl of salt, a jar of dried chiltepines. The kitchen without chairs. The table with flies. The woman served the beans and meat in plastic bowls and she stood by the brazier watching him eat. When he asked if she would join him, she said no, later, with the boy. When he asked the boy's name, she said, "Epi."

"¿Epi como Epifanio?"

"Sí," she said.

Retch nodded. "My name is Retch. Retch Barter. And you?"

"Dolores."

Retch ate. "And your husband, Dolores?"

"None," she answered.

"Dead?"

Her shrug said that if he lived, his life was unknown to her.

Retch waved at the flies. He asked who had dug the well.

"El viejo."

"The one in the grave?"

"Sí."

"Did you bury him?"

"Sí."

Retch ate. To his best calculation the grave lay far enough from the noria not to ruin the water. "Did the well salt after you buried him?"

She nodded.

He took in the sleeping boy, dark-skinned and bony like his mother. His genitals hosted the most flies. "Who made the cactus still?" he inquired.

"Yo," she replied.

Retch nodded, thinking he had met no other woman who had made one. "And your family?"

"The boy," she answered.

When he asked how the old man had died, the woman said he drank. She stirred the brazier coals with a firehook. Retch mopped his bowl with a tortilla before pushing it away. Not his business to inquire further upon the death of a man he had not known. He knew what drink did.

He spoke to her of using the storebought milk before it soured. He said the cheese would hold if left where the dirtfloor was coolest. Then he left.

That afternoon he assembled the tripod from three lengths of steelpipe welded with a chain shackle and eyebolt hanger for suspending a single-whip tackle. The pipes and tackle part of his transaction with the scrapdealer.

He pumped and rested the well in uninterrupted cycles, the extracted water pooling at the lower end of the clearing. He pumped through the night, haunched by the well, smoking Faros, Dig's brand. He watched the cold cascade of stars drop below the rimland, dawn unbraided. He walked to the gravemound where he scuffed the dirt. He wondered if the woman had dug the grave with the same tools her father had used to dig the well.

At sunup he tasted the pumped effluent, the water still salted.

With townwater heated in pots, the woman bathed the boy in a rusted washtub, sudsing him with soaptree yucca, his first bath since the well had ruined. She righted the stock trough and filled it, herding the goats into the stakewood corral, letting the dames drink first. She pailed water to the kitchen where she scrubbed the linoleum-topped table, the crockery. She boiled formula for the boy. Her own thirst she quenched directly from the drums, tasting in the traveled townwater the corroded pipes of La Fortuna, its dirt streets, the life once lived there.

After lowering the ladder into the noria, Retch climbed to the bottom where he retrieved the broken sledge, using it to test the basalt's hardness. The saturated rock with a dank cellar smell. He returned to the surface to cut the sledge handle clean before he placed it in a bucket tied to a length of rope threaded through the whiptackle on the tripod. He pumped the well dry before he lowered the pail, following after it with a shovel and the old man's chiselbar. He hammered the basalt floor, filling the pail with black mafic rock. When the well refilled to his knees, he ascended the ladder, raising the pail with the handcranked winch. He pumped again, descending to pound the bottom with sledge and chiselbar, filling another pail, raising it when the water rose.

He breakfasted on egg tacos bundled in a dishtowel brought to the noria by the woman. The boy wore the new shorts. He suckled milk from the formula bottle. "¡Mira!" he cried, seeing the lakelet of pumped water.

"Agua," Retch said.

That afternoon while the boy slept the woman returned to the noria where she peered down at the rusty-haired gringo who pounded the rock bottom. She touched the ladder. It occurred to her that if she lifted it from the well, the gringo would not ascend again to daylight. He might grab for the rope, but when she released it from the crank, the rope would join the pail to which it was tied. If he tried to climb out, she had rocks to throw until he drowned.

Later she would lower the ladder and descend to rope his body. She would crank him out of the well and roll him off the ranch in the wheelbarrow, dig his grave with the tools he now held. The day the scrapdealer returned she would say he had departed to parts unknown. She would say the other gringo—the bald maniac—had come for him. The truth mattered not, only the story told from it. She would take what belonged to him—the pumps, motors, tools, the money he surely had—and she would make a deal with the dealer, the old snake. His business to buy such things. She would pay him to truck the goats to market in La Fortuna. So financed, she would rent a room, find work, raise the boy far from the accursed ranch.

Retch lifted his gaze, seeing her backlighted silhouette. He smiled. "¿Qué pasa?"

"Nada," she said. "Nada pasa."

Not like the old man, she thought as she departed. No steelbellied varmint this one. Soft inside.

She toasted the green coffee, glazing the beans with sugar, cooling the mix into a hardcrack slab that she ground in a burr mill. Early the next morning she boiled the grind. She filled a lidded jar and carried it to where the man slept. She stood over him, making no sound. His slumber measured before she left the coffee.

Retch awoke to the howl of coyotes, their banshee cries to the departing night. He unlidded the jar and sipped, savoring the smoky woodfire flavor, the metalline heat. Memories stirred of coffee drunk over the cutting-camp fires of a dissolute youth. He observed her in the kitchen, her figure moving before the glow of a burned-down fire.

He thought about how the choices of others left us in places not of our own choosing. So it seemed the woman had been left. When he considered the possibility that the noria might not surrender its salt in spite of his battering, he wondered what choices such an eventuality would leave him.

He turned east, watching the sky pale above the jagged hem of the Madrean mountains. All outlines on the landscape momentarily grew sharp, as though newly cut from some cloth made of itself. Then the desert dawned.

By the fifth day he had deepened the well three feet, the water salted. On the sixth the weathered basalt gave way to crystalline granite so hard the chiselbar bounced when struck by the sledge. Retch laid by his tools and inspected his blistered hands. He watched the seeping brine rise around his legs.

In the kitchen he washed a coffee jar, wiping the inside dry with his sleeve. He descended into the well to dip the jar into the water, lidding it before he climbed the ladder. He swirled the jar. When the water stilled, he removed the lid and decanted the liquid. The fine grains left in the jar he rolled between his fingertips before he tasted them.

Midmorning he removed the bottom bung from an empty drum, fitting a nippled valve into the hole. The drum he elevated on bricks stacked to a height that allowed a pail to stand beneath the valve. He wheeled the barrow to a drywash gully two kilometers distant from the ranch. With screen and shovel he sifted the arroyo's maicillo into the barrow. At the ranch he washed the sand with townwater before he layered it inside the drum atop a cloth barrier. He bailed water from the well and poured it into the filter, dispersing it across the sand until it percolated to the valve and ran into the pail. Retch dipped the coffee jar and swirled the water, inspecting for precipitate. Nothing settled. He sipped, tasting the salt. Twice more he filtered the water, each time tasting it. A third percolation completed before he rinsed his mouth with townwater and raised the ladder from the well. "Shit!" he said to the cloudless sky.

He gathered the tools and rope. He unrigged the winch and tackle, dismantled the tripod. He dumped the sand from the filter and rethreaded the bung. To make a cover for the noria, he pulled mesquite posts from an unstrung fenceline. In the corral he found sheets of rooftin, the same glinting atop the rooms, rooftin first spotted by Retch from the rimland. He laid the tin over the posts, shoveling extracted rock onto the cover. The circumference he embanked with a revetment of stones.

In the kitchen he told the woman the wellwater could not be made potable. "No sirve," he said. He waited for her to ask what he would do in accordance with the scrapdealer's imminent return, but she said nothing. He said the noria was sealed for the day the boy wandered, that he might not fall in, as was known to happen. He said he regretted the condition of the well. More water would be brought to the ranch, he added, arrangements made.

Dolores silent, face a mask. Well-intentioned men as foreign to her as the land she had come to live upon. At once she read advantage and opportunity in the stranger's solicitude. In such a place a man with good intentions stood lost and lampless in an aniline night.

She smiled, her black and carious teeth revealed between twisted lips. "No hay problema," she said. Then she fed him and served him fresh coffee.

. . .

That night Retch was awakened by the tug of his pantszipper. He felt the grip of a hand between his legs. When he reached for himself, her head there.

He started to get up. "¡Espera!" he blurted.

Her lips gave a tentative nibble.

"Hold on!"

Then she bit him and wrenched her head.

"Sonofabitch!" Retch with the sudden remembrance of a brown dog on a dirt street, the dog bleeding from where Digger had shot off its penis with a gun borrowed off a judicial cop who had bet such a feat could not be accomplished between copulating dogs. The dog ran with blood squirting from its underbelly. The penis stump protruded from the copulated bitch who circled on herself, trying to bite it. A crowd of men laughed at the spectacle, Retch among them, new to this cold measure of cruelty.

"Sonofabitch!" When he tried to push her off, she bit harder, her purchase on him further secured by a two-handed grip on his testicles.

"Okay, okay," he bleated.

Her fingers pressed his lips. She unbuttoned his pants and shimmied them to his knees. Drawing aside her undergarment, she straddled his loins and lowered herself upon him.

Retch reached for her breasts. His mouth searched for bare skin. But the woman leaned rearward, pivoting upon his penile fulcrum, her pubes lifted to the night sky in angled coitus.

Like rutting beasts they fornicated into the early morning hours, copulating repeatedly without caresses or kisses. At dawn she rose to answer the boy's cry, departing in silence. Retch slept without dreams, curled on the ground.

A man's voice broke the silence. "Hace falta un perro."

Retch squinted at the penumbral figure standing above him. "¿Qué pasó?"

Rolando guffawed. "Not much. I came. I stole. No dog here to warn you."

Retch gripped the scrapdealer's outstretched hand and stood, legs gelatinous, the rest of him crushed. The taste of last night's coffee clung to his mouth. Rolando asked if he was hung over. Retch nodded.

The dealer retreated to his truck, returning with cans of beer yoked in a plastic ring. Retch chugged the first, the beer warm. He drained the second. From the rooms no sound came.

The scrapdealer observed the covered well. "¿No sirve?"

Retch shook his head. Both men stared at the noria. Neither spoke to its past or future. Retch felt the lift of the beer. The steelbright daylight fixed him to the ground. He took in the scrapdealer's empty truck, no drums loaded. "¿Y el agua?"

Rolando raised his hands in dramatic despair. La Fortuna had been without water for two days, he explained, the potablizer pump broken. But he had come to the ranch on the appointed day, as agreed upon.

Retch asked when the pump would be fixed.

"Mañana," the dealer replied.

"¿Mañana?"

"Sí, mañana en la mañana."

Damn sharp, Retch thought. In coming today without water, the dealer had found a way to charge for a trip when the pump was fixed.

He stared at the truck. One load tomorrow. Another next week. In the clearing empty drums lay on their sides. He knew now was the time to walk, no harm done. At least he had saved them from Digger. And the boy would not fall down the well, though he might die of thirst.

His gaze fell on the rooms. He had returned for the right reason only to give himself no right way to leave. *Then there was last night.*

He asked Rolando to reverse his truck so the empty drums might be loaded. He drained a third beer before he went to speak to her.

The boy stood naked in the kitchen. "¿Y tu mamá?" Retch asked, peering into the unlit room, black as a crypt. He heard a trickle of water. He looked down to see the boy urinating on the dirtfloor. The boy pointed to the puddle. "¡Agua!" he said.

Retch nodded, their connection to the word affirmed. He stepped past the boy and stood inside the doorway. A dense heat filled the windowless room. Where the rooftin had lifted from its nailing, pinholes of daylight vectored into the darkness. Retch discerned a space empty of furniture, bare of adornment. No bed. No hammock. No wardrobe. At the far end of the room, the woman lay on the floor. Only her face showed from under a cover.

Retch stared. He still felt her teeth, her vicelike grip. He informed her that he would be leaving with the scrapdealer. "I will return with water," he added. "Tomorrow."

Her gaze remained fixed overhead. "Go with God," she said.

Retch paused in the doorway. "Do you want to come?" he asked, the invitation made without taking measure of its consequence, just the decent thing to do. "I will get you and the boy a room at the hotel," he offered.

She turned to look at him. When she sat up, the cover fell from her shoulders to reveal the slope of her neck, the outline of her bared breasts. She gazed at him, not covering herself. "Vamos," she said, her black-toothed smile lost in the darkness.

She wore walkworn huaraches. Her faded poblano dress exchanged for a weaved huipil. The boy sat shirtless in the gifted shorts.

"How barbarous the sun," remarked the dealer as the truck climbed onto the rimland. When he asked the boy's name, the woman didn't answer.

"Epifanio," Retch said.

The dealer chortled. "Like his grandfather, eh!" So encouraged, Rolando chronicled his acquaintance with the old miner, recounting in detail their mercantile transactions. "A good man," he said.

Dolores held the boy, silent. Unknown to her the goodness of the old man in life, much less in memory.

The scrapdealer said he possessed in his yard an assortment of shopmade crosses for Christian burials and wayside shrines. Credit available, he said, if a cross was desired to mark the old miner's grave.

"Ahorita no," Dolores replied.

When Rolando asked how Don Epifanio had come to end his days, Dolores stared at the reticent land as though it might surrender an answer in spite of the truth. "Murió de viejo," she said.

Rolando nodded his approval. Dying of old age, he said, is much preferred to dying of anything else sooner. "Así quiero irme," he added.

Dolores said nothing. She kept to herself the hope that the dealer would not get his wish to die old but be crushed under the weight of his greed at God's earliest convenience.

Retch listened, resisting the urge to interject his wisdom—that to die young was the best way to escape corruption—unsure how this would translate in the company he kept. At each sway of the truck, he glimpsed the woman's reflection in the sidemirror—her pockmarked skin, the ribboned cicatrix—a grim and ill-favored face belying the lascivious creature within.

"I have stove irons," Rolando offered without preamble. "Five pesos."

Dolores said she had no stove.

"Charcoal irons, then."

"Gracias."

The sun beat on the truckcab. The windowwind blew gritty. An hour from the ranch, they overtook a foursome of women afoot with bundled firewood on their heads. Each carried a machete. None looked up when Rolando honked the horn. "Adiós," he greeted.

They passed the town brothel, a lowbuilt, windowless structure, its wallfront painted with voluptuous figures, the roofline festooned with lightbulbs. Dolores turned to look. The scrapdealer hummed. Retch recalled the nights spent there with Digger. No one spoke.

The road widened onto a silica flat hazed from the smoldering trashpiles of La Fortuna's garbage dump. When they drove by the town cemetery, Rolando crossed himself. "Que Dios nos cuide," he declared. Dolores stared ahead, her mother buried there.

A pavingstoned street brought them to the town plazuela—a grassed square enclosed by a promenade and shaded by ceiba trees. Marketstalls lined one side of the square. A whitewashed church stood on another. Storefronts, a bar, and La Fortuna's only hotel occupied the north side. On the south end sat the town waterworks—a corroded assemblage of pipes and tanks, the largest with a faded waterdrop painted in cerulean blue. Here the scrapdealer stopped the truck. "Venga," he said to Retch.

They left the woman in the cab, the boy asleep. Retch followed the dealer onto the grounds where a circle of men stood watching a mechanic at work on the town wellpump.

"So you see," Rolando explained, "why your water was not delivered."

The pump unbolted from the wellpipe and suspended by a chainhoist tracked on a cantilevered I-beam. The mechanic, a squirrelly, grease-stained man, worked installing an armature.

"Se desgració," said the dealer, invoking disgrace in the pump's ruin.

Retch approached. The town well not a handdug noria, rather a machine-drilled hole cased with a steel sleeve. When he asked for the well's depth, the onlookers shrugged, not knowing the particulars of the well from which they drank.

The mechanic said he could not speak to the nearness of water, being a mechanic who repaired wellpumps, not the wells themselves. Retch selected a gravelstone from the backfill. He dropped it into the annulus, listening as the stone chinked twice before it plunked. He reckoned the time of its fall, doing the math with a formula dimly recalled, calculating the water's depth at four hundred feet. "Como cien metros," he said.

Men nodded at this cipher.

"Él es un ingeniero," Rolando announced, introducing Retch as an engineer. The concocted title caused the circle of men to widen, as though professional utterances needed space to ventilate.

It occurred to Retch that a well of this kind, drilled and cased to the same depth, could yield clean water on the woman's ranch. When he asked for the driller of the well, several men answered as one. "Fue El Güero." Others repeated the name.

The scrapdealer explained that the well had been drilled years before by a man known as El Güero, so called for his fair skin and sunbleached hair. He had been contracted by the Ministry of Hydraulic Resources in Hermosillo to drill wells in the eastern municipalities where potable water was hauled to the towns in tanker trucks. El Güero had come to La Fortuna to drill the town well. He had arrived in his rig, hiring a local man for his helper.

"Chalino López," someone added, remembering the helper.

"Pobre Chalino."

Men shook their heads gravely.

"Sí, Chalino," concurred the dealer, who provided further particulars about the driller. El Güero, he said, had chosen the wellsite with a forked dowsing rod. He had circled the plazuela many times until the stick picked the spot they now stood upon. During the job he had camped next to his wellrig. Some said he never slept. While his machine drilled into the night, he could be heard singing above the roar of the drill motor. Sometimes he called out in an indecipherable tongue. "Un poco loco," Rolando concluded.

Onlookers nodded. "A big man," said one. "Short-fingered," added another. When Retch inquired where the driller could be found, Rolando said the whereabouts of a man once departed La Fortuna became known only from those who saw him somewhere else. So it was with the driller. After leaving La Fortuna, El Güero was seen next in Huásabas on the Bavispe River where he had commenced a new well. It was here one night, while drilling in a chubasco downpour, that he was electrocuted when the rig derrick was struck by lightning. Local authorities called in the announcement of his demise to LA KALIENTE radio in Hermosillo, which broadcast the death notice together with others of its kind as a service to relatives wishing to claim the remains. This, said Rolando, was when he learned of the driller's whereabouts.

"Dead then," Retch said.

The dealer shrugged. "Se supone," he replied, unwilling to confirm beyond the alleged. He said a year later he was visited by a fellow yarder offering to sell twenty-five lengths of new wellcasing. The yarder told him that he had received the casing as payment on a debt. The casing, he said, lay in Huásabas. It was from this yarder that Rolando learned new particulars surrounding the driller's whereabouts, among them the revelation that the body of the driller, whose presence atop the derrick had been witnessed by onlookers in the selfsame light of fulguration, was never retrieved. His remains were presumed lost down the borehole, propelled and compacted there by the thunderbolt—a phenomenon of extraordinary force known to launch men like projectiles, sending them great distances in uncommon trajectories and sometimes fitting them into narrow spaces.

Rolando pointed to the well, its dinnerplate diameter. "Imagínense," he added, shaking his head at the prospect of such a passage.

He said that in the days following the radio announcement, no relatives of El Güero arrived to claim what amounted to a body vanished down a hole. According to the yarder from Huásabas, the absence of next of kin made it convenient for local authorities to leave the driller where God had interred him. A week after the accident these same authorities capped the borehole with a plug of rocks and concrete. They announced that any water extracted from the site would be unsanitary. No new well was drilled in Huásabas, the populace preferring to continue their purchase of trucked tankwater though it came from a distant well whose history remained unknown to them.

"Algunos dicen que no se murió nada," added Rolando, his voice dropping. "Some say he wandered off lightning struck. Some say he drills still."

Men nodded. The dealer spat. Retch eyed the well. So much for El Güero, he thought. "Did you buy the casing?" he asked.

Rolando shook his head, saying he had declined the offer from the yarder in Huásabas though the price was fair. "Pipe with such a history is not a thing to have around," he added. "It carries bad luck."

When Retch asked what became of the drillrig, the dealer replied that he did not know. "Probably appropriated by an opportunistic soul. The world is full of such men."

"¿Y Chalino?" Retch inquired, thinking the driller's helper might offer assistance.

"Muerto," replied the dealer. "Killed crossing a street in Cuauhtémoc. I was hired to bring back his body."

The mechanic, who had suspended his repairs to listen, said Chalino's widow was his wife's cousin.

Silence was observed for Chalino's widow before Rolando asked loudly when in fornication would the pump be fixed and potable service restored. He said that washing without water was damn inconvenient for anyone intent on whoring.

"Mañana," the mechanic answered. "Mañana en la mañana."

The boy pointed to the dog that peed on the scrapdealer's truck. "¡Mira!"

"Perro," barked Rolando, who had given no thought to leaving a woman and boy in a shadeless spot while men talked at leisure under the trees.

Retch paid him what was owed, the dealer promising to return to the waterworks in the morning to fill the drums and transport them to the ranch. "By God's favor," he said. Retch unloaded the ice chest, his satchel.

The deskclerk at the Hotel Posada remembered Retch from previous stays. He also remembered Digger. "¿Y el Topo Loco?" he inquired. A thin youth with delicate hands, the clerk did his best to look disappointed as Retch explained that he no longer partnered with the man known as the Crazy Mole. In their last stay Dig had destroyed the greater part of two rooms after the manager requested he refrain from urinating out the upperstory window onto the street. An enraged Dig had removed the lavabo from the wall and used it to batter the toilet tank, flooding their room and the one below it. Before the manager could call the police, Dig had stuck a wad of bills in his face. Then he had requested another room, one with a garden view where he could piss in peace.

"Qué lástima," lamented the clerk, as though the rampage of a drunken guest a thing to be missed, like a handsome gratuity.

Retch requested two rooms away from the street. He wondered if Dig had buggered this ectomorphic youth in some hidden corner of the hotel. Those green eyes had allured not a few into the shadows.

"¿Dos?" the clerk queried, looking past Retch to the woman and the boy who stood in the hotel's narrow, dimlit foyer.

"Dos."

The roomkeys hung with plyboard handles, their painted numbers faded. Retch motioned for Dolores to follow.

"Bienvenida, señora," welcomed the deskclerk, his gaze lingering on her scarred face before locking onto the boy's red hair. Dolores ignored him, her eyes downcast, not liking the man's serviceable effeminacy. It confirmed her opinion that deskclerks were but women inside men's bodies.

She followed Retch up a tiled stairway and across a second story gallery lofting above a garden courtyard. Years before, the hotel had been the home of a mining hacendado who had brought from distant coasts the cultivars of mango, banana, and coconut palm to be planted in his highland desert patio, there to be irrigated from rain cisterns by his peón houseworkers. The cisterns now empty, the gutters fallen. A waterless fountain stood in the yard's center.

The woman's room with a highbrick ceiling and screenless windows curtained with battenboard shutters that opened inward. Above the bed hung a three-bladed fan wired to a rotary rheostat on the wall. Retch showed the woman how to start and stop the fan. Then he handed her a one-hundred-peso bill, telling her to buy shirts and a pair of shoes for the boy.

At the mercantile Dolores held leather sandals to the boy's feet, selecting a size larger than his measure. In the checkout line she read the sign. SE SOLICITA MUCHACHA. She pointed to the sign and asked what the work paid. The checkout woman eyed Dolores, the boy. She said a girl had been hired, the sign's removal overlooked. Dolores paid and took the change, discarding the receipt. Outside, she buckled the sandals on the boy's feet. She pulled a new shirt over his head. Epifanio tugged at the shirtfront to view its serigraph of balloons. He lurched as he walked, staring at the shoes. She led him to the plazuela where she bought steamed corn served in a nut cup with a plastic spoon. They sat on an iron bench under the ceiba trees where her mother had sat with her on the promenade years before, laughter between them. The memory fresh, a world unspoiled, the old man off at the mine.

She watched the boy eat.

Two years her mother gone, no day since the same. When the sickness had first come, her mother had refused to visit the town doctor, a man whose wife had died from lockjaw. "I will not see him!" she protested. "His own woman dead from what he could cure!" Dolores took her to the curandero in Bavispe, a healer who diagnosed a patient's ills from the death throes of a wrung chicken. "Cancer," the curandero announced after completing his study of the dead bird. He treated the sick woman with a snake egg, the egg rolled over the affected area to incarnate the illness into a deformed embryo revealed to them once the egg was cracked.

Weeks later, her mother's suffering undiminished, Dolores led her to the church so she might touch the black feet of San Martín de Porres enshrined within. Dolores took her by the arm and left her inside, the church empty of priest and parishioners. Her mother performed her devotions before a chipped plaster statue. She kissed the painted feet. Dolores stood near the door, silent, unhallowed by the place, waiting for her mother to finish.

When the pain worsened, Dolores used the last of their money to visit a local reflexologist, an aged Oaxaqueña living in a thatchroofed bungalow at the edge of La Fortuna. Her thumbwork on callused soles lifted bad humors left by illness, snakebites, and spoiled water. The old woman rubbed her mother's feet, grunting as she drew the cancer into herself. At the end of the stroking, she pronounced the patient cured and ready to return home to live a long life.

That same evening her mother died in her bed, Dolores the sole witness to the agony. She kissed the woman's cold cheek and removed from her neck the pewter crucifix hung on a steelchain. The chain she kept, the pendant she put in her mother's mouth. Five days later, when the old miner appeared—his drunken disregard the final indignity—Dolores cried for the darkness to come as much as she cried for the loss. Not since had she wept.

She rose from the bench, took the boy's hand. They returned to the hotel, walking sidestreets without hurry, her thoughts on the gringo stranger whose name she could not pronounce. Of all possible intercessions, this the least expected. As unlikely as rain. His fight with the crazy bald gringo. His return with water and food. His working the salted well to no purpose. Now he had brought them to town. Tomorrow he would take water again. To what end? What advantage? Something wanted. Some prize. No man so selfless. No man she had met.

For now, take what he had, she decided. He would not stay long but perhaps long enough to get them off the godforsaken ranch. The road to another life best sought by keeping him close, no guile spared. Ride him, let him think the gift belonged to him. For the boy, she thought.

Back at the hotel, she counted the man's money, separating what to keep, what to return. While the boy napped, she lay on the bed and waited for him to knock. She lay smelling the bedsheets, their crisp laundering. She watched the fan twirl overhead. A good place to lay, she thought, his mistake to bring her.

Retch opened the faucet in the tin showerstall. Then he remembered. "Goddamn it!"

When Dig had ripped the lavabo from the wall, heaving it against the toilet tank, Retch had sought to dodge the spray from broken pipes. He had cursed his wet clothes, soaked shoes. Now he stared at the showerhead's fenestrated disk, the sprayholes choked with mineral deposits. His world a journey from one waterless corner to another, and Dig off to heave lavabos in a world where deluge perturbed no man's slumber.

He sniffed his nakedness. Her smell on him. The miasmic spoor of copulation, their commingled ejaculate. His foreskin glared red with her teethmarks. His scrotum itched. He dressed and descended to the lobby where he asked the clerk for bottledwater. "¡Híjole!" replied the youth, his delicate hands a flutter of helplessness. "Un momento plees."

An hour later the houseboy delivered a bag with glassbottles sealed with crown caps opened with a churchkey not in Retch's possession. He inverted one bottle above another, interlocking the pleated metalwork caps, opening each in turn. Mineral water sprayed between his fingers as he emptied the bottles into a ceramic pitcher. The last one he opened with his teeth, saving it to drink. He wet his face and shaved, returning to the shower to wash under his arms. He rinsed between his legs, the mineral water drying with pellicular tautness. As he dressed, he considered anew the woman's situation and what might be done to improve it, and whether he should be the instrument of that remedy.

He knew what was wanted on the ranch, the same seen at the town waterworks. A deep well. Machine drilled. Steel cased. A well bored into freshwater aquifers where no salt had leached.

No more hauling water.

A driller and drillrig needed. Casing. Wellpipe. A truck. Retch stared out the window at the palms shading the courtyard. He tried to imagine the woman's ranch with water, and he tried to imagine himself living there with the woman and the boy.

Hard to picture.

The better part of twenty years he had spent free from attachment, his world without corner or center, his life led without commitment or calling. A fugitive's trail left to the few who remembered him. Then he had dropped off the planet with Digger, another miscreant orphaned from a nameless, placeless past.

He drank the mineral water, thinking of last night, what wickedness. Most men stuck for less. She was something caught from the wild.

When he finished the bottle, he read the label, its claim that water from the mineral springs of Tehuacán had fortified the great Moctezuma before his epic battle with the brutal Cortés.

Right. He threw the bottle into the trashcan.

One thing certain, he told himself. A drilled well would give the ranch drinking water. What else, he couldn't say.

He turned from the window and pulled a leather billfold from the knapsack. The billfold a zippered purse handtooled with images of fighting cocks. Retch opened the purse and counted the money into stacks. Dig had been generous, a generous asshole in an ungenerous world.

Payola, bud, for whatever hell comes next.

After he hid the purse he clapped his boots together, shaking loose the crumbles of mafic mud.

Drink. That's what you'd do. Drink, piss it away. Like him.

Then he locked the room and walked the arched gallery to the woman's door.

She handed him the coins, leaving the sandaled boy to speak to expenditures. "¡Mira!" he exclaimed, pointing to himself.

Retch took them to a sit-down fonda where they ate plates of noodle salad and enchiladas sided with rice. Retch drank two beers, the first quickly, the second with his food. He watched them eat, the woman new to public dining, the boy new to fork and knife.

At a corner abarrotes he led the woman inside, telling her to set on the counter what goods were needed. The woman gathered bags of rice, sugar, and beans, bottles of cooking oil and vinegar, cans of pickled chilies and tomato sauce, and tinned lard. The shopkeeper boxed the goods. When Retch observed the woman's choices, he added cereal, sliced bread, jam, toothpaste, brushes, barsoap, toilet paper, a flyswatter, and Mercurochrome. For the boy he bought a bottle of bubblemix with a wirewand. Retch asked the shopkeeper to deliver the boxes in two hours' time to the Hotel Posada.

They walked to the plazuela where Retch showed the boy how to blow bubbles off the wand. At the waterworks he observed the mechanic at work on the pump, onlookers bearing witness to the repair. He pointed to the well and told the woman the surest way to have good water on the ranch was to drill a deep pozo such as the one that watered the town—an undertaking he was willing to pursue if she agreed. He asked her what she thought.

The woman looked to where he pointed. She knew that men like him lived in the making of their destinations but made not their destiny. To keep him on the ranch was to keep him from going somewhere else. Soon he would tire of the land, watered or not. "Bien," she said, giving a black-toothed smile.

"I will have to hire a driller," he explained.

"Bien," she said.

That night while the boy slept she came to his room. She found the door unlocked, the man lying naked in his bed. He tasted of salt not sweated. When he touched the scar on her face, she pulled away. "¿Quién?" he asked.

"Shh," she said.

"¿Quién. El viejo?"

"Sí."

She let him do what he pleased. Soon he slumped beside her in exhausted sleep. Lying in the darkness, she soothed her throbbing scar with wetness from between her legs. Later, when the spatter of running water came from the showerstall, she rose and left the room, not waking the man, not closing the faucet he had left open.

In his dream Retch stood in a clearing on a forested hillside, gun in hand, listening to the windblown hush of grass, the storm's approach. He looked upon a vast and rolling land darkly verdant, its coniferous canopy broken by pastures. Below him mottled cattle grazed by a stream, their solid bovinity aligned before the storm. As he lifted the gun, taking aim at the nearest, the land suddenly darkened. Large, tear-shaped drops hit his hands. Before he could pull the trigger, rain encircled him, the cattle gone. Then the sky fell in metal sheets.

Daylight seeped between the shutters. Retch awoke to water running in the shower. He rose scurfy, broken-bodied, his first business to check the purse. In the stall he soaped under a spray of chilled groundwater unheated by the hotel boilers. He remembered the night. *So the old man had cut her. Her own father!* He recalled the scar's carinated feel. The runover grave stuck in his head. The machete hung in the kitchen. *And the boy with his name!*

In the gallery the woman leaned on the balustrade watching the boy play. Her hair damp, face washed, the lavandin smell of hotelsoap on her. A thin chain without pendant hung on her neck. Not half bad, Retch thought.

They breakfasted streetstand tacos of marinated pork, the woman ordering without words, holding up three fingers, sharing her softdrink with the boy. Retch drank glasses of limeade prepared while he watched. The limes squeezed into a plastic pitcher filled with water drawn from a sidewalk barrel, the same barrel used to dampen streetdust in front of the stand. La Fortuna's revival complete, even its streets drinking.

The woman and boy waited in the plazuela while Retch took the cooler to an icehouse where he bought a chipped block. In the market he purchased fryers and hangersteak, milk and cheese. He left the cooler with the woman while he retrieved the boxed goods from the hotel.

At the waterworks the dealer backed his truck under the discharge gantry. He filled the drums with a length of relay hose suspended from an elbowpipe. Retch climbed into the bed, capping the drums with canvas covers. Rolando announced it was a good morning to haul water, there being water to haul. After the drums filled, Retch inspected the repaired wellpump. His hand rested on the manifold, feeling the water's venturi pulse, the cold steel. He told Rolando of his intention to sink a deep well on the woman's ranch. He said he did not wish to inconvenience him any longer with the hauling of townwater. His plan, he said, was to purchase a truck to transport the drums until a well was sunk.

"Bien," agreed the dealer, thinking the gringo a greater fool than he had supposed. He looked to where the woman stood. She's got him now, he thought before he smiled. "Buena idea," he said, adding that a drilled perforation would be a godsend to the ranch if freshwater was found, though the drilling of it was a trickier proposition than the hauling. Men had lost all they owned down a dryhole. Lost, too, what could not be owned.

Retch said that while this was true, the hauling of water had no end, but the drilling of it did. Then he asked the dealer if he knew where a driller and rig could be hired.

"Hermosillo," Rolando replied. The capital was full of rigs, he said, one parked on every corner, the city populated with welldrillers lined up for work, any one of whom would come to the ranch for hire.

Retch was mildly encouraged. "Qué bueno," he said.

Taking sidestreets, the dealer routed his truck to the pavingstoned road. He threw wet kissing sounds at the women he saw. They passed the house where the woman had lived, a stuccoed house with screened windows, a front door. Dolores gazed at the yard. The laurel tree taller, its shadow shading the porch where she had sat with her mother smelling the verbena in the garden. She said nothing as they passed, waiting for the dealer to speak of the house, but he only whistled.

They drove by the town slaughterhouse, its corrals crowded with cattle on the hoof until dawn, the next killing hour. By the road a tire mechanic pounded senseless a wheelrim with a sledge. The truck stopped at the dealer's yard where Rolando descended without a word, disappearing into a fenced lot with twisted pipes, stacked drums, and the rusted remains of broken and discarded machines in craggy piles. No office, no sign, but odd specimens of automotive seating set adrift among the ferric outcroppings. The yard's background murmur of advancing rust suddenly broken by the barks of dogs, three hounds charging the chainlink fence.

"¡Mira!" cried the boy.

"Son perros bravos," bragged the dealer. He emerged from the yard carrying a gravecross. He held it up for the woman to inspect. The cross with the channel openings unwelded. "Para Don Epifanio," he intoned gravely.

Dolores stared, face a mask.

"To complete a Christian burial," Rolando added.

She almost spat. A cross to mark the grave of one she hated in life and loathed in memory? A man she had buried face down? She nearly laughed. He was plain stupid, this heaper of metalshards who forged crosses from bargained scourings, this fool who believed that the weight of years was enough to kill a man overdue for death.

"Después," she said, looking away.

"Don't pay me now," he offered.

"Después."

The dealer nodded. "Bien," he said, returning the cross to the yard.

Retch said nothing. Let deaddogs lie an opinion he kept to himself, his thoughts on the hire of a driller, how to proceed. Hermosillo first. If no luck there, he would write Tex Hinton. Tex would know a driller.

As they departed, the woman observed the silver Daxara parked in a corner of the scrapyard, recognizing it as one seen before, the same trailer towed by the gringo's yellow truck the day they had descended on the ranch. She looked again to make sure.

The boy climbed onto the man's lap and fell asleep. Dolores stared out the window. A thing not much thought about until now. How this gringo who held her son had struck the green-eyed driver with the metal bar, struck him then drove away, the maniac slumped in the seat, his bald head bloodred. But now she thought about it. When next she looked at the boy, she saw the gringo fallen asleep as well, his mouth open to the untelling day. His jeweled watch told the hour.

Hellfire's Heap

Driller kept to roads less traveled, his journey unmapped and without haste. In the Capitan Mountains he waited out a proxigee moon to better hear the tidal slosh of aquiferous currents risen below the granite intrusion. Crossing the Tularosa Basin, he lingered on the Carrizozo Maplais to walk the ropey lava flow in search of pea-size lapilli, their basaltic flavor his fancy. He stopped north of the Oscura to survey the distant playas, land without outflow to river or ocean, its saltpan bottom sealed to water beyond the reach of the augers he bore. In Pie Town he detoured to a local café where he sat at the counter and ordered piñion pie. The waitress said the New Mexican apple was the only pie with pine nuts, and not many.

"Picked by the Washoe?" Driller inquired.

"Heck if I know," said the waitress. "Picked by someone."

He drove west to Quemado where he stopped for diesel at a service grocery. In the towyard stood a Christmas tree of deer antlers assembled in an arboreal cone with blinking lights strung on the points.

A razory wind blew past the pumps. The old man who dispatched fuel studied the rig, its balloon tires, the unhoisted derrick. He asked Driller if he was headed to Gallup. "I got a brother lives there. Says they ain't got water."

Driller didn't answer.

"Haven't seen one of these in a coon's age," the dispatcher continued, eyeing the cabdoor with its scratched-out lettering. "What year is she?"

"Year the Mack brothers met the Wrights," said Driller.

The dispatcher laughed. "And I thought I was an old-timer." He noticed the man's missing fingers, the odd way he parted his hair.

Driller studied the antler tree. "Who shot the bucks?" he asked.

"Boss man. He's the hunter. There's an elk rack in there. Pretty, ain't it? Like having Christmas year-round."

Silence stretched beyond the guzzle of diesel fuel. The pump shutoff triggered.

"And Jesus, is he coming?" Driller inquired.

The dispatcher hung the nozzle. "Say what?" he asked.

Driller grinned. "I said, is Jesus coming? To be born here in Quemado, this scoria you call a town?"

The old man looked to see if Driller was joking, but his grin too toothy for that. He noticed the man's eyes, grayblue like the Gemblade of his razor. "Well, I'm not sure what you mean, mister. I was talking about the tree." He pointed to the pumpmeter. "That'll be forty-seven dollars."

Driller removed from the cab an oversize wallet carried by routemen. He handed the dispatcher a new bill. "Keep the change, old-timer."

The dispatcher held the bill to the sky. "We don't keep change here."

Driller climbed into the cab and started the rig.

"Hold on there," the old man protested. "I've got to check this money."

"Gallup sits on sandstone," Driller said from the window. "Late cretaceous. It's got artesian water. Tell your brother he's a liar."

The dispatcher stared. The wind tugged at the bill in his hand. "I'll tell him no such thing," he said, watching the rig depart, surprised at how quickly it took to the highway, quiet for a diesel. The wind made more noise. Or the wind carried it. Something wasn't right.

"Had a burr up his butt," he told the boss back in the grocery, the bill authenticated. "Crazy to boot. Driving hellfire's heap. Damnedest thing I've laid eyes on."

After acquiring the rig in West Texas, Driller refit it to his purpose and destination. Cab markings effaced. Flotation tires added. The drilltable retooled with a four-drum drawworks. New seals snugged the cylinders of the mudpump—a Failing Power Slush with mudmaster pistons. A Hughes tricone bit rode on the platform. Driller calculated the rig could sink five hundred feet of drillsteel into the Gaean basement and sodomize a catamite angel while he slept.

He drove south off the Mogollon, past the blockfault Galiuros, a white sun unleashed above the desert sprawl. On the Old Nogales Highway he stopped in Amado where he ordered steak tartare marinated in limejuice. The young waiter stared at the stranger. "We don't sell that," he replied.

Driller grinned, all teeth, eyes sliding sideways as though to find a thing to light on. He changed his order to the house sirloin, blue-rare. "Cold," he said. "No sides."

At the border crossing a customs agent halted him. "What's your final destination in Mexico?" she asked.

Driller said his final destination was unknown to him, as it was to all who traveled beyond borders real or imaginary."

"Your destination, sir?"

"Points south."

"Are you transporting weapons or ammunition?"

"This rig," Driller said. "An assailant of Mother Earth."

"Answer the question, please."

"No."

Other agents approached, curious, friendly. One led a sniffer dog. "Man, where are you headed in that thing?" the handler asked.

"Infernal regions, brother. Land of shortlegged men driving big trucks."

They laughed. The dog sniffed the rig's undercarriage and tires before it heeled at the handler's side. It gazed intently at Driller. When Driller extended his hand, the dog dropped its tail and crouched, ears laid back.

"Don't touch the dog, sir," the handler said. "It confuses him."

Across the border, the Mexican aduana officer offered no small talk. The braided visor of his cap shaded a practiced eye for smugglers guised as anything else. "¿Qué trae?" he asked, his voice wearied by the question, one asked many times that day and days before. He did not inspect the rig. He hardly looked at it. Neither did he ask for papers or permits. What business this foreigner had bringing into Mexico a machine to violate Zapata's sacred land and sovereign waters was not his concern but the concern of others down the road—if they wished to make it their concern—if, indeed, he was a foreigner and not a big

Veracruzano or some moreno from Costa Chica—matters best left to immigration agents and the police. He wished to know only what the man brought to Mexico that no man should bring without bringing money to explain it.

"Traigo lo que usted está viendo," Driller replied effortlessly. He shook the officer's hand, leaving there a one-hundred-dollar bill crisply folded.

"Adelante," said the officer, waving him forward.

Driller drove ahead, tasting the dust of Mexico, licking his lips. So he advanced, at home upon God's land given to a brown-skinned race, the first to eat dahlias and smoke their woody stems, the first to trade in the carmine of cochineal blood. They who ran toward death with faith.

El Agua y El Hombre

"Ándale," Retch urged, speaking in the manner of men who coaxed endurance from their machines. The old truck ascended off the rutted caliche road and wound its way over black-rock hills dotted with saguaro skeletons and the sunbleached skulls of cattle. Each switchback rose steeper than the one before it, the pulverized roadstone crunching under weighted tires. In the truckbed water sloshed from open-topped drums.

In his twelfth month of hauling, Retch knew the road and he knew the pitched desert scrubland through which it ran, dry as bonemeal, bleached of green. Twice a week he trucked water from La Fortuna, a roundtrip of forty kilometers, the Fargo showing the wear. Nose-heavy. Muffler lost. The burnt smell of a slipping clutch risen inside the cab. Retch had purchased the truck—Canadian iron with a stakebed body—from a Mennonite dairy farmer in Ciudad Cuauhtémoc for five thousand pesos. Another six hundred pesos had delivered it to Hermosillo on a Ferromex flatcar. He considered it a truck that listened well for its age, it being two decades older than he and truer to its calling. Why he spoke to it.

"Ándale."

At a drywash arroyo the road narrowed to wheelworn ruts crisscrossed with the tracks of javelinas come to snuffle the drum-spilled dampness. Retch slowed the truck. The summer before, machete in hand, he had widened the crossing, but the thornscrub had since retaken the arroyo. Spined branches clawed the truck. The cabmetal screeched.

"¡Puta madre!"

Retch found the native expletives welltailored to his circumstances. He never cursed the truck, but he often cursed the woman. Mostly he cursed the old miner buried at the ranch. Retch cursed him every time he thought of him, which was every time he hauled water, every time he saw the grave.

He ridged above the basinland and eased the truck down the bajada, braking with the motor, the clutch slipping badly. From the outrun he coasted into the clearing of Rancho Anguamea where he stopped the truck beside a stocktank bought the summer before to cistern water.

The scrapdealer's claim that drillrigs and drillers abounded on the streets of Hermosillo proved an exaggeration. Retch found these machines and their operators to be as elusive as honest answers in a whorehouse.

He had begun his search at the Ministry of Hydraulic Resources where a clerk referred him to a perforator of local repute. Retch followed the lead, finding the man to be a jackleg waterpuncher who drove wellpoints into softsoil with a twenty-pound sledge. Next he consulted the cattle growers association. The president of the association informed him that the waterwells on the oldest ranches of eastern Sonora had been drilled by a man known as El Güero—so called for his pale complexion and blond hair. Retch said he had heard of El Güero, heard, too, that he was dead. "Asi es," the president agreed. He explained that the new ranches in need of water hired Pozos Sonora for their drilling. This enterprise employed rigs capable of perforating the rock substrate that made up much of the state.

Retch visited Pozos Sonora. The owner, a youthful man with no dirt under his fingernails, not a driller but the son of one, told Retch that the charge to survey a prospective wellsite was six thousand pesos.

Retch stared. That was more than he had paid for the Fargo.

The owner informed Retch that he would charge twenty thousand pesos to transport a rig to La Fortuna, plus two thousand pesos per meter of borehole cased and another thousand pesos per hour to develop the well, should that be necessary.

Retch laughed. "I'm not a rich gringo," he said. "Or a fool."

The owner smiled. He said in Mexico poor fools outnumbered rich ones, which was why the terms he offered were not negotiable. He said an advance was required, 50 percent the standard arrangement. He added that finding freshwater was not guaranteed, dry holes being common.

Retch stood. He told the owner that he would haul his water for now, but the day he found the buried silver of a dead hacendado, he would return to pay the advance, though the finding of such treasure was not guaranteed, such luck uncommon.

That afternoon he went to the local newspaper where he placed an ad for a drillrig and an operator. Pago en Efectivo. Estancia Garantizada. Ocurre Retch Barter. He designated the Hotel Posada in La Fortuna as his domicile. The same for messages.

. . .

Two months passed before he wrote Tex Hinton care of the University of Oklahoma. A former drinking buddy, Tex had worked as a leadhand on Gulfcoast oil platforms. Now he was a geologist, a professor, and a drip-dry Baptist. In his letter, which included a map to the ranch, Retch asked for the name of a welldriller willing to come to Mexico with his rig. Six weeks later a postcard arrived at the Hotel Posada. The card with Tex's phone number. "Call me," he wrote.

Wailing vocals and the cataracts of accordion poured from a cantina adjacent to the public callbooth where Retch dialed on a rotary phone. Over line static the two men caught up.

Tex said, "I hear music."

"There's a cantina nextdoor."

"Sounds like you're in it."

"Not yet."

"Seeing is believing. I'll have to visit."

"Do that," Retch said. "Bring Rose. She'd love it." Rose was Tex's wife.

"Hell no!"

Retch laughed. "So what have you got?"

"Good news. I got you a driller. I don't know him personally. His name is Peterson. Bill Peterson. His rig is in West Texas. I told him what you wanted and he said, 'No sweat.'"

"Did he say how much?"

"Eighty a foot, bored and cased. You supply the pipe and fuel."

Retch did the math. "Sounds reasonable."

"You might have to help him, be his mudman."

"No problem."

"He'll need advances. Going-to-town money or whatever."

"Not much to go to."

"I'm hearing different on this end. Is that polka music?"

"Yeah."

"Do they still dance the polka in Old Mexico?"

"I wouldn't know. Is the man coming to dance or drill?"

Tex Hinton cackled. "Well, I imagine he has expenses. Maybe you can feed him. Keep him close that way."

"Okay."

"I haven't met the man, like I said, but sinking holes in the West Texas Estacado means he can sink one anywhere."

"When can he start?"

"In however long it takes him to get there. So he said."

"Give him the go, Tex."

"Okay. Will he need this map?"

"Yeah. Tell him to take the road to Rancho Anguamea."

"Anguamea? Is that your place?"

"Sort of."

"I'll come when you get water."

"Do that, Professor. It's a snowball's throw from damnation."

Tex laughed. "Finally settling down, are we?"

"Sort of."

Eight months gone and Bill Peterson hadn't appeared. When Retch phoned Tex for news, his friend offered replies of increasing perplexity. "I sent him the map." Then, "He must be on the road." Most recently, "Hell if I know, Retch . . ."

Retch figured the Fargo had hauled two hundred drums of water since his last call to Tex Hinton.

* * *

The boy came first, followed by the dog, a short-eared mongrel that had followed the truck from town the year before. Retch had let her stay, hoping she would ward off coyotes and warn of strangers. The dog yet to bark.

Epifanio ran naked to the truck. "¡Papi!" he screeched.

Retch climbed onto the truckbed and siphoned the drummed water into the cistern. Radio music blared from the kitchen. The woman called the boy to eat.

"No!" he shot back before he sat under the truck's dripping tailgate.

The smell of burnt asbestos rose from the Fargo's clutch. Retch stared at the anemic land. When he looked down, the boy threw mud at the dog.

The woman shouted from the doorway. "¡Niño, que te vengas a comer!" The boy jumped up, slamming his head on the tailgate. Retch heard the thump, the howl. He watched the woman give chase, their stubbornness played out in the clearing. The boy as hardheaded as the mother. The mother as hardheaded as the old man who had squatted the thirsted ranch.

"Hay comida," she said as she passed him, the crying boy slung over her shoulder.

Retch lifted the siphon hose. "Dámelo," he called.

She returned and raised the boy for him to take. Retch held him over a drum of water before dropping him, his cry drowned. When the red head popped up, Retch dunked him again, the boy with screams of joy.

He watched them retreat.

After the cistern filled, he siphoned the remaining drums into empties rowed beside the kitchen. At the corral he drained the water from the baptized boy into the trough. When he restarted the Fargo, a calamitous metallic clang rose from the clutch. Retch got down and stared at the truck.

In the kitchen he silenced the radio. "Voy a Hermosillo," he said.

She stood at the brazier. The boy slept on the floor. "Trae la estufa," she replied, a reminder of promises unkept from his other trips to Hermosillo.

"You'll get your stove soon enough, Dolores. I've got a broken clutch." He had observed it recently, her willingness to assert. "You want a clothes dryer, too?"

"Bien."

He shook his head. "Of course. I'll bring the electric poles."

A month after his arrival, he had bought an absorption refrigerator and a set of kitchen chairs. The chairs with seat bottoms of weaved tule. The fridge with dual jets to burn kerosene. On subsequent trips he had bought a metal wallpantry, kitchen utensils, ceramic dishes, and castiron cookware. He had purchased mattresses and pinewood bedframes as well as a liquid-fueled lantern and a barrel chair made from pigskin leather stitched to cedar slats with red osier withes. Retch had imagined himself seated in the shade of a porch he intended to build on a new ranchhouse.

He ate. She stirred the coals with a firehook.

"How about this," he said. "First the old man. Then the stove."

The woman silent.

"I'll do it when I get back. Dig him up and haul him off."

Her ribboned scar darkened. "Te lo dije," she warned.

"Promises, woman. Yet there he lies waiting on a shovel."

When he had first mentioned exhuming the old miner, she had spat at his feet. "Pura madre lo saca de ahí," she had hissed. Expecting the driller Peterson to arrive, he had told her that a rotting body could not stay in the ground to spoil pricey, machine-drilled water. "¡Déjamelo a mí!" she had replied, as though she knew the days for the driller to arrive were many.

"You will dig him up?" Retch had asked.

"Sí."

"Rebury him?"

"Sí."

"Onward, girl!"

But she had done nothing. Weeks turned to months.

Retch finished his plate, lit a cigarette. He intended to be rid of the remains no matter what the woman said. The stove but strategy.

"How badly do you want gas cooking, sweetheart?"

She stood at the brazier.

"Enough to smell the old goat when I dig him up?"

With the firehook she stirred the coals.

"Come. Say you want it. Open that pretty mouth."

She glanced at the sleeping boy.

"What's to be afraid of? He won't cut you again."

She spun and brandished the firehook in his face. "¡Chinga tu madre!"

Retch smiled. "She speaks!"

"¡Déjamelo a mí!" she said. Then she lifted the boy and carried him from the kitchen.

Retch stubbed his cigarette. He called out, "Water's coming, honey."

* * *

She laid the boy on the bed. Good, she thought. Let him fix the worthless truck. Soon it would break again. Water its ruin. And his.

A year now waiting for the burned land to consume his folly. She cooked. She rode him. She took what he brought. She stole what she could. At the beginning she had half expected the bald maniac to show up. Or the police. When neither appeared, she knew he wasn't leaving until he gave up on the well. His delusion large. His plans futured for her to hear. How they would prosper on watered land. The gramineous hectares. The herds of cattle.

But no driller came, the man becoming like his truck: worn, dirted, broken. At night she added unflagging fornication to his bones. Drain him, her plan. Suck his marrow and pockets. Each week of water hauled a week that withered him. Months now since the boy had started calling him "papi," red hair their only likeness, the end of this journey begun. The day the thirsted land swallowed the last of his money, no choice would be left to him but to take them off the ranch. The man without balls to abandon a boy who called him father.

More than before he slouched at the kitchen table, the sickness clung, the bad seeds boweled. Of late she purposely burned his food—a new dagger in his gut. Now the stove thrown in to weigh on him. How better to burden his load than to nag him for another convenience from town.

She stood by the window and eyed the old miner's gravemound. Leave it to me, she had said after he spoke of exhuming the bones. On and on the gringo fool went about sparing the land, its sacred water, as though he knew the curse if not the secret. Soon she would see it done.

Retch had moved into the miner's room in accordance with unspoken hominal rites. Gone the old man's bed, his clothes, burned by the woman. At night she came to him with her woodsmoke smell, her safflower taste of cooking oil. Retch right with the choice, biding the driller's arrival.

His first business had been to carry off the trashpiles and liquor bottles. Next he had pounded out the mudbricks to make windows, framing and screening them. He had poured concrete floors. He had hung staveclad doors. With a tarred pole-swab he had sealed the rooftin and then he had dug a pit latrine. He had constructed a plywood showerstall with a pullchain valve, the discharge fed from an elevated drum. He had bought two dozen Creole pullets. A coop framed. Nest boxes built. With the old man's mattock he had turned the ground to plant pinto beans.

Then one evening he fell ill in a new way. Vomiting. A bloody bowel discharge. Chills and a breakbone fever. He suspected bad water. A week he lay in a febrile stupor, lifting himself to void into a five-gallon pail. On the fifth day he swallowed the last of the enterovioform bought by Dig in an Obregón pharmacy, dirty yellow tablets traveled beyond the sell date. Retch reckoned his chances of climbing into the Fargo and driving to a doctor in La Fortuna the same as crawling there. He kept to the floor in a fitful gray-out, plagued by delusions of a faceless woman standing over him winding his viscera onto a winching spool. Sometimes he heard an inquisitive presence in the room. When he opened his eyes, he saw no one.

Later he drank boiling tea brought by the woman. He vomited, then slept, waking again in a fierce sweaty panic, his thirst large. He drank water from the bule and slept again, each day outlasted. By the seventh morning he slept more than he retched.

When Dolores saw how far she had sickened him—wanting to empower herself but not kill him—she boiled tea from dried manzanilla flowers and muicle leaves, herbs stored in jars that sat beside the ones holding the toloache and coyotillo seeds she had mashed with his beans.

While he slept, she rummaged his room, looking for the leather purse not seen since the man had bought the truck. The purse etched with gallos. She searched his clothes, finding loose change, packaged condoms, a pocketknife. His wallet with small bills. His knapsack with workclothes. The jeweled watch still strapped to his wrist. Inside a pair of vaquero boots she found two bottles of liquor but no purse.

At the bottom of a pail under a jacket, she uncovered the pocket pistol and the box of bullets. The pail with a smokey smell. When she took the gun, her finger kept far from the trigger, her breath held. A new feel the coldsteel grip of what killed a man by making a hole. She counted six shells in the wheel.

"No tan pendejo," she told him as he lay sick in the room. Then she returned the gun to the pail. No longer did she look for his money.

To remove the Fargo's clutch, Retch reassembled the tripod from the wellpurging. With the winch he lifted the flathead motor and separated the clutch assembly from the flywheel. He found the plates worn to the rivets, the chattersprings broken, the release fingers gone, a perfect mess of a clutch that could have left an unluckier man on the road. He tied the parts in a seedbag, fitting it into the knapsack. Then he filled his jug thermos from the cántaro. He told the woman he would return no sooner than three days. "Water the beans," he said before he walked onto the hurling land.

The doctor he had seen in La Fortuna examined him in the back bedroom of his house. Retch lay on the cot looking at a Virgin of Guadalupe wallcalendar two decades old. A short man with raccoon eyes and garlic breath, the doctor listened to his chest before peering into his mouth with a flashlight. When Retch described his symptoms—diminished appetite, exaggerated thirst, sudden feverish sweats—the doctor asked if he had been bitten by a dog. Retch said when he was ten. "¿Y los moscos?" the doctor asked. Retch said no mosquitos lived where he lived. The doctor inquired if he drank cold liquids instead of ones at room temperature. He asked Retch if he washed his hands after manual labor or waited for them to cool first. Retch said the colder the quicker, the quicker the better, except for women. And what water did he drink? the doctor asked. Townwater, Retch replied.

Now as he climbed onto the rimland with the clutch parts, Retch recalled the doctor's diagnosis. Bile sickness. Desert rheumatism. The doctor had told him to abstain from digging in the dirt, especially alkaline dirt, of which there was considerable in the region. He had told Retch to avoid ice.

Retch knelt in the shade and drank from the thermos, an aluminum-bottomed jug with a button spigot and a bail.

The water with ice. When he resumed the road, the sky cloudless, the sun high. Before him the untenanted surmise of desert shimmered under a large and unfocused radiance as though mirrored by an ethereal form of itself.

The farthest he had walked until that morning was a nine-hour trek between thumb rides west of Holbrook, Arizona. Three hours he had watched traffic speed past his felonious aspect before he had begun to walk. Six hours later, within sight of Winslow, the rideless drought made sense. Before him the sign read: STATE PRISON—DO NOT STOP FOR HITCHHIKERS. He had leaned on the signpost and stuck out his thumb, baring his teeth in a maniacal grin. "Not this prison!" he had shouted as drivers sped past.

Water sloshed in the thermos. Retch kept to the road, thirst endured, his mind on the brandy back at the ranch. There's the cure, he thought. Get drunk. Purge the mal. Restore old chemistry. When the doctor had asked about dog bites, Retch hadn't mentioned the hooch-hound that had nipped at his heels years before, the little doggie in the bottle that had chased him from job to job back when he pissed away work as often as he pissed in public.

His youth largely blurred by drink. The days with painted houses, bused dishes. The nights not long enough to dry his liquored mind. Only a few memories saved. The howl of wolves in a pulpwood camp. Puking his guts on a scallopboat. Such was his marathon inebriation that twenty years passed in the surly anonymity of a sober self, his liver doing laundry while the rest of him darkened in a slow quotidian eclipse. Then one night, blind drunk behind the wheel, he ran down a woman in a crosswalk. White uniform, dark face, her shoes taking flight. Suddenly she lay splayed on the pavement and he was speeding away, his shriek torn from a fiery place. Nineteen-year-old nursing student pronounced dead at the scene. Local Indian community mourns. Only daughter of . . . So wrote the papers. Driver sought. Another fatal hit and run. And run.

Stunned sober, gutted by panic, he drove through dawn to another city, the windows down, clear calculation streaming in with the cold morning air. He ran the car through an autowash before leaving it in airport parking, returning in one week to drive it out, pay the metered ticket, and drive it in again, parking in a different spot. A month later he sold the car off the street to a Mexican who saw the sale sign on the windshield, their transaction completed in Spartan English. Cash dolar? Ok. Retch used the money to purchase a three-week bartending course, learning to mix drinks from bottles filled with colored waters. Keep it close, he decided. Salaried sobriety the safest path to a slow return. No better prophylactic for drunkenness than to bear abstemious witness to the outrageous lunacies of other drunks.

Of the young woman killed, no news reached him. No longer did he read the papers. She was dead. He had lived. Death and deliverance saving some other who would have crossed his path. His father had taught him well not to cry, and he soon forgot the woman's name. No nightmares woke him.

He bused to the darkside of a westcoast city, finding barkeep work in an all-night dive, meeting Digger, a green-eyed replica of his once future self—the Retch whose liquor-stoked train continued to hurtle ahead. Dig the only person with whom Retch shared his secret. In doing so, Retch found that he was able to drink again. Drink and not get drunk with craziness. As though sharing with the monster-to-be freed him from the one left behind.

. . .

He climbed off the road and squatted under a guamúchil tree. Beneath the tree fallen fruitpods. Retch plucked the flesh from the ripest, savoring the tartness, spitting the black seeds. He threw the empty pods into the scrub before he sipped from the thermos, weighing the water left. When he stood, he kicked dirt over the spat seeds.

On the backside of the guamúchil, he pulled a hooked branch from the hollow that extended into the trunk. With the hook he reached into the cavity and lifted a plastic bag. He removed a leather purse from the bag, opening a zippered pocket thick with Dig's drugdollars turned to pesos at a Tijuana changehouse. The purse secreted in the tree after the woman had begun to pilfer money from his pantspockets, thieving like a rodent come in the night.

He counted out pesos to buy clutch parts, pay travel expenses. After pocketing the cash he counted the remainder. Bill Peterson better show up, he thought. Some driller. This bank not bottomless.

He zippered the purse, bagged it, and returned it to the hollow, using the branch to snug it inside. He scuffed his prints as he retreated, cutting a new direction to retake the road.

After leaving Digger he had driven to the scrapdealer's yard to sell the Willys. Retch reckoned that a man who traded in metals of dubious provenance would be willing to blindeye matters of prior ownership.

Rolando Arenas declared himself too poor to buy a fancy yellow truck. His cash, he lamented, was bound in scrap and whores. He looked apologetic before telling Retch that he could recommend a buyer for the Willys. "I will take you," he said, "as a favor." Then he made an offer on the Daxara.

Retch recognized the shrewdness of a bandit who bartered. The dealer's oldboy affability and breezy collaboration dissembled a ruthless mercantile opportunism. His yard crammed with the wealth of what others filched or discarded. A deal was struck for the Daxara, Retch wanting to be rid of it. Inside the trailer Rolando observed the goldpanner. "¿Lavando oro, eh?"

Washed a lot of rock, Retch admitted, but not much gold. When Rolando asked about Retch's friend, the bald gringo seen chasing whores in the town brothel, Retch said their prospecting partnership had dissolved, his friend departed, each man taking his share.

On their drive to see the buyer, Retch told the dealer his plan to take townwater to Rancho Anguamea where he had found the woman and boy. He spoke of his intention to purge their ruined noria and to deepen it until good water was found. He said he would need steel drums and a tripod for the job.

"Qué bueno," remarked the dealer, making no sense of the project. Something done for strangers? Done for free? "¿Una buena obra, entonces?"

"Un favor," Retch corrected. A good deed what good men did, he said.

"Ah." Rolando smiled. He offered his services. His yard was wellstocked, his truck available. "I am at your orders, friend."

Retch thanked him. He said he would need transport to the ranch once the Willys sold.

They washed the truck at a ramp-lave before driving to the edge of town. On a street paved with crushed tezontle, they stopped outside a highwalled residence with a tiled roofline. Concertina wire topped the wall.

The dealer stated their business to a guard at the gated entrance. The guard spoke to two sandaled men playing dominoes nearby. Retch and Rolando were asked to step down from the Willys. The sandaled pair emerged, one of them dropping to the paved drive to examine the truck's undercarriage while the other searched the interior—Retch presumed—for weapons of the kind that showed from under their untucked shirtfronts.

Inside the compound the visitors were instructed to wait behind the truck. Retch counted nine vehicles parked in the porticoed entrance, none yellow. He heard the shouts of children playing.

The young man who met them had a hard, boyish face. Wearing shorts and a baseball cap, he might have stepped away from a backyard barbeque. He took their hands without interest, asked how much, and then agreed with a nod before he was gone. Within minutes another man—el licenciado, the dealer called him—appeared in buffed vaqueros to pay Retch out of a selvedged pocket. He instructed the sandaled pair to drive the sellers to their destination.

Back at the yard, Retch asked nothing about the buyer, his business. A truck bought with dirty money had sold for the same. All he needed to know.

Rolando loaded empty water drums onto his truck. "Call him one of the fortunate of La Fortuna," he said of the young buyer, his own luck considered in this assessment. Hauling townwater for a gringo—as a favor to a woman— made him fortunate, too.

. . .

Retch walked. What passed unnoticed from a truck ambushed him on foot. Cat tracks. The chamiza soapsmell. A scattering of roadside bones, their cortical apatite bleached by the sun. Retch recalled the story of a mojado picker whose skeletal frame had defied such dispersal. A dark-skinned man with a heatshriveled voice, he had crossed the desert, abandoned by his guide, scourged by the sun, stumbling ahead without water. Retch remembered how the picker had described his demise. Blood vomit. Black urine. Craziness that turned dirt to water. When Retch asked the man if he had seen death close enough to embrace it, he said he had seen the face of a longdead brother smiling at him. He said what had worried him was not death, death but a moment. What had worried him was the fate of his remains, that they endure unburied under the annihilating sky. To be interred, he said, even in godforgotten ground, was every man's due.

Retch gazed at the roadside bones. He thought of Digger and how he had been given his due. How hard the godforgotten ground.

With the gorilla bar Retch had loosened the calcrete ouklip solid as cement. He had chiseled the hardpan layer until it broke, excavating the sandy subsoil with a shovel. For Digger no shallow grave of the crimenews kind but a crude oblong hole trenched deep to the shoulders. After three hours' digging, Retch's blood-blistered hands too slippery to grip the shovel—true to the saying that a gravedigger's spade turns red. Late afternoon when the hole was dug, the distant cordillera shadowed in its folds, the sun ginning spectral threads of crimson and gold. On Retch's wrist the deadman's watch. On his belt the leather purse. Dig's shitcaked pants emptied of loose change, a pack of cigarettes, a pocketknife. Shaken from Dig's boot a condom in its yellow wrapper.

He kicked in the boots before he rolled the body, Dig landing face-up, green eyes with a look of surprise, lips rucked in a strange curve—Dig in death searching for a drink. Retch reminded of a ranch wake attended the month before where mourners had poured bottled whiskey over the casket, dousing the acrylic pane above the man's head, the whiskey seeping past the seal to drip onto the dead man's lips. The deceased a shadetree mechanic who had died drunk, crushed when the Willys had slipped off its screwjack, the man making repairs beneath it. Though strangers to the family, Dig and he had attended the man's deathwatch as the consolatory spectators of his last moments, and they had borne witness to his sepulture.

Retch stood over Digger, witness anew to death and interment. "Bottoms up, bud," he said, draining the bottle of Moctezuma White on the rucked lips. He dropped the bottle into the hole and pushed the excavated soil with his boots, sparing his blistered hands. His thoughts not on dirt but water—finding enough to drink. The bule empty. The jerrycans filled with salted wellwater from the woman's noria. How this end began.

He backed the Willys across the grave, tracking both wheels until he felt no hump, no trough. Then he drove to where he had unhitched the Daxara. From there he took a route different than the one that had brought him, traceless on the weathered waste.

The thermos empty, caliche dirt underfoot when he heard the engine whine. He looked back to see a dustcloaked vehicle turn onto the road. As it sped past him, Retch glimpsed a short wheelbase, a blur of yellow. Men with guns held to the Willys rollbar.

Retch waited for the dust to settle. *Damn small desert.*

He stopped next before the town brothel. In the graveled parking lot Retch spotted the scrapdealer's truck, it's bed loaded with rusted waterpipe. "Now there's a piece of luck." He hadn't seen Rolando in months, but he was glad to see his truck. He slid off the satchel and set it in the truckbed. Busted clutch. Rusted pipe. Saturday night at a whorehouse. Life was good for the king of scrap.

Inside the bar a smell old to Retch, the air hazed with cigarette smoke. He found the dealer whore-clung in a booth. Rolando lifted his beer. "Canelo!" he greeted.

Retch sat. Beside him a whore slid into the booth. Pimple-faced, her red dress shimmering, she put her hand on his leg. Retch asked the barman for water.

"Water with what?" the barman replied.

"Ice," Retch answered, handing him the thermos.

Rolando laughed. Retch explained the broken clutch, his walk from the ranch, how he had spotted the truck. He said nothing about hiring the dealer to take him to Hermosillo.

"Pinche cloch," Rolando commiserated.

"Yes, a good for nothing clutch," Retch agreed, taking in the room.

The barman returned with the thermos and a shooter glass. Retch raised the diminutive glass, too thirsty to call the barman back. He put the thermos spigot in his mouth, the water cool, tasting of lead pipes. The pimple-faced whore wiped the trickle from his chin. Retch warned her not to touch him again. She moved closer. She desired him, she said, her breath clung with semen. She desired him now. Retch said his only desire was for her to leave.

"Dos," ordered Rolando, tabling an empty beer. His whore lifted the bottle for the barman to see, signaling two fingers.

Retch owned a pair of shoes older than the dealer's whore, a girl young enough to be his granddaughter. Someone's granddaughter. The barman brought two beers. Rolando allowed the girl whore to pay with money pulled from his shirtpocket, the man of hardmetals showing himself pliant. Retch tossed the empty shooter onto the barman's tray, telling him that only an imbecile would bring such a glass to a thirsty man. The dealer handed Retch a beer. He raised his own. "Mi canelo."

"Mi amigo." Retch drank quickly, not tasting it. He ordered the next round. When Rolando followed the girl to a room, Retch told the pimple-faced whore to leave.

"Cincuenta pesos," she offered, a fire-sale price.

He shoved her from the booth, the whore grabbing the table to keep from falling. "Pinche maricón," she teethed, off with disheveled dignity.

Retch set the thermos on the seat. Not after a twelve-hour hike would he abide the likes of one he had left at the ranch that morning.

He held to the beer's bottled iciness, careful not to stare. His gaze measured as he surveyed the room, not seeing her. He ordered porkrinds laid on a plate with sliced limes. The beer risen to his head from an empty stomach. He looked at his watch. No desire to hoof clutch parts to the hotel at this hour. However long it takes, he decided. He tried to shake any imagining of Rolando's ruststained hands on prepubescent nakedness.

Later he spotted her sitting alongside another, her face thinner but her hand pushing her hair back just so. As she had done with Digger.

He rose, taking his beer, the thermos. At a nearby table he waited. Then she stood before him. Retch kicked out a chair.

She smirked, sat. She asked for Dig.

A year passed, the intervening nights of what she did. His name come first. "Se fue," Retch said.

"¿Se fue?"

"Sí, se fue."

"¿Dónde?"

Retch shrugged. Dig's whereabouts unknown to him, he replied.

"You wear his watch," she said, pointing to his wrist.

Retch kept his eyes on her. "He gave it to me."

She smiled a smile that said men's lies meant nothing here, even truth a lie. Her lovely iodine skin what made Retch ache. How wholesomeness hung by a thread. At the beginning he had pursued her. Then she had chosen Dig. In succeeding visits he had kept her for himself, teasing Retch with details, telling him she never charged, claiming to know her Christian name. Now Digger gone, taking the name but leaving the whore.

Retch reached into his pocket. He asked how much.

"I will go with your fat friend before I go with you," she said.

"Mil pesos," Retch offered.

Her head said no.

"Dos mil."

Silence.

"Tres." More cash than he carried, but he wanted to tempt her where it hurt. When she started to rise, Retch dropped it on her cold as a corpse. "Está muerto," he said.

Her face gave away nothing, the bitch within steeling the bitch without. "Deader than you?" she scoffed.

Retch said that though he might be dead to the cold-blooded charms of a whore such as she, he was not as dead as Dig, who most certainly rotted.

She rose. "¡Chinga tu madre!"

Retch smiled. "Cinco," he said, removing the wadded bills from his pocket, holding them out for her to take. Digger's money to Digger's whore.

After she retreated, he pocketed the wad and swallowed the rest of his beer. His evening made, the wait worth waiting. He had owed it to Dig.

When the dealer reappeared, he looked smaller, shriveled, the spryness sucked from his gait. "Vamos," he croaked to Retch.

Dolores waited out the dayheated interval before she fetched the mattock and shovel. Rimland shadows stretched across the clearing when she stood over the old miner's grave.

She had buried him with the same mattock and shovel, tools bought by him and bound to his interment. No barrow then to haul off a body. Instead a length of braided ixtle used to drag him behind the latrine. Three days to dig the hole, taking breaks to milk the goats and nurse the boy, her hands blistered and bleeding. Behind the latrine flies swarmed. A blue tongue protruded from the miner's mouth. When she towed him to the hole, the grotesque tuber between his legs burst from his pants. At the grave she aligned him beside the slotted ground. His eyes agaze at the world departed, his brain blossomed from a smashed skull. With the pick mattock she pried him into the hole, the ixtle left tied to his legs. She spat on him before she pushed in the gravedirt. The hole half filled, the soil tamped. So the layers added, the earth mounded.

Now as she disinterred him, Epifanio watched. "¿Hoyo, mamá?"

"Vete," she said, sending him to play with the mongrel dog. Later she carried him to the kitchen. She washed and fed him before she lay with him until he slept. When she returned to the grave, the land dusked, the night not to be wasted. No sooner than three days, the gringo had said of his return.

She dug in the dark and later she dug under the risen moon, its liquid light. Crouched on the gravedirt the dog sniffed the taphonomic reek. The hole deep to her shoulders before the shovel skidded on his bones, the putrescent smell close. She climbed out and went to the kitchen where she lit the lamp and checked the boy. A dishtowel found to tie around her neck. From the gringo's truck she took work-gloves, rope. From the latrine a wastepail. At the grave she tossed the pail into the hole and knotted one end of the rope to the lamp bail, lowering the lantern into the grave. His bones scraped clean where the shovel had skidded. The ixtle still bound to his legs. She tied the rope to the barrow to suspend the lamp above the hole and then she masked her face with the dishtowel before she descended to dig again.

His corpse not something raw, rather the dry turd of a man raised in rude relief. Flesh gone, the miner mined, his bones bedded on a waxlike layer yellowish in the lamplight.

With the shovel she chopped the sinews that wired him. His cranium a small skull befitting mean-mindedness but not malice so largely lived. She stared at it. The frontal bone cratered where eight pounds of a flathead sledge had struck the skull. So she had swung it to end his miserable life, the impact breaking the hammer's handle. Later the sledge tossed into the noria. There it lay until the gringo had pumped the well dry and used the sledge to pound the same rock pounded by the old miner. So passed the tools of man's unmaking from hand to hand.

Let him dig now. The fool.

With the mattock she shattered the skullbowl, his brittle pottery. The shards shoveled into the pail, evidentiary of nothing. Then more of him. The bone bucket raised, its contents dumped into the wheelbarrow before she descended again. The sound of her breathing loud to her. The night otherwise silent. So the old man quarried in three bucketfuls. With gloved hands she loosely roped the ribbed vertebral column, a piece too large for the bucket. She dropped it atop the other bones, cutting the rope with the shovel tip, leaving the gloves in the barrow. When she returned to the rooms, the dog lay with the boy.

She pushed the barrow into concessionland, the moon large above her, the desert white, the old man's oleaginous shards wheeled on a squeaky axle. She pushed quickly, her serpentine trail weaved through thornscrub. The smell of chamiza strong, the howls of cóyotls distant. When she looked back, the dog trotted behind her.

Not her first run into concessionland. Other nights she had come, heavy with the unborn boy, fleeing the old man whose bones she propelled. His drunken rage. His broken bottle brandishing. "Ven mi Paloma Negra," he had taunted.

To escape him, she had weaved through the thornscrub as she did now, the old man falling behind, dizzied by the sinuous chase. Then one night, sobered by scalding water thrown at him, he had outwaited her return, hiding in the scrub near the ranch, ambushing her with his machete. His rabid swing meant to sever her head, the blade gashing her face instead. Avoiding a second thrust at her belly, she had retreated into the concessionland where she had waited out the night.

So she had come to know it.

The cóyotls alerted by the squeaky axle. She saw their gray backs frosted white as they raced toward her across the moonscaped basin. She tipped the barrow, spilling the miner's spine. She pushed ahead and when she stopped, the thornscrub with dogs.

They stood with jaws hung in silent pants. Their leanfaced snouts scenting the air. The ones nearest moved to flank her. Others crouched. The mongrel dog appeared at her side, teeth bared, ears laid back. She growled but did not bark.

Dolores started the barrow toward them. She shouted. The cóyotls jumped, recoiled. She grabbed the handles from behind, retracing her path, tipping the barrow from side to side as she hastened, spilling the bones, the gloves. She saw the mongrel dart ahead, then disappear into the scrub.

After the barrow emptied, the sound of dog fights behind her. Minutes before she stopped to catch her breath. Near the ranch she heard the boy's cry. She dropped the barrow and ran. In the clearing she saw the mongrel atop the gravedirt looking into the hole.

Three hours on the road to Hermosillo, the dealer's talk of whores and scrap. The day ablaze. A sky dried of azure.

Retch drank iced water from the thermos. He gazed out the window at the taciturn land conversant with its own mystery.

Rolando said what a shame El Güero wasn't around to sink his well. "That one could drill."

Retch silent. Yes, a shame, he thought, considering El Güero was dead.

"A bad break for you, my friend," Rolando added.

Retch tipped the thermos to drink. Apparent how the dealer saw him. A luckless fool with a broken truck living on a thirsted ranch. Retch spat out the window. "Actually I've got news," he said "A driller is coming."

Rolando showed surprise. "¿De veras?"

"The truth," Retch replied. True as hell. Hired and on his way to the ranch as they spoke, driving from west Texas across the cordillera backbone.

"Qué bueno," the dealer said, adding that Retch had run into goodluck afterall. "Perforators are not found on every street corner, you know."

"Así es," Retch agreed. Drillers were hard men to hire, but thanks to an old friend he had succeeded. Retch said he planned to call his friend from Hermosillo to check on the driller's progress.

Rolando nodded. He said that in the event materials were needed—pipe, casing, anything—he was of service.

Retch savored the water's iciness. "Gracias," he said, the tedium of a long drive agreeably broken by sharping the sharpie. It mattered not where a driller came from, only that he come. The world to change when he did.

He stared out the window at the xeric scrubland, his thoughts turned to west Texas, one truth spoken. He would call Tex from Hermosillo. Call him on the chance there was news of the driller. This man Bill Peterson.

. . .

In Hermosillo the parts manager at the Dodge dealership said he no longer stocked the clutch for a Fargo truck, or any part for a Fargo truck since the days when Methuselah drove. "Buscan usado," he suggested. They searched the city for a used clutch, visiting repair shops and junkyards. One garage owner reported the known world of Fargo owners to be growing smaller by the hour, a man having come to him the day before, traveled from Tiburón Island, in search of a Fargo axle.

At the hotel Rolando lay on his bed drinking canned beer iced in the bathroom sink. He predicted the clutch would not be found in Hermosillo or anywhere in Sonora. Maybe in Chihuahua City, he said, where men drove relics, or in Cuauhtémoc among the Mennonites, who rode Farmall tractors to church. Retch reminded him that the Fargo had been bought from a Mennonite farmer. He said he planned to advertise for a junked Fargo in the local paper.

They ate tacos at a corner streetstand. Back in the room, Rolando finished the beer. The empty cans he carried to his truck, these to be added to the ones piled in his yard for sale to a crusher in Guaymas.

Retch stood before the bathroom mirror, surprised at how thin he looked. The reflected self honed by illness, bad cooking, and relentless copulation.

Damn, what a year does.

"Come, let's buy a bottle," suggested the dealer. "It's early."

Retch said he preferred to save his hangover for another day and thereby guarantee an early rise.

"There is good Bacanora here," Rolando insisted. "You will like it."

"Not as much as I once did," Retch replied. "You go if you want."

They lay on their beds without smalltalk, the dealer soon asleep, Retch awake with the clutch and the world without one. When he slept, he dreamed he was standing waistdeep in the darkwater of a mountain pool stone-bottomed and fed by a high cascading falls, the cataract crashing on him, washing from his nakedness bloodstains dried black.

The next morning at a boneyard off the Sahuaripa highway, they found a clutch with resurfaced plates and a relined disk, the seller asking scrap price. "Qué suerte," said the dealer, who saw in Retch's goodluck the seller's ignorance. They loaded the parts and drove to the citycenter where Retch bought a gasplate stove with enameled burners and porcelain valve handles. The stove used to boil water for washing napery and bedlinen in a local hotel.

Rolando nodded his approval. "Tired of a woodfire, is she?"

Retch said he was tired of burnt food.

He purchased a butane cylinder and connection hose for the stove. *That'll shut her up.* He planned to exhume the old man as soon as the truck repairs were completed.

At a Telmex callbooth he phoned Tex. He listened for the Hinton drawl, willing his friend to answer with news of the driller Peterson. No one picked up.

Damn it, Tex.

Back in the truck, Rolando said El Güero would have been the man for the job if he had been alive, which some say he was.

El Güero can go to the hell, Retch nearly said. Instead he asked to be driven to the newspaper office. At the classified desk he placed an ad for a drillrig and operator, the same ad placed on earlier trips.

In the truck Rolando slept.

The afternoon sun still high when they drove the flatlanded road west out of Hermosillo.

Her sandals fell from her feet as she leapt. She landed hard in the grave, a bone shard sinking into her heel. She lifted him, his nakedness, his screams, his swiveled arm. The dog sidled atop the gravemound, dislodging dirt into the hole. Dolores saw no way to ascend with the boy clinging to her. Then she saw the dog. She used her free hand to pull dirt into the grave, the dog watching. She stamped the dirt, added more, and when she stood waisthigh, she cajoled the boy to release her, setting him on the cleared spot. His screams turned to exhausted sobs when she carried him to the rooms.

Lanternlight revealed his body smeared with the waxy deathsoap. Two knobby burls grew where the forearm had broken. Fractured bones a recent sight to her, but still she gasped. "¡Dios mío!" She clothwashed him with pailed water and barsoap. The yellowish wax worried her as much as the arm. The accursed power it could possess, rendered from a wicked man. Under the lamp she examined his scrapes. When she asked him how he had fallen, he said he fell. Had he come to find her? He nodded, no words to explain how, asleep in the room, he had not walked to the hole but only dreamed of walking, beckoned there by a man's voice that called his name. Then his arm caught on fire. Then he awoke.

"Hoyo malo," he cried.

She wound a wet towel around the arm. Between the wrappings she laid a greenwood stick. An hour later the towel taut with the swelling, the splint bowed. She removed the wrapping and sponged the arm with cane vinegar before she applied árnica del monte, the boy protesting in a cryworn voice. In a pot she diluted molasses in water, boiling it with oregano, making a tea for the boy to drink, her mother's recipe to dull the pain. Nearby the dog cleaned herself.

So passed the remains of the night, the morning unrolling bright without clouds. To help the boy sleep, she decocted the broth of boiled yucca roots, stirring spoonfuls into a glass of goat's milk, making him drink it. His arm thick like a gourd, the redness run to the elbow. She covered his head to keep out the malignant aires, and when he slept at midday, she painted his scrapes with the Mercurochrome. At the grave she retrieved her sandals before backfilling the hole. Her cut heel throbbed. She mounded the dirt, leaving it untamped, satisfied with its lay. The rope she returned to the man's truck, the pail to the latrine. She was about to wash herself when the boy cried out, a wail shrill like his infant cries of thirst. She fed him tea. The swelling large above his wrist, the skin turned black where the bones parted. When he slept again, she bathed, exchanging the poblano dress for a grainsack shift. She roasted tlacámel leaves, squeezed the juice, boiled it, and poulticed the arm with the fibrous lamina. So the nighthours passed, the boy exhausted from his cries, the woman rendered deaf. At dawn she reckoned the hours until the man's return and whether the boy's arm would endure. A world hinged upon his acts. She scrubbed the barrow and wiped it dry before she lifted him from the bed, the boy weighing nothing. She laid him on a blanket in the barrow and rolled him off the ranch, taking water in a bule. The dog trotted behind them.

They came upon her at dusk. "¡Híjole!" blurted the dealer, first to see the boy in the wheelbarrow. Retch saw the woman limp.

Twelve hours trekked. Arroyo climb-outs. Steep descents. The boy grown heavy as cement. Twice she nearly dumped him. At every jolt he cried. Midday she rolled the barrow into the shade of a guamúchil tree, giving the boy pulp from the fruitpods. Her cut heel pulsed hotly. The dog circled the tree, sniffing the trunk. After they rested, she retook the road.

In the truck Retch cradled the boy. The swathed arm slung in his kerchief, the boy pale, groggy, almost voiceless. "Hoyo malo," he whispered. The woman silent after her brief account of events, two words. "Se cayó."

"Fell where?" Retch asked.

"The ground," she replied.

Rolando said the town doctor would fix him.

The dog left to follow or to return to the ranch. The wheelbarrow bounced in the truckbed. Nighted the hour they arrived at the streetfronted house, its only window stenciled with MEDICINA GENERAL. The light on.

"Hector, you raccoon," greeted the dealer. "We brought a broken boy."

The doctor remembered Retch from his visit the year before. Retch remembered the outdated wallcalendar.

Epifanio screamed when the swathe was removed, the woman holding him. An excellent counteractant, the doctor said of tlacámel leaves after he learned that she had poulticed the arm. He did not ask how the arm had broken. With the boy sedated, the doctor tied his elbow to the cot frame. He asked Retch to pull on the boy's hand with a slow but steady force. The hand small in Retch's, the first time held. The doctor aligned the bones, holding them in place as he wrapped the arm with a crepe bandage. He mixed gypsum plaster in a coffee can, submerging a second bandage in the slurry before winding it over the first. Then two more. He smoothed the plaster, sculpting the excess. He said the arm would mend straight, the cast to be removed in six weeks, the boy to be brought to him at that time. When he asked the woman why she limped, she said she had thorned her foot.

"May I see it?" the doctor asked.

She shook her head. "No es nada."

The doctor gave her an antiseptic cream. "Keep it clean," he said.

Dolores said nothing. This doctor the same doctor her mother had refused to visit, the one who had let his wife die of something he could cure.

The dealer drove them to the Hotel Posada, promising to return in the morning with the stove and wheelbarrow. "He's a good doctor," Rolando said. "Even if he buried two spouses, one my sister."

"He is your brother-in-law?" Retch asked.

"I think of him so," Rolando said. Then he asked Retch for an advance on his fee. "Not much," he said. "For drinks, a whore. Maybe just a whore."

That night Retch purchased beer and two orders of tostadas from a cenaduria. He brought the food to the woman's room. She took the plates at the door. The boy asleep.

"Knock if you have trouble," Retch said.

In his room he drank the beers. Later he slept and dreamed that he clung to a tree high among dead branches. Then he was falling, the ground turning to water as he hit, the water cold and sweet to drink.

At the ranch they unloaded the stove and carried it to the kitchen. Neither man observed the reworked gravemound, the dead buried to their eyes. Retch paid the dealer what was owed. Rolando wished him luck with his drilling.

That morning the boy came to where Retch worked beneath the Fargo. He pointed to the old man's grave. "Hoyo malo, papi."

"Hombre malo," Retch corrected.

The clutch installed before dark, the truck test driven. In the kitchen the boy said it again. "Hoyo malo, papi."

Retch shook his head. "Hombre malo."

"No," said the boy. "Hoyo malo."

Retch looked at the woman. "What damn hole?"

She said the boy had broken his arm after falling into the redug grave hole while she had disposed of the old man's bones. As promised.

Retch stared. "No time lost, woman." He asked how the boy was left to fall. Dolores said he awoke before she returned.

"At night?"

"Sí."

"How deep was the hole?"

"Suficiente."

Retch asked where the remains had been taken.

She pointed in a direction different from where they lay.

"Did you bury them? I don't want the coyotes baited."

She nodded.

Retch said it would be well to know the spot.

"No," she replied. "Es mi negocio."

"Your business was to water the beans, woman." Retch said he was glad not to have been born her father or die as such.

The woman silent.

"Go burn something. You got your miserable stove."

That night she dragged the brazier behind the kitchen. When the dog returned, she fed it beans warmed on the stove. A week passed before Dolores walked without a limp, her cut foot healed. The doctor's medicine she had thrown into the hotel trashcan, no reason to trust it.

On his next trip to La Fortuna, Retch stopped at the guamúchil tree. He stared at the sandal prints and wheelbarrow tracks in the dirt. "Shit!" he shouted. He inspected the hollow, finding the hooked branch as he had left it, the purse secreted, the money untouched. He counted it. So close to screwed, he realized. So close. Yet not screwed.

Damn blind of her.

With lengths of galvanized channel Retch hung a guttered roofdrain with downspouts and a barrel collector. When monsoon clouds rushed east to the cordillera, he watched the distant etching of mercurial drops. He smelled wet earth. Then the sky cleared, the ranch without rain.

A month passed. At the frontdesk of the Hotel Posada, no messages arrived for Retch. His calls to Tex Hinton went unanswered.

The coyotes descended in plainday to drag off the kid-goats, the dog not barking. Retch fetched the pistol, revealing it to the woman even as he suspected the sight of it not new to her prying eyes. He fired at the retreating pack, hitting distant dirt. Then he pointed the gun at the mongrel, asking what poor excuse of a dog didn't bark at coyotes. A week later Retch off trucking water when they returned to ambush the hens. The woman called in the dog. She watched from the doorway. Blood and feathers met Retch as he drove into the clearing. Hens roosted on the roof.

Late that afternoon he walked into the concessionland with pocketed ammunition, rope, and the spotlamp Dig had used to jacklight hares. Distant from the ranch, he found their run cut through a dry arroyo. He waited until dark, wishing the pistol had a longer barrel, hearing their yips before he saw them. When they halted in the washout, lifting their snouts, he hit them with the light, freezing the frontrunners. He fired, dropping two, hitting a third. He reloaded and shot the heads of the fallen dogs before he tracked the one that bled. The coyote found panting on its side. He shot it in the neck and looped the rope over its hindlegs. As he dragged it to the ranch, he lighted ahead, spotting desiccated bones and the remnants of a chewed glove not recognized as one of a pair belonging to him. At the ranch he took out his knife and slit the dog's ventral to the anus, the bitch fat with pups. He dragged the coyote into the clearing, its entrails spilled, its scent wetting the dirt. He circled the coop and corral before he left it at the fenceline, the mongrel watching. This remedy to daunt coyotes Retch had learned from a Gallup sheep rancher who festooned his barbedwire with carcasses of shotgunned coyotes.

Before his next trip to town, Retch penned the poultry.

As soon as the boy spotted the saw, he began to scream. The doctor shortened the retractable blade to the toe. He angled it before cutting a thin kerf in the cast. Retch held the boy to keep him from hitting the doctor.

The arm mended with a slight crook. Straight enough for life's hardknocks, the doctor predicted. He wrapped it in a bandage and told the woman to wash the arm daily before rewrapping it. He advised her to keep the boy off highplaces from which he might fall and rebreak the bone. When the doctor inquired about her foot, Dolores said the soreness was gone. Retch studied the old wallcalendar. One date circled.

That night a fullblown tromba dropped off the heat-stoked cordillera. A fast, dustchoked wind lifted the kitchen roof and knocked over the wallpantry with a crash of pans. The next morning Retch found the plywood showerstall flattened, the cactus still gone. Crumbled sheets of rooftin lay scattered across the clearing. In the kitchen the radio smashed.

On a roll, Retch told himself, the old miner still sucking luck from the land. He studied the repairs to be made, deciding to replace the kitchen roof with sawed joists and channeled asbestos sheeting.

Dolores saw the latest misfortune as a means to more quickly unhouse them. "Qué pendejo," she said when the man spoke of rebuilding the kitchen.

Retch told her to shut up.

She asked when the fool in him would see the ranch for what it was, salado—a place meant to bleed the lives of those who lived there.

Retch pulled the stringers from the collapsed roof. Cursed the ranch might be, he shot back, though she knew better than he why. A shame the old man was not here to ask.

Dolores smirked. She said he was a fool for waiting out the son of some fornicating driller who would never come.

"Ye bitch of little faith."

"Hablame en español," she said.

"Mujer de poca fé."

The only driller who would come, she said, was the thief of a scrapdealer—a man who drilled holes in gringo pockets.

Retch said he would let Rolando know her high opinion of him.

"Tell him," Dolores replied. "It matters not. What matters is no good will come to this place. It is not meant for water. It is meant to ruin lives."

"Careful with that tongue of yours, darling. Now that it's come loose, it might spill those pretty teeth." Then Retch told her a driller had been hired and was on his way.

The woman guffawed. "¡Cómo no!"

Retch said the day the ranch had drilled water, he would watch her choke on it. "Don't think I'm walking away. Not now."

She spat. "Is this driller coming by burro?" she asked. "Because if he is, please tell him to hurry. I do not want to die first."

Retch laughed, the woman not to be out-lied.

"Laugh," she said. "Your crazy bald friend laughed when he came, but is he laughing now?"

Retch clung to a smile. "Are you threatening me, woman?"

She shrugged. "You have the gun. I have but a boy."

He watched her walk away before he resumed pulling poles and twisted tin from the collapsed roof. He threw the smashed radio into the scrub. "Finally, some quiet!"

The next day he purchased pine joists and asbestos roofing. As he worked rebuilding the kitchen, he sipped the

Madera brandy, a bottle pulled from his boot. He called to the woman. "Nothing wrong with this kitchen. Just like town."

The boy stood beside him, watching.

"Tell your mother she's a bitch. Dile a tu madre. A bitch."

"Beetch?" the boy repeated.

The Madera's taste sharp as glass. Already the woman had called him a drunk. Retch replied that he was distant from those shores, but she would be the first to know when he sailed.

No more calls to Tex, he decided. No more newspaper ads. He would travel to Chihuahua to find a driller. Juárez. El Paso. West Texas, if necessary.

"Mommy a bitch. Dile."

"Mami Beetch."

"You'll go far with women, lad."

Retch took another drink, the brandy tasting better.

The Devil Be Not Drowned in His House

In Magdalena de Kino, at a highway eatery known as El Árbol Caído, Driller ordered a plate of yearling lamb. He ordered tripe, brains, and moronga. The lamb wrapped in maguey leaves and buried in a burned-rock midden dug in the stump of a fallen strangler fig.

Driller sucked the marrow from the yearling bones, wiping what dripped from his mouth with a folded tortilla. He had stood beneath the strangler tree in the years when it had shaded the eatery, then named El Macapule, and he had warned the owner that figs of this species attracted fulgurous groundings that made their sap vaporize and explode. So it had come to pass. Within days of Driller's departure, lightning had struck the fig. Later the tree was felled, the trunk too large to move, the eatery renamed.

When Driller finished his plate, he asked the server boy if any forked branches remained from the tree. The boy returned with a pronged stick used by the pitman for fire tending. Driller inspected it to ascertain that its wood had come from the fallen tree. Then he tipped the boy and paid for the meal, leaving with a toothpick clamped between his large teeth.

At the crypt of Eusebio Kino, he stopped to view the priest's unearthed remains. Driller recognized the deformed gabbro in the excavated tomb as burial dirt daylighted twice. Catholic peregrines from Colima prayed before the relics. When their devotions ended, Driller told them that he had known Chevo Kino as a padre who had fathered many mestizos with Pima women. Children of a holy man, he said, whose descendants had paid for his rampant fornication with blood spilt on the desertfloor by the massacring Seri. Driller said that if holy bones unearthed were to be venerated, then the bones of these, too, should be made relics, being of Kino's blood.

The pilgrims crossed themselves and departed in tight formation, leaving the stranger to solitary communion with the sacred remains. Driller waited for them to leave before he flicked his toothpick into the tomb.

He drove south, routing through Opata territory, past Querobabi and Carbó, refueling in Pesqueira, known to Driller as Mátape. At a corner grocery he purchased cigarettes and a package of double-edged razorblades. Idle men seated on streetfront benches squinted at his passing, their sun-thinned eyes stretched by efforts to fully appreciate the stranger's size.

He bypassed Hermosillo, heading east on the Moctezuma Highway, a dustswept and deserted strip of broken asphalt running with the Sonora River. Above El Molinito he parked the rig and set off across the riparian scrubland. At the river he removed his clothes and waded into the water, bending to drink. He tasted the ancient limestone washed from Madrean flanks. He savored the dysenteric urine from upstream villages. His thirst quenched, he defecated deeply into the river before returning to the rig.

East of Ures the high desert thornbush thinned, the gray land broken and rock-strewn. No birds flew in the pale sky, but a dozen men stood on the highway, obstructing passage. They wore ski masks and held their weapons with cavalier prepotence.

"Judicial," shouted the frontman. He ordered Driller to descend for a search.

Driller recognized ruthlessness made flesh, these men the sinister minions of blood brought to the Indianland by those who had stood with Cortés, their faces also hidden.

One of them frisked Driller, checking his pockets, finding nothing. Others scrambled onto the rig and inside the cab.

"¿De dónde eres?" asked a burly man, voice of the boss.

Driller said he came from nowhere and everywhere, but most recently he had come from bathing in the luxurious waters of El Molinito just off the scenic highway.

The boss eyed the big prieto who spoke like a native. "¿Eres paisano?"

Driller met his gaze. He grinned.

New ground for the burly boss, an old hand at outstaring those he sent to their graves, his masked face seared onto their lifeless foveae. He found it hard to hold the stranger's gaze. The prieto oversized him, forcing him to look up. Something odd in his eyes, no fear. And that grin. Was he crazy?

He turned to the rig. "¿Y esta chingadera . . . qué es?"

Driller said the machine drilled holes for extracting water so the thirst of men might be quenched and the devil be not drowned in his house.

Crazy, the boss thought. An imbecile. "¿Eres un perforista?"

"Sí, señor."

When the boss addressed the searchers, asking what they had found, they held up empty hands. "Ni madre, jefe," answered one.

The boss clutched his weapon. "So where's the stash?" he asked.

Driller grinned. "I hide nothing, friend. I drill what is hidden."

His interrogator drew near. "Do I look like fool?" he barked.

Driller shrugged. "That is difficult to say," he replied. "A face behind a mask cannot be looked upon and so the fool not seen."

"¡Hijo de tu puta madre!" screamed the boss. He pushed the gunbarrel into Driller's gut, waiting for him to flinch. But Driller moved closer, the barrel seeming to shorten, his grin broad. The smell of something dead washed over the boss. He felt inexplicably short of breath, his ski mask hot.

"Why do you grin, you whoremothering son of fornication?"

Driller stood unfazed. "I grin because I rejoice," he replied. "I rejoice to see that banditry flourishes in Mexico, that men steal in broad daylight. Men like you. Everywhere else they are caught or killed."

The boss saw the stranger's mouth open, lips thinned to reveal enormous molars and bloodred gums. He saw himself fall into the fiery yawning of hell that was this man's mouth, his life swallowed, its deeds, the taking and sparing of lives, all of it engorged, crumbs to an abysmal appetite. Then he saw only a grin.

"I congratulate you," Driller said.

The boss released his weapon and backed away. "Déjalo," he commanded, waving his men off the rig.

Driller removed a fifty-peso bill from his pocket. He handed it to the man who had frisked him without finding it. "For drinks," he said before he climbed into the cab and started the engine. "Adiós," he called, the rig rolling forward, the men stepping aside.

So he advanced, as night advances upon day, as darkness eclipses an imagined land. Across the parched cordillera flanks and the basalted folds of igneous flows, he drove unhurried, time but another destination, his world without hour or dimension or end. He stopped in the Mulato Range to search the black scree-slopes for seashells left on ancient oceanbottoms uplifted by the gyrating bowels of the planet. He detoured on rutted sideroads to taste the noria water of solitary ranches unmapped on man grids. He ate the beans served in the mudbricked chozas of these same ranches, paying for his posada and for the water. The days not hot enough to warm the shape he took.

In the municipal seat of Moctezuma, known to Driller as Oposura, he left the federal highway and climbed east into the Madera Range past Tombabi and La Palmita, the road dropping out of the Silla Mountains into the Bavispe basin. He stopped at the plazuela of Huásabas to inspect the town's condemned waterwell. He stood on the plug of cyclopean concrete to read the cemented inscription—one word fingerwritten by local officialdom—CLAUSURADO. He scuffed the untroweled finish that topped two hundred feet of rubble masonry hurriedly poured by godfearing men. He bent to sniff the untapped aquiferous swell beneath him. "So much for El Güero," he said to curious onlookers.

From the plazuela Driller drove to the local scrapyard. Knowing its owner to possess twenty-five lengths of wellcasing, he purchased the pipe at salvage price, paying cash and paying for its delivery within a week to the boneyard of Rolando Fermín Arenas in La Fortuna, there to be called for. The owner of the Huásabas yard counted Driller's money. He kept to himself his amazement. Many times he had tried to sell the wellcasing, offering it to scrapyards as distant as Hermosillo, including the yard of Rolando Arenas. "I know Fermín," he said.

Driller watched him count the pesos paid for pipe not his to sell. When the yarder finished counting, Driller took him by the shoulder, drawing him near to advise that if the pipe was not delivered as agreed upon, he would return to take his life and those of his offspring, which numbered six, including the newborn girl.

The Huásabas yarder felt his hand grasped. He looked into the stranger's eyes where he saw his newborn held by her feet. He saw her head swinging toward the guava tree in his yard, an old tree planted by his father, the child's brains dashed on the trunk. Then he saw a bloodied, short-fingered hand picking a ripe guava from the tree.

"I swear on my sainted mother's grave," he promised, crossing himself. He smelled guava on the stranger's breath.

Driller nodded, licked his lips, thanking the man for favors unpaid. Then he returned to his rig and departed Huásabas at dusk to drive the deserted Bavispe road north into the sierran night.

La Nochebuena y La Navidad

DAWN BROKE IN A windowed sky when Retch heard the dog bark. He rose, finding his pants and boots, feeling for the gun beneath the bed. Outside, night's delirium washed from the east. The low-slung gibbous moon shrunk to a centavo. In the clearing the dog stood stiff-tailed, barking at the rimland. Her graveled bark new to Retch.

He sighted up the basinslope to the ridgeline where a craggy silhouette rose in relief, backlighted by the dawn. He stared, trying to make shape of it. When he looked behind him, he saw the woman and boy in the doorway.

The sound of an engine startup silenced the dog. She cocked her head. Headlights switched on, their beams plunging down the bajada. The dog backed past Retch, barking from where the woman stood with the boy. In Retch's hand the pocket pistol raised. At this hour what came if not his past. The vehicle turned into the clearing and bore down on him. Retch shot high into the daybroke sky, five rounds fired in quick succession, their discharge swallowed by the motor's roar. Headlighted dust overtook him before the vehicle braked, then went dark. Retch kept the gun raised. In the dead-engine silence a doorhinge squeaked.

"That's no way to welcome a pilgrim," bellowed a deep voice.

Retch discerned the outline of a large truck with an unhoisted derrick. "Goddamn," he blurted. He lowered the gun.

The driver closed the cabdoor and moved toward him. "Goddamned we are indeed," said the voice. "Even that boy there. Like the catamite grooms of Rome. Like the baby Jesus soon to be feted."

A big man with a lumbering walk, his grin strangely white in the leaden light. Retch gripped the gun, one round chambered. He called out. "Are you the driller?"

"The same, friend."

When the stranger stood before him, Retch saw why his grin gleamed. A thing Tex hadn't mentioned. The driller was black.

The dog growled. Retch shook the man's hand, something missing in its grip. "It's Bill, right? Bill Peterson?"

The driller eyed the dog. "Sure as shooting it is. Your shooting."

"I'm Retch. Retch Barter," Retch said. "Sorry for that."

"Expecting another, were you?"

"Not expecting, you could say."

"A surprise, then. A good one, I hope." The driller leaned in, his voice low. "You'd best holster that pistol, amigo, unless you plan to fire it again."

Retch slipped the gun into his pocket. The dog slunk near to sniff, then backed away.

"Buenos días," he called out to the woman and boy.

"Días," echoed the boy. The woman silent.

"Yours?"

Retch started to nod. "Not exactly."

"Is that his mother?"

"Yeah. She's standoffish."

The driller chortled. "I'm partial to standoffish."

Dolores took the boy into the rooms. The dog followed. In the clearing the drillrig daylit. Retch took in the trussed derrick, the assemblage of spools and hoists.

Shitfire, Tex.

"Are you hungry, Bill?"

"I could eat a ky-oat." The driller grinned, big teeth awash in the light.

"Come," Retch said.

The driller looked about an empty kitchen. When the woman appeared, he said, "Señora, me dicen Negro."

"Dolores," Retch interjected after the woman failed to respond. "Her name is Dolores."

"Dolores? La Virgen María de los Dolores. She who is too pained to speak. A good name, but not one I'd give my daughter."

Retch said if they waited long enough she might talk. He told the woman to make food. Then he offered the driller water from the cántaro.

"I drink only what I drill, pard. I brought a carboy from my last job."

With the gourd jícara Retch dipped from the cántaro. "Any trouble finding the place?"

"I followed the wheelruts."

Retch said he had sent Tex a map.

"Never got it, but no matter. I'm here. In time for Christmas, too."

Retch looked up from the dipper. "Today is Christmas?"

"Christmas Eve. Bad night for inconsiderate innkeepers."

No calendar on the ranch. The days and weeks beyond count. "We've lost track of holidays," Retch said.

The driller grinned. "Hard to celebrate what don't come, right? My last Nochebuena was twenty years back. I was drilling in Tierras Coloradas at the time. They served me salted codfish stewed with red chilies."

On the table Dolores set a bowl of beans, plates of fried eggs. The chiquihuite she stacked with tortillas. The driller studied her. He said he remembered the eggs in Mexico having standup yolks. He served himself and began to eat. "What happened to her face?" he asked.

"Cut," Retch answered, thinking the question asked too soon.

"Does she chew fine?"

"I suppose." Retch noticed the driller's scarred scalp. He observed the missing fingers.

"In the Kathputhli slum of Jaipur," the driller said, "I met a gal with a hole in her face from toothwork gone awry. She had two mouths, not one. She became a pukka whore who blamed Krishna, not the dentist, for her calling."

Retch ate. Nothing came to him.

"Got stories for you, chico. Traveled the continents I have, going and coming." He sat large at the table, his gray-blue eyes sliding sideways as he spoke. Big teeth. Oilstained clothes. Some cut of a driller, Retch thought.

The woman twice refilled the basket with tortillas. The boy and the dog watched from the doorway.

"Vente, niño," the driller called. He pulled a furry fob from his pocket, holding it out to the boy. "Feliz Navidad."

The boy didn't move.

"¿Cómo te llamas?"

The boy didn't answer.

"Epifanio," Retch said.

"He's got your hair."

Retch nodded.

"Does he know Christmas?"

"Probably not."

The rabbitfoot fob fitted into a tarnished metal crimp strung with a gilded beadchain. "Tenga," the driller offered.

The boy approached, his gaze narrowed on the fob.

"Pata de conejo," the driller said. "Buena suerte."

"Pata," Epifanio repeated, taking it.

"That's no storebought trinket, boy. It's the left hind-foot of a graveyard rabbit caught in a darkmoon on a rainy Friday and cut by a cross-eyed man while the animal was alive."

"Pata."

"Powerful luck. Lifesaving luck of the kind you can't have too much of. Cuídalo, Red. That's what I'll call you. Red."

Epifanio dangled the charm. "¡Mira!" He brought it near the dog, the dog retreating from the room.

The driller pushed back from the table. "¡Qué rico!" he declared. He told the woman that for a man to eat that many tortillas they had to come from the hand of temptation itself.

The woman silent. Retch watched her. *What now, cabrona,* he wanted to say. He turned to the driller. "In light of the occasion, Bill, how does roast goat sound for dinner?"

"That's white of you, sport," the driller said.

When Retch told the woman she was to butcher a goat for dinner, she didn't answer. He smiled. Son of a fornicating driller, she had called him. Son of a fornicating driller who would never come. Now she would cook him goat.

. . .

They stepped beyond the kitchen, took out cigarettes.

"It's Retch, right?"

"Yeah."

They smoked, the sun on their backs.

"We're all wretches, Retch. Don't you think?"

Retch forced a smile. "You could say so, I guess. Living without water."

The driller took in the Fargo, the rusted drums. "Hauling it, are you?"

"A year."

"Cattle?"

"Goats and chickens." Retch said he hoped to raise cattle.

"Wanting prosperity, are we?"

"Just water."

The driller's gaze swept the tenantless land. "You got yourself a view, I'll say that. Not every man can look upon the face of God, not every day, not from his door. You got yourself a nice watch, too." He pointed to Retch's wrist.

Retch said it was a gift.

"Like time itself," the driller said. He scuffed the dirt with his bootheel.

Retch eyed the toe rands and buckles. Boots of a dandy, he thought.

"You live on an orphaned seabed," the driller said, studying the scuff mark. "But I've seen worse. Places so dry the maggots of Beelzebub shriveled to quickdust with no tax rendered from the dead. Places where a man sells the souls of his children to wet the soles of his feet. Places where the thirsted do anything to see a puddle that isn't piddle. Wretchedness the price, Retch, that's what I'm saying."

This driller a real slinger, Retch decided. "Speaking of price," he said, "I understand from Tex we have an agreement."

"Of the kind gentlemen make?"

"Of terms."

The driller grinned. "What cipher did this Texas fellow pass along?"

Retch quoted the price without casing. He mentioned room and board.

The driller bent to sniff the dirt. "I don't lodge, but I do eat like a nigger. You feed me and buy the diesel. As for the casing, I bought twenty-five lengths from a yarder in Huásabas, which I shall pass on to you at cost. They are to be delivered to a boneyard belonging to Rolando Fermín Arenas in La Fortuna. Do you know this man?"

"Rolando? Sure."

"Fermín. Rhymes with vermin. A sharpie and finagler say the loose tongues. Scrap the metal off a deadman's eyes. We best fetch the pipe before he sells it. You'll have to truck water, too. Need water to drill water."

They smoked, staring at the land.

"I'll want an extra pair of hands. Are you hiring?"

"I told Tex I'd help."

"It's mudman work. Do you know it?"

"Not really."

"You'll embrace God's clay. Mix it, shovel it, scrape it from inside your buttcrack, and wash it from your teeth. Mudman and factotum, that's the job."

"What's the pay?" Retch quipped.

"Blisters. Body aches. Broken teeth. A knock upside the head. Some pay with their lives." The driller grinned.

Retch asked how he should settle up.

"I'll need an advance. Then we'll see." He dropped his cigarette into the bootrut. "Welldrilling is monotony. Hours of mud and jouncing steel. Days of it until something goes bad and your bunghole puckers. Are you up to it?"

"You bet."

"Do you drink?"

"Drink?" Retch repeated.

"Spirits, local or imported."

Retch said not enough to matter.

"Just asking. I like to know what thirsts a man before I find what quenches him." He stretched, broke wind. "Well, let's do us a walkaround."

In the clearing the driller pointed to the grave. "Who lies yonder?"

Retch said the woman's father, an old miner, had been buried there.

"Smells fresh dug. The topdirt was bottomed."

Retch explained that the remains had been exhumed months before. "That's some nose you've got," he added.

The driller grinned. "When you drill as long as I have, you smell where the dead lie and where they don't. Who buried him?"

"She did."

"And she reburied him?"

"Yup."

At the noria he kicked at the cover. "How deep?"

"Thirty feet."

"Salty as cedar sap, I bet."

Retch nodded.

"Who dug it?"

"Her father."

The driller guffawed. "There's a life—going from one hole to another. Squatted the place, did he?"

"Yeah. Concessionland."

"Now it belongs to your woman."

"Right."

"But you're the one wanting water?"

"We both want it," Retch said. He watched the driller walk onto the noria cover. "Careful. That could give."

"Never fallen down a well yet, chico." His boot cleared the dirt until he found where the tinsheets abutted. He knelt. "Did you purge it?"

"I did. Deepened it, too."

He sniffed at the cover. "Reeks of dead water." He stepped off. "No bedrock aquifer smells so. Only the phantom tides of Neptune's pisspot."

Retch shrugged. "I'm not sure what that means."

"It means she could have buried him here and saved herself the trouble of digging a grave. The well was ruined from the day it was dug."

"She said it didn't salt until after she buried him."

"Salted from this side of the grave or beyond, the same water. I've tasted the shat of dermestids from wells dug a day's trek from burial dirt." The driller looked distantly. "Are there runs on your land?"

Retch said he knew a dry arroyo where coyotes came.

"Any seeps?"

"I haven't seen any."

"When did it rain last?"

"It hasn't."

The driller gave him a side-glance. "Have you prayed to Judas Tadeo?"

"Who?"

"Jude Thaddaeus, the saint of lost causes and desperate situations."

Retch laughed. "Why would I do that?"

"For water, budro. Rain or any other. He's partial to the blighted of Mexico on account of all the causes lost and situations beyond hope."

"I don't need that kind of help."

The driller grinned. "Well, yours is a popular notion." He looked to the rimland. "Time to take a hike. I'm getting a drink before we set off. You may want to bring some water if you're a man who thirsts on foot."

She watched them from the kitchen. On and on they talked, no end of saying more than less, standing like deciders of their fate. Their dirtkicking, their cigarettes. The stranger with that queer way of eyeing things, as though to see around corners. So big, so black, so oddly shaped. She had heard of Negros, but she had never seen one. She had heard rumors of their great strength, their large genitals, their great appetite for food and fornication. Already she had seen how he ate.

Her gaze turned to the drillrig, a machine as strangely contrived as the man who brought it. She knew what it could do. More than bleed the land, it could bury her dream.

¡Chingado!

So close to quitting the vile ranch. Calamity and a cloudless sky her conspirators. The gringo all but given up.

Now this perforator come. Built for work. Blackened by the sun. He would drill the land, and if water rose, then what?

The dog lay at her feet. The boy played with the rabbitfoot, a trinket the blackman had called buena suerte. Take care of it, he had said, as though luck a thing to be kept.

When the man entered the kitchen, she watched him draw water from the cántaro. The gun bulged in his pocket.

"The perforator eats with us," he said.

She stood by the stove. "Bring food," she answered. "He eats for three."

He laughed a laugh unheard for many months. She watched him enter the room. He reappeared without the gun in his pocket.

"Didn't I tell you he was coming?"

She said nothing.

"Pata, papi." The boy held up the rabbitfoot.

"Our luck has changed, Epi."

The man started to leave.

"Where he sleep?" she asked.

"In his truck, woman."

He joined the blackman who stood by his machine. She watched them depart and then she went to his room and took the gun from under his bed, secreting it in a new place. When she returned to the kitchen, the dog had left.

They hiked. The driller told Retch to look for nature in alignment—pitaya patches, depressions, ant mounds. "Ants smell hell's blood rain." From the rimland he pointed to the vegetation's trellis design. "Reads freshrock."

Retch stared, evidence new to his eyes. "Does that mean water?"

"There's always water. Always."

When Retch asked how deep, the driller said he would not guess, not wanting to be held to it. "I've bored holes where there's water aplenty but no bottom to drilling it. Sometimes a hole in the ground turns into a hole in the pocket. Then drilling is about how deep you want to go."

Retch said he was willing to go as deep as it took.

The driller grinned. "Spoken like a man with deep pockets."

"Just thirsty," Retch said.

The driller lit a cigarette. "Be advised there are detours in drilling. Accidents, collapses, bits stuck, bits lost. Craziness, too. I want a man to know what he's in for."

Retch nodded. "I've been detoured already."

"So I see." The driller smoked. He studied the basinland. "Detoured but not dead. That's the good news."

Below them the dog lay in the rock-spilled shadows. The driller's short-fingered hand swept the panorama. "How many men have met their end out there? How many do you reckon?"

"No idea," Retch said.

"A guess?"

Retch shook his head, smiled. "I don't want to be held to it, Bill."

The driller grinned. "Fair enough. Ain't about the dead you know but about the ones you don't, right? Your woman buried one. Buried then reburied, you said. So there's a start."

"I suppose," Retch said.

"Just an example."

Retch said he hadn't thought much about it.

"You buried any?"

"Excuse me?"

"Have you buried any dead? Added to the land?" The driller's skewed gaze fixed on him.

Retch laughed. "What kind of question is that, Bill?"

His grin large. "Nothing personal, pard. When you dig holes like I do, you ask what the land gives up that ain't water."

"Makes sense," Retch said, though it sounded like nonsense.

"Shut me up if I get to digging too deep."

"Okay."

Retch drank water. The driller put out his cigarette. "Time to find a site," he said.

The dog followed them off the ridge, then ran ahead. Neither man spoke. Impossible, Retch thought. No way could Bill know about Digger, his desert burial. No one knew. This driller fallen on his head.

The yearling wagged its tail as Doloras bladed its throat. She strung and gutted it, letting the dog drag off the entrails. In the kitchen she rinsed her blooded hands. Then she set about chopping the meat with the machete.

"Cut from a strangler fig struck by a thunderbolt," the driller said of the forked stick he held. "Best witcher there is."

Retch took it. The stick heavy, the ends charred. "Lightning did this?"

"The Fulminator himself."

Retch thought the stick smelled of something cooked.

"Fancy apparatus don't work out here, amigo. Witching is what works."

He held the stick before him as he approached the noria. "The figwood thirsts for the water eye," he called out. "It fancies your dugwell." He followed the fenceline to the cornerpost before he returned to the clearing. He circled. When the rod rotated downward, the driller gripped it as though to impede its descent. He bent backward, muscles tensed, face grimaced. Then the stick dropped to his feet. "Unholy teeth," he blurted. He dragged his bootheel across the dirt to mark the spot. "Here it runs like white river from the loins of Gaea. The limb tells no lie."

The driller stood in the center of the clearing.

"Well, that's convenient," Retch remarked.

"The stick knows no convenience. What's convenient is you ranching atop this spot and not some other."

"Lucky, then," Retch amended.

"Luckier than he who squatted and cleared this ground, nothing but a salted hole to show for it." He broke the stick across his knee. "Fig witchers have but one find in them," he said, tossing the pieces into the scrub.

He backed his machine to the site and raised the derrick. Retch stood by, taking in the rig. No fenders. No mirrors. The tires without tread. The cabdoor lettering scratched-out. A cryptic remainder read:

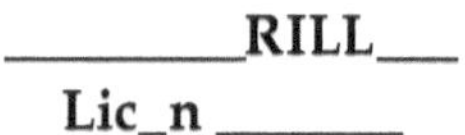

Like its owner, Retch thought. Odd.

To level the platform, the driller released a weighted cable from the mast. He bled air from the tires until the pendulating cable centered inside the rotary. "I taught this trick to Failing," he said, pointing to the letter *F* cast into the mudpump covers. "George Enid Failing. Drilled his first well at Salt Fork with me and Burt Garber. We fought the Madeley fire in '33."

Retch nodded. That put the driller north of old.

"You're the first to hear it. Keep it close."

"I will," Retch said. He stared at his hands. *Yup. Tex sent a loon.*

The sun overhead when the driller traced the mudpits with his bootheel. Two pits, flat-bottomed and deep to the knees. Retch dug with the gorilla bar last used to bury Digger. He softened the caliche hardpan with cistern water. The driller watched him dig. "That big one is the suction pit. You'll be mixing mud there. The other is to settle cuttings. Make sure you leave some grade in the channel. I don't want my slurry backflowing."

The boy came with the dog. "¿Hoyo, papi?"

"Sí," Retch said.

"You ought to teach him English," the driller opined. "Red. Dile 'hole.'"

"Ol."

"That a boy. Do you have the rabbitfoot? La pata?"

Epifanio pulled it from his pocket.

"Say 'foot.'"

"Oot."

"Good."

Retch told the boy to bring water. "Dile a tu mamá."

When the boy left, the driller sat and smoked. "Didn't I call it?" he said. "Hell on the hands. Next comes mudmixing. Hell on the back. Then cleaning the pits. Then mixing again. Altogether hell with a shovel. Blisters and blood. You'll sweat the fat drops."

Retch watched for the boy. No water brought.

"Are you sure you don't want to hire out?"

"I'm sure, Bill."

The driller stretched his legs. "You got slacked lime?"

Retch said he could buy it.

"Good." He walked to the cab and filled a tin cup from his carboy. "You want a drink?" He held out the cup.

Retch shook his head. He shouted to the rooms. "¡Mándame agua!"

The boy brought the thermos, then retreated. Retch drank. The driller gazed at the sky. "Don't you love a sunny day," he said.

Retch wiped his brow. He continued to dig.

The kitchen table set with plates and cups, bowls of diced onions, chopped cilantro, and sliced limes. The woman piled chunks of roasted goat on a platter. She filled a pot with steaming broth. The tortillas she served inside a folded dishtowel. They rolled tacos, dipping them in broth. The goat tasted better to Retch than others the woman had prepared. After the driller served himself a second plate, he pulled a bone from the meat. "Give," he said, handing it to the boy, pointing to the dog.

They watched the dog sniff, then back away. The boy returned the bone to the driller. "No quiere," he said.

The driller finished the meat, the last of the tortillas. When he told the woman it was a fine Nochebuena dinner, she left the kitchen, saying nothing.

Retch said that was the most they'd hear from her tonight.

"A woman of few words. Is she healthy?"

"I suppose."

"Some women have hidden ailments that keep 'em quiet."

"She's got bad teeth."

"I noticed. But that don't always keep 'em quiet."

They sat at the table. The boy and the dog gone. "Damn if the black thirst isn't on me," the driller said. "What do you have to drink?"

Retch pointed to the cántaro.

The driller chortled. "I figured you for a man fond of spirits."

"Was fond," Retch rejoined. "Now only my spirit thirsts."

"Not a teetotaler, I hope."

"A sipper."

"Thank the Lord. That means you've laid in for the journey."

"I'll see what I got."

Retch fetched the opened bottle of brandy. Alcohol not part of the arrangement, but a contented driller was. Four fingers left in the bottle. He brought two glasses, pouring into each.

The driller examined the label. "Missionary brandy."

"You know it?"

"I drilled Parras Valley. Sits atop the Lagunera aquifer. Good water."

Retch with a newfound appreciation for the unopened bottle in his boot.

The driller lifted his glass. "To Christmas and the heir apparent."

"To water."

They drank, the driller sucking his large teeth in a noisy aftersavor. "That's Madera all right. Spanish pox and Barb horseprints."

Retch found the driller's skewed gaze an awkward engagement. He stared into his glass, the brandy shimmer easy on his eyes.

"Does your woman want to join us?"

"She doesn't drink."

"Good. It doesn't become a woman." He poured himself another round. "Was her old man a drunk?"

"He died of it, so she says."

The driller emptied the second glass. "Is that his mark on her face?"

Retch sipped, nodded.

"Pitiful what drink does to men. You ever go crazy with drink, budro?"

"Some, when it didn't matter."

His black face glowed in the lamplight. He poured another. "Ever hit a woman?"

Retch tossed back his glass. *Hit a woman?* He studied the bottle. *Did a runover student nurse count?* He studied the bottle. Two drinks left. If he didn't pour, the driller would. He poured. "Are you drilling again, Bill?"

The driller threw back his head, roaring a laugh that seemed to come from beneath him. "That's good, pard. Drilling Retch. You got me there." He emptied the bottle. "Pay it never no mind."

Retch nodded. "So where do you hail from? Where's home?"

He smoked, looking at Retch. "Everywhere and nowhere."

"Seriously."

He swirled his glass, nursing the last of the brandy. "Born and raised a stone's throw from the old Acheron landing, closed due to lack of freights."

"And where's that?"

"Don't matter, does it? It's one planet in either direction."

"Right." The brandy talking, Retch guessed. He finished his glass. "So how did Tex find you?"

The driller grinned. "A blackman ain't hard to find among drillers."

"He told me you were in West Texas."

"Yup. On the Ogallala. Red caprock and sandstone."

Retch said it was goodluck for him, their finding each other."

"Welldrillers is a small world. Marble size. You can hold the lot in one hand." He inverted the empty bottle, shaking amber drops into his glass. "You don't have another, do you?"

"That's it," Retch lied. He let the bottle sit. "You want coffee?"

The driller wheeled his glass by the rim, shook his head. Then he rose from the table. "Mañana we fetch the casing from Fermín."

Retch stood. "Good."

"We'll buy more of this brandy. Bring your money."

Outside, moonwash risen behind the nigrescent rimrocks. The rig black in the clearing. "Do you have something to sleep on?" Retch asked.

"God's tiniest turd," the driller replied. "Don't need more."

Retch made for the latrine. A long day since the dog had barked. A drinking driller to end it. Half crazy and meddlesome. Weirder than words. Still, an improvement over no driller.

While the man slept, she cleared the table of plates piled with gnawed bones. She dropped them on the floor, the dog taking some, not others. She worked by lanternlight, stacking platters with a ceramic clash. The waterglasses she left to soak, their stale ester smell of brandy making her gag. The empty bottle she heaved beyond the kitchen.

Moonlight awash the nightscaped land at the hour she stood at the window of her room looking out. The spired shadow of the machine a trussed skiagram splashed largely on the ground. Somewhere in its shadow the stranger slept, his blackness melted, his bulk lost in the monstrosity. She stood for minutes, watching. Then she went to bed.

The yarder from Huásabas delivered the twenty five lengths of wellcasing to Rolando Arenas two days after its sale. His truck idled on the street at the hour the scrapdealer arrived to open his business. The yarder escorted by three men.

"Tú y tus pinches perros," he greeted.

The dogs barked at the fence.

"¡Son bravos como yo!" Rolando shot back. He recognized the pipe as the same offered to him years earlier by the Huásabas yarder. "¿Eran del Güero?"

The man nodded. "To El Güero the pipe had belonged."

"And now?"

"Another driller. I'm only delivering it."

Rolando recalled the rusty-haired gringo, his talk of a Texas driller. "¿Lo compró?"

"Sí. Lo compró."

Rolando took in the men—muscled, rough-looking. Not mere handlers of pipe. "Who will call for it?" he asked.

"I suppose the driller," replied the Huásabas yarder.

"Does he have a name, chingado?"

The yarder said the driller had not given his name. "Even so, there is no confusing him with another. He is a blackman."

"¿Un Negro?"

The yarder nodded, adding, "Somekind of black devil."

"What?"

"He threatened to kill my family should I not deliver the pipe."

The dealer guffawed.

"Go ahead, laugh. God knows you won't be laughing when you meet him. I saw it happen. I saw him kill my youngest, dash her brains against my guava tree. I saw it play in his eyes."

The dealer's smile vanished. "Whoreson of a fornication!"

"A big man," continued the Huásabas yarder. "Always grinning, showing more teeth than a caiman. Fingers gone from his hand, too."

Rolando stared. The yarder pointed to the men. "Do you think I brought them to move pipe? I could have hired cheapos here for that. I don't want that devil getting near me. He might ask me to do another job."

The scrapdealer grimaced, realizing that the Huásabas yarder traveled with a false sense of security. As tough as these men looked, they had no chance against the devil. "Listen," he said. "It's El Güero. I'm sure of it."

"Who?" the yarder asked.

"The owner of the pipe, man. It's him."

"Are you crazy? El Güero is dead."

"Dead by some accounts," Rolando replied. "But his body wasn't found."

"He went into the hole, you fool."

Rolando grunted. "Only God knows for certain."

They stared at the pipe as though it might speak to the mystery.

"What's more," said the yarder, "they called him El Güero for a reason. He was white. This mandevil is blacker than a cricket's ass."

The dealer shook his head. "Un rayo lo chamuscó. No lo mató."

The Huásabas yarder struck silent. This possibility hadn't occurred to him. He wondered if lightning could do such a thing.

Rolando said, "It burns a man black. Remember, El Güero was short-fingered, too."

"But," began the yarder, looking at his hands. "But why would he buy back his own pipe? It doesn't make sense."

The scrapdealer shrugged. "Don't expect the devil's work to make sense." He pointed to a spot on the street outside his yardfence. "Unload the pipe there," he said.

"Wait!" the yarder protested. "Not on the street. What if it gets stolen? He'll come for me."

"Not my problem," Rolando said. "He paid you to bring it, but he didn't pay me to keep it. Not in my yard. It's bad luck."

"Puras pendejadas," the yarder replied, throwing up his hands. He told the men to unload the pipe on the street.

The dealer locked his yard, boarded his truck, and drove off. Damn gringo fool, he thought. Hiring El Güero to drill his water. Trouble for him.

"Buy larder," she said, "if you want him fed."

Retch sat at the table. "Cook beans, woman."

The driller appeared in the kitchen. "Feliz Navidad," he sang out, his toothy grin wedged with scraps of goatmeat. "Alleluia, he is born."

His appetite undiminished as he downed bowls of beans for breakfast. Tortillas disappeared as fast as the woman cooked them.

That morning they drove to La Fortuna for the casing. Retch silent until the driller asked if he had come to Mexico for his health.

"My health?"

"So they say when you come to a place you wouldn't come to otherwise unless you're running from something bad for your health. Like bullets, jail."

Retch said he had come for the adventure.

"Adventure? There's a sport for the hopeful. Find any?"

"Still finding it," Retch replied.

The driller nodded. "You come alone?"

Retch said he had partnered with another to pan gold in the highlands, but it hadn't worked out.

"Prospectors, then."

"And none the richer for it," Retch added.

"Did he preserve his health?"

"Who?"

"Your partner."

"I guess."

"And you settled down, got yourself a spread and a woman."

"I wouldn't call it a spread."

They passed the guamúchil tree, the driller looking. "Have you married her, Retch?"

"No."

"Lewd and lascivious cohabitation they call that. Outlawed in parts." The driller grinned. Retch said nothing. More damn nonsense, he thought.

At the edge of town they passed the day-shuttered brothel.

"Is that the lair of the pretties?"

Retch nodded.

The driller gazed at the rowed buildings. "It's my experience that the ugly ones lay better. Beauty beneath the skin." He chuckled, spat. Before they reached the pavingstone road, he lifted his nose, remarking on the slaughterhouse. "'Tis the killing hour."

At the scrapyard they found twenty-five lengths of casing stacked on the street. The yardgate locked, the dealer not answering hoots or hails. The dogs charged the chainlink fence, barking.

"Should we load it?" Retch asked.

"I reckon that's what Fermín wants." He approached the fence, extending his hand to the dogs. They shied off, suddenly quieted. "Good pups," he said.

Retch eyed a chainhoist crane locked inside the boneyard, no way to use it. "Maybe he took off Christmas."

"No holidays for sharpies, pard. Likely he saw no money to be made."

They loaded the pipe. The driller with the strength of two. When Retch cut his hand, the driller said blood was part of the job. "There has to be blood before there's water." After the casing was loaded, he took in the yard. "That varmint Arenas knew the kind of fun he was missing."

Retch said they were sure to run into him before the well was finished.

"Looking forward to it," the driller declared.

At the plazuela they found La Fortuna's liquor store sold out of brandy. The driller purchased warm beer at an off-license depository, block ice from a hielería. He picked the ice with a screwdriver, layering it into a pail with the beer. Retch bought soupbones and boiling fowls at the market.

On the road the pailed beer rode between them.

"Help yourself."

"Maybe later," Retch said.

The driller emptied a can. "Can't guarantee later."

They offloaded the pipe at the ranch. Retch reloaded empty drums to bring water. The driller drank beer in the shade of his rig. "Buy diesel," he called out.

Retch sweatsoaked when he set off for town. At the guamúchil tree he stopped for the driller's advance. The sun down at the hour he retook the road with water. Lanternlight illuminated the ranch in the desolate dusk. When he entered the kitchen, he saw empty beer cans aligned on the table.

"I warned you, chico. Beer's gone. But we saved you mole. Dolores fixed a brace of your finest."

Under the table the dog crunched chicken bones. Retch washed his hands before he drank from the cántaro.

"The boy liked it—didn't you, Red? "

"Ed."

"He understands more than you think. You ought to speak to him."

"I'll do that," Retch said. He sat, waiting for the woman to serve. The folded bills he placed on the table. "There's the advance."

The driller leaned in his chair. "Thanks. No trouble, I hope."

Retch silent, watching the woman. Epifanio pointed to the bills.

"¡Mira!"

"Money, Red. Say money."

"Mooni."

"The root of all evil, boy. What rings the bells in hell. The big wind that brought Jesus to town and knocked him down."

"You may want to count it," Retch said.

"I'll take your cipher. Neither of us are going anywhere."

The woman brought a plate piled with rice, bathed in sauce. Retch eyed the food. He saw no chicken.

The driller took the money from the table and peeled off the top bill, holding it out to the boy. "For you, Red."

Retch ate, listening to the dog crunch chicken bones.

"¡Mira!" the boy said to his mother, holding up the bill. The woman looked but said nothing. Then she left the kitchen, taking the boy.

"Kid's a hoot."

"Don't spoil him."

"Money don't spoil, Retch. Desire does. You know that." He pocketed the bills, emptied his can.

Retch ate, thirsting for a coldbeer. "So tomorrow we drill?"

The driller abruptly stood and stepped outside. "Hell's hot trickle, budro. Tomorrow we seek it."

The heavy splatter of urination sounded from beyond the kitchen.

Retch finished his plate. When the driller didn't return, he pushed back from the table. *Too much beer. Beer and craziness.* He waited until the woman came to clean. "Be it the last time," he warned, "that no food is saved for me. Do you hear?"

The woman swept, silent. In her pocket the money gifted to the boy.

Retch left the table. "Feliz Navidad, bitch!"

That night he slept and dreamed of walking through high grass, parting it as he walked. Suddenly a snake rose at his feet. Eyes glazed, fangs white, it struck between his legs. Retch awoke grabbing himself. "Damn, woman!" he gasped, his gaze fixed on the darkness, seeing nothing.

Bottomless

THE FADED BLACK-AND-WHITE photograph showed a workline of grimed men standing shoulder to shoulder before a mudfilled crater of enormous size. Rows of flattened trees receded from the crater. Beyond the trees rose smoke plumes horizoned in the grayscale distance. The grimed men stood at the crater's edge holding shovels and picks, their faces weary and oil blackened, their lives threadheld. MADELEY AT CONROE 1933 read the caption.

"Those were most of them," Tex Hinton told the student. "On the left is Stanley Hinton, my granddad. The fire blinded him in one eye and he lost his rightside hearing from the roar."

The student approached the framed photograph on the office wall. "Who are the others, Professor?"

"The wildcatter Strake is standing next to him. At the other end is Failing. Abercrombie is there. Harrison, Garber, Kelly, Barker, Juergens, Theo Slade. The textbook players. Harlan Eastman—"

"The father of directional drilling," the student quickly interjected, hoping to impress her professor.

Tex smiled. Even his wife knew Eastman. Rose knew the inside of a mudpump. Still, this student was defying the odds, breasts be damned. He didn't have the heart to tell her that this two-fisted fraternity of buggering drillers would have made her their cook.

"Did you know him?" she asked.

"Eastman? No." Tex chuckled. "That was before my time, younglady. My granddad was twentysomething then. Not much older than you."

The student examined the photograph. "It's hard to tell," she said. "They all look so old."

Tex searched for the book the student had come to borrow. "Aged by oil and blackened by smoke," he agreed. "Everyone of them is burned. Only Failing and my grandfather left the fields to go into waterdrilling."

"I can see why," the student said. "That's one nasty-looking crater."

Tex nodded. Geology of the prosaic, he called this language of science turned subjective. "That field, Miss Sanders, lies on a faulted salt dome of the Eocene age. An unconsolidated formation with a high-pressure reserve under shallow, gas-charged sand."

She looked at him. "Really? Wow!"

"Really," Tex said. "What you see there is hell risen from a runaway well. All the spudded holes ignited, their casings shattered, a piece of ground swallowed under men eating breakfast. Whole derricks sunk from sight. That crater might as well be bottomless and those men might as well be dead."

Her gaze returned to the photograph, her face close to the glass. "And who is this?" she asked, pointing to a corner of the picture. "He's not with the others."

Tex found the book. He studied the student from behind. "Who?"

"This man." She fingered a figure perched at the rim of the crater, his presence obvious under her painted nail, but otherwise he blended into the charred landscape.

Tex stared. A big fellow, he guessed, if sized by the trees. As many times as he had shown this picture, not once had he noticed.

"He looks black, sir."

"Yes, of course," Tex began.

"African American, I mean. His face."

Tex looked over his glasses. A black-faced man, yes, but a Negro?

"He has like a grin," the student observed, her finger shifting on the glass. "You can see his teeth."

Tex brought his face close, trying to ignore her perfumed scent. He saw something white above her nail. "It's the light," he corrected.

Her eyebrows lifted. "Oh. Okay."

"Why on earth would the man be grinning, Miss Sanders?"

She shrugged. "No reason I can think of, really."

"Hardly a congruent response to the gravity of the situation. Deadmen lost. The living burned."

"Like dancing at a funeral."

"Yes, like dancing." He almost shook his head. Instead he handed her the book. At least Rose is smart, he thought.

"Thank you, Professor. It's very interesting. I really like your class."

Tex nodded. Was it because she mentioned dancing that he suddenly remembered his friend Retch Barter living in Old Mexico? Footloose Retch in the land of the fast-stepping polka and lovely señoritas. Lucky dog.

"So you don't know who he is?" she asked, stopping at the door. "No one from your books, Professor?"

He turned to the photograph. "As to who he is, I cannot say. A latecomer, maybe. A disoriented soul. He could be one of the crew. He could be black. But I don't know his name."

After she left, his gaze lingered on the photograph, the black-faced figure lost once more in the devastation, gone without the underline of a painted nail. Funny I hadn't noticed him, Tex thought. Funny how he disappears.

El Hoyo y
La Perra

GENUINE WYOMING BENTONITE. Words written large on the sacks, but the fine print told the truth. *Made in Billings, Montana.* Retch stared at the label. He had been to Montana. He had raged in Billings. Billings where he had rundown the student nurse.

He opened a sack and dumped its contents into drummed water. He stirred the chunked clay with a shovel.

The driller watched. "That's Benton shale cut from the Bighorn Basin and carted to the Magic City. Ever been to the Magic City, Retch?"

"Yup."

"Pretty Indian girls up there. Daughters of the largebeak bird." He stuck his hand into the barrel and squeezed the clay. "A shovel don't dilute it. This mud has to be manhandled, busted up. You have to get it on you."

Retch broke the chunks with both hands, the clay cool and slippery.

"It needs to cook before it circulates. What you educated pards call hydrated. Otherwise it swells in the hole and wreaks havoc on the pump." He sank his arm into the drillfluid. "You'll be mixing in the pits, so put the feel to memory. Mud too thin, the cuttings won't lift. Too thick, they won't settle. The slacked lime is for fine-tuning. All about viscosity. Another fancy word for you school pards."

"Actually I'm a dropout," Retch said. "If that raises your opinion."

The driller grinned. "You might make good yet, but I won't guarantee it."

Retch stirred the mud from Billings. Some coincidence, he thought, Bill's talk of Indian girls.

He unloaded drillsteel from the cradle bays, laying them across two wooden rails. He counted twenty-five joints—enough drillsteel to bore a five-hundred-foot hole.

"The old horny has a long one," said the driller, slapping Retch on the back. Retch felt an odd sensation, as though the hand passed inside him, a touch cold and probing. "No job for pantywaists, this blind business. Be prepared for craziness. It's a wildride screwing the salted firmament with a steel pecker."

He sent Retch up the derrick with four tiedowns hooked on his belt, the stay wires dangling to the ground. Retch clung two-handed to the derrick's trussweb. The masthead with pipes and hoses, a crown block, a traveling block, winchcables, and chain sprockets.

"This mast killed the first man who climbed it," the driller shouted. "The front stay broke with him atop— just where you are—and down came the whole shebang. Threw him on a laid-up jackshaft that skewered him like a jumbuck shashlik at a MayDay picnic. He was from Bosier City, I think."

Retch located the masthead eyebolts where the stays attached.

"One helluva mess. Him bleeding, me bleeding, my headbone split . . ."

Retch hooked one arm inside the trusswork to free his hands. He lifted the first tiedown from his belt. The wire fitted with a shackle and clevis bolt fixed by a splitcotter.

"But be not feared. Lightning never strikes twice."

The mast swayed. The trussjoints creaked. Retch straightened the splitcotter, pulling it from the shackle to free the clevis pin. He placed pin and cotter between his teeth. After he aligned the tang with the eyebolt, he inserted the pin and locked the cotter. He fixed the second and third tiedowns. When he reached for the last stay, he heard the rig motor crank. Suddenly a combustion roar shook the derrick. Diesel smoke engulfed Retch. "What the hell!" he shouted, hugging the mast.

A loud silence punctuated the engine shutdown. Black smoke drifted in a cloudless sky. Retch looked down. He saw the cabdoor open. He heard the big man's laugh. "Warming her up, Retch. No harm done."

"Thanks for the warning," Retch called.

He fixed the clevis to the last eyebolt. *Crazy sonofabitch.* If scaring the crap out of him had been a test, so be it. Now he knew what he was in for.

On the ground he waited behind the rig. The driller whistled inside the cab. When he appeared, his face freshly shaved. Retch stared.

"Don't fret. I'm still a nigger." He grinned before he looked up at the mast. "What are you waiting for? Get thee to anchoring these stays. The sooner, the sooner. Don't want the mast moving on us, do we?"

He threaded the six-inch rollerbit to the kellybar, tightening it with long-handled Stillsons. Retch emptied the drummed slurry into the suction pit. When the driller started the mudpump, the slurry rose into the pump through a drafting hose laid in the pit. "Stir, man, stir!" the driller ordered before he set the rotary in motion.

Retch waded into the pit, mud to his knees, the submerged hose sucking at his legs. He stirred with the shovel, watching the bit descend into the ground. The driller stood on a narrow perch at the rear of the rig. He began to sing.

> Early one morning 'bout 7 o'clock,
> Twenty tarriers working on the rock.
> Boss came along and said, "Boys, keep still
> and bear down harder on the cast iron drill.
> Drill, ye tarriers, drill!
> For it's work all day for the sugar in yer tay
> Drill, ye tarriers, drill!"

Damn fine voice, Retch thought. He looked to the rooms and saw the woman and boy in the doorway, the dog crouched beside them.

The kellybar sank swiftly into the hole, one song sung. The driller halted the string and backed out the bit. "Whorerock, budro. First dip is always the quickest." He directed Retch to reel out a braided steel cable fixed with a swivelhead hoisting plug. The cable recoiled and twisted as Retch unwound it off the drawworks and over the mast's crownblock. When he reached the stacked drillpipe, the driller appeared at his side with the Stillsons. He threaded the hoisting plug into the drillcollar. "This is the mudman's job," he said. "Connect my steel." He cinched the plug with the wrenches before he stuck his short-fingered hand in Retch's face. "Count 'em! Pipe falsely winched done this. Make sure this hoister is tight." He handed the Stillsons to Retch. "I call these my bobbejaan spanners. That's Afrikaans for baboon grabber. In case you didn't know."

Retch nodded. "I didn't. Thanks."

"Walk the steel as I lift it. Don't let the threads drag." He returned to the rig and disengaged the drawworks clutch to reel in the cable, lifting the collar from the stack. Retch raised the unhoisted end and walked it to the rig. He watched the driller maneuver it over the platform and into the rotary.

"Fetch the bobbejaan spanners," he shouted.

Retch ran for the wrenches. He knelt in the mud to hold the bit while the driller cinched the collar. Then he sat in the mud with the Stillson gripped to the collar as the driller threaded the kelly. Mud filled his pants. He wiped it from his eyes. When he looked to the doorway, he saw the woman's black-toothed smile. "Water's coming!" he yelled.

She had stepped to the doorway to hear him sing. His voice heavy with cojones, darker than his black skin. The devil's voice.

The last man she had heard sing was the old miner as he lay in his bed drunk on Bacanora. His thick-tongued croon of *Paloma Negra* suddenly transformed into a strident wail when he saw her bearing down on him with the flathead sledge raised in both hands. His last song sung before she caved his skull into his brains.

Now alone in the room, the boy asleep, no eyes watching when she removed the man's pocket revolver from where she had secreted it three days before. Nothing said yet by the gringo fool. The walnut grips wellfit to her small hands as she aimed the pistol, a good feel. She took it to the kitchen and wrapped it in a dishcloth, laying the bundle in a pail, filling the pail with beans poured from a sack. She set the pail beside the stove and set about boiling a pot of beans.

Let him walk by it, she thought. Let him eat beans cooked from its pile. Not a place he would look.

Later she added soupbones and cilantro to the beans, her mother's recipe for wakabaki. Then she kneaded three kilos of tortilla dough, calculating the blackman's appetite by the loudness of his shouts.

"Granite!" he hollered when the bit struck felsic rock. The rig motor pulled down. The kellybar chattered. "Plutonic piecrust!"

Progress, Retch thought. The same rock had bounced the chiselbar off the noria floor.

Late afternoon the woman brought beanstew and tortillas. The driller secured the pulldown lever with a springcord. He wolfed tortillas and threw his soupbones to the dog. When the dog approached, he reached to pet her.

"She bites," Retch lied.

The dog spun and snapped without a growl before running to the rooms. The driller grinned. "Fresh dirt confounds her. She'll come around."

At dusk he powered the platform lamps, the rig awash in dirty yellow light. When the masthead bulb failed to incend, the driller sent Retch up with a replacement. "Watch your hands," he said. "Watch that fancy watch." The bulbsocket mounted between the sprockets of the shuttle chains.

Retch changed the bulb. After he climbed down he listened to the driller tell of a mudman whose pantscuff had snagged on the quill swivel, his trousers torn off, underwear caught, the fabric ensnaring the man's genitals. "Skinned him like a freshkilled rabbit. Foreskin shucked. Scrotum scalped. No more getting hard like Christmas candy."

Retch hitched his pants. He had skinned rabbits.

"Are you cut, chico?"

"What?"

"Circumcised."

Retch shrugged. No question too personal for this man.

"You don't have to say. It's your business and the missus."

Retch retreated to the latrine. The beansoup gone through him. Some spice the woman had added. Or the heat. As he squatted, he stared at himself, thinking of the unlucky mudman.

The driller called out. "Budro!"

Back at the rig, the drillstring raised, the collar out of the hole. "No time for a long dump, man! Get the bobbejaan spanners."

Retch ran for the wrenches and reeled out the winchline, threading the hoistplug into a length of drillpipe. He fetched the grease bucket and wiped lubricant into the collar and then he gripped the collar with the Stillson while the driller snugged the new joint. Once the string rotated again, Retch stood in the mud, catching his breath. *Christ, this is work!*

Darkness walled the clearing. The rig an island of light. Retch's shadow stretched beyond it, tethered thinly to his weariness.

"Put diesel in her, pard."

He unscrewed the bung from the diesel barrel and poured fuel into a pail. He inserted the funnel in the truck's fillpipe, emptying three pails into the tank. Unsure whether to add a fourth, he opened the cabdoor to check the fuel gauge. "Get the hell out of my cab!" shouted the driller.

Retch closed the door, tightened the fuel cap. Damn private, he thought, for such a prying bastard.

An hour later he revisited the latrine. When he returned to the rig, the driller's grin gilded in yellow lamplight. "You got the Moctezumas, sport?"

None of your damn business, Retch almost said. He shook his head.

"Happens to every mudman. The suction pit tugs the innards."

Retch stuck with bad soup. "I'm fine."

"Boiled tarbush tightens a bunghole. Hojasén, they call it here."

"I'm fine."

The rig jounced. The bit ground granite. The driller savored a cigarette, his gaze fixed on Retch as though to ponder deeds yet to pass. "Won't add steel 'til morning. Don't need mud. Get thee to bed."

Retch silent, gut twisted.

"Otherwise you won't be worth a pissant's turd come morning."

"I'm okay. Just thirsty."

"Go to bed. Diddle the little woman, if you're up to it."

Retch retreated to the rooms, too diminished to offer more than an eyeroll. He flopped on his bed. *If you're up to it* . . . What a bastard!

He slept and dreamed of nothing, his bowel knotted. Later he rose to drink from the cántaro. When he looked to the site, he saw the driller on the rig. He spotted the dog in the lamplit clearing, crouched, advertent.

Five days a sunstrided sky, a thirst that nagged, a bowel that ran. So Retch worked. Five joints strung, the borehole wide as a waterpitcher, the mud black with cuttings. The driller sluiced them in his hand, showing Retch the groundpepper granite. "Enough of these and you can make yourself a tombstone."

Retch said he hoped not to need one anytime soon.

"For a loved one perhaps? Some other fondly remembered?"

No one he loved that much, Retch replied. None to remember.

"Adrift ye are then," said the driller. "Adrift upon the living water."

Retch silent. The truth strangely put, he thought.

One evening, the driller gave the boy a dogcollar fashioned from a leather cinchstrap. The collar with a rope leash. "Say 'dog,'" he instructed.

"Ogg."

He showed the boy how to align the holes with the split pin. He lured the dog to the table with food scraps. When he cinched the collar, she yanked at the rope and tried to bite it. He handed the leash to the boy, who pulled the dog. "Tame the two at once," he joked.

The next day he sent Retch to town for drummed water, diesel, and lime. "Bring monkeypods. The sweet and sour hankering is upon me."

"Bring what?"

"Sweet Ingas. False tamarinds. There's a tree on the road. Guamúchil, they call it. Gather some fruit, like a good budro. Buy my missionary brandy, too. Take it off my next advance."

On a sidestreet in La Fortuna, Retch met the scrapdealer in his truck.

"Can't talk!" Rolando blurted as they stopped window to window. "I know about your driller and the casing. Got to go. I'm late."

Retch wanted to say, *I told you he was coming.* Instead he said, "We're down one hundred feet."

"Bueno," Rolando replied, starting to pull away.

"Seems like he knows you," Retch added.

The dealer stopped his truck. "Who?"

"The driller."

Rolando stared. "What did he say?"

Sharpie, the driller had called him. Finagler. Retch said the driller had mentioned his name in a professional context.

The dealer's face one of intent thoughtfulness. He bit his lip. "Ten mucho cuidado," he croaked grimly. "Mucho, mucho cuidado."

Retch smiled. That was a lot of caution.

"Don't smile," Rolando said. "It's a serious matter."

"Okay."

"El es un . . . un . . ." Rolando searched for the word.

"¿Un Negro?" Retch suggested.

"Yes, he's a blackman, but he is also something else."

"¿Un poco loco?"

"No, no. Es alguien más," he amended. "No es lo que él dice ser."

Such could be said of any man, Retch thought. That he is not who he says he is.

"He's strange bird all right," Retch agreed.

"No more will I say," Rolando said.

"Okay."

He repeated his advice to be careful. Then he pulled away. Retch watched in the sidemirror. He had never seen Rolando in such a rush.

He visited the icehouse to buy a fractioned block, which he chipped into the cooler. At the market he purchased stewmeat, cold cuts, fresh fruit. At the mercantile he bought sliced bread, elbow pasta, jars of instant tea, the slacked lime. When he paid for the brandy, he asked for a cash receipt.

He loaded diesel and water before he stopped at the callbooth to phone Tex Hinton. He wanted his friend to know Bill Peterson had arrived.

"Hello," answered the female voice at the other end.

"Rose?"

"Yes."

"This is Retch, Rose. Retch Barter. I'm calling from Mexico."

"Oh, Retch. How sweet of you to call."

He could see her smile, hear the teacup charm. "How's everything, Rose?"

"Just fine, hon. We're waiting on rain."

"Same here. And the professor?"

"He's out buying a lawnmower. The man can't stand to see grass grow."

"I called to let him know that Bill arrived. Bill Peterson. If you could pass that along."

"Who's that again?"

"Bill Peterson, the driller."

"That name sounds familiar."

"Yeah. Tex sent him to drill my well."

"I think he called here a while back. Had a nice voice, as I recall."

"You should hear him sing."

She laughed a full-bosomed laugh that made Retch smile. The way a woman should laugh. "You want to leave a number where Tex can reach you?"

"I don't have one, Rose. This is a paycall. I need water before a phone."

She cackled again, finding this funny. "I'll give him your message."

"Thanks, Rose. You'll have to come visit when I get the place fixed up."

"You tell him to take me. The man doesn't want to travel except to shoot birds. I'd love to come. But you tell him. Promise me you'll tell him."

"I will." Then Retch hung up.

Lucky Tex, he thought. Grasscutting, duckhunting Tex. Living in a place with water enough for both. But lucky the most for Rose. She had dried him of drink and pointed him toward prosperity, not letting him look back. The way a woman should.

Midday he left the plazuela. At the town brothel trucks parked in the graveled lot. The roofline bulbs blinked. Retch slowed the Fargo, a cold beer considered, an hour of dimlit respite. Since the driller's arrival, canicular days. He checked his watch, the shouts of "Budro!" imagined.

He advanced on the road before stopping at the guamúchil to pick the driller's fruitpods. Keep the loon happy, he decided. When he arrived at the ranch, the driller not on the rig, the motor shutdown. The dog lay by the mudpit, tied to a water drum.

He sat large at the table, the mudcaked boy beside him. The woman stood at the stove.

"Jammed the bit, pard. Been waiting on you."

Retch set the cooler on the floor. He told the woman to unpack it. "How bad is jammed?"

"As bad as a pederast's prick at a Sundayschool picnic. If that's jammed enough for you."

"Okay."

"Waiting on fuel. We took a beanbreak, me and the boy."

"Boy," said the boy.

The driller laughed. "You're a boy all right, one who needs a bath." He ruffled the red hair. "I've been training him as my new mudman. Giving him a taste of what his daddy does."

Retch told the woman to make noodle salad. He dispensed water from the cántaro into a pitcher, mixing the tea, adding chipped ice from the cooler.

"Where's my brandy, Retch?"

"In the truck with your fruit." He pulled the cash receipt from his pocket and laid it on the table.

The driller ignored it. "Put it on my tab. One of these days I'll go to town and do my own shopping."

Retch drank the tea.

"Refresh yourself. We'll get to extracting that bit directly."

While the woman cooked the pasta, Retch prepared sandwiches with layers of ham and cheese. The driller watched him. "That ain't going to stick to your ribs. A working man's food needs fire for a proper tuck-in."

Retch sat to eat the sandwiches. The noodle salad warm when she set it on the table. He drank more tea. "Who tied up the dog?"

The driller grinned. "She got into the mudpit. I didn't want her rope sucked by the drafting hose."

Retch nodded. He studied the mudcaked boy. "I guess we'll have to tie up both of them."

"There you go." He laughed. "The darndest things get grabbed by a suction hose. Once I was drilling government water in Kassala when a half-blind woman fell into a mudpit.

By the time I shut off the pump, the hose was on her face like a leech. Sucked out her good eyeball. Left her full blind."

Retch silent. No story too outrageous for this driller.

"That's why I made the collar. Dogs go wandering."

"Did he get in?" Retch asked.

"Who? The boy? No. He played at the edge."

Retch finished the sandwiches, the salad. He emptied his glass before he reached across the table and took the boy by the ear, lifting him from the chair. "Mírame," he said. He told the boy to stay away from the pits or he would get a whipping he wouldn't forget. The boy ran crying to his mother.

"¡Es peligroso!" Retch shouted. Then he told the woman to keep the boy away from the hole.

The woman left the kitchen, taking the boy.

"Damn, budro, I reckon they got your drift."

"Save your opinion, Bill."

"Okay."

"And if you'd do your part to keep him clear."

The driller grinned. "Count on it, Retch."

The jammed bit broke free as soon as the driller reversed the string. "Luck hangs with us," he declared. "The rollers cooled and shrunk."

Retch silent. Luck, science, craziness. Did it matter what governed a jammed drill bit? He untied the dog and kicked it. It ran to the rooms dragging the mudcaked rope.

An acetylene-lighted sky, white and gold, paled in the west. The driller stood on his perch eating guamúchil fruit. "Make mud, Retch."

In drummed water he mixed the bentonite from Billings. At dark the driller went to the cab and returned with the brandy. "I drank yours—you must share mine," he said. "It's New Year's Eve!"

A week already, Retch reflected. Bill's stay seemed longer. "I'll pass," he said.

"Come. A toast. Get the glasses."

Retch went to the kitchen. *One drink. One.* On the table the plates left with food. The beanpot astir with flies. He fetched the glasses.

The driller poured. "To doors and gates, chico. To beginnings and ends. To this portal we drill."

"To water," Retch said.

The driller emptied his glass. Retch sipped, the brandy truckheated.

"Madera up, man. No drink for señoritas."

Retch drank.

"Another. Come."

"I shouldn't."

"One more. Then a night off for you. Last call for me."

Retch held out his glass. "Half."

The driller filled it. He raised the bottle to toast. "To mudmen."

"To mud."

"A prosperous New Year."

"The same."

They drank, the brandy tasting better to Retch.

"One day I must see you drunk."

"You would not like me drunk, Bill."

The driller laughed. He handed the bottle to Retch. "As promised. Hold it for me, pard." He pulled a handful of guamúchil pods from his pantspocket. "These will get me through the hours 'til ladyday."

The boy cried until he ran out of breath. Then he began to wheeze, lips turned blue. The woman pushed a glob of VapoRub between his teeth and she held his mouth shut, a remedy learned from her mother. The boy tried to vomit. His eyes bulged with the camphor burn. The mentholated fumes dug inside him. He sucked a breath, then another. His color returned.

The woman rubbed him with the ointment. She lay beside him. The room dark when he spoke. "Papi malo."

She caressed his face, her only tenderness.

"Me pegó," he mewled.

"Sí."

"Papi malo."

She stroked his hair.

"No quiero papi," he said sleepily.

She put her lips close to his ear. "¿Lo mato?" she whispered.

He closed his eyes.

"¿Lo mato?" she asked again. "¿Con la pistola?"

"Sí," he murmured.

When he slept, she kissed him and rose from the bed.

In the lamplit kitchen she cleaned plates. Retch set the driller's bottle on the table. The brandy warm inside him. Liquor sweetness on his lips. He saw the stovepot with flies.

"Cover those beans, woman!"

"Screw your mother," she replied.

Retch smirked, sat at the table, his gaze on his empty glass. The woman washed plates, ignoring the beanpot.

"I told you to take care of those beans, chingado. I don't want my driller foodpoisoned. It's bad enough your cooking makes me sick."

Dolores covered the pot. At her feet the pail of beans, the buried gun. She turned from the stove, her face dark. "If you ever lay a hand on him again, you will be more than sick."

Retch shook his head. "I'm trying to protect him, you ignorant fool."

She reached into the pail, lifting a handful of beans. "All the same," she said, "and be that as it may, do not touch him again."

Beans dropped from her fingers into the pail, their sound like the ticks of a clock. "Que no lo vuevlas a tentar, te digo," she repeated.

Retch poured from the bottle, drank. "Fine," he said, refilling the glass. "Go bury another Epifanio."

She flung the beans at him. "Shut your mouth. I will see you dead first!"

Retch finished the drink, set down the glass, a bean at the bottom. "You think?" Then he was up and at her side. He saw her hand dig into the pail. "Beans won't do it," he snarled, grabbing her arms. He wheeled her against the table, the jolt sending bottle and glass to the floor. Her poblano dress wrested by the collar, the overwashed garment pulling off like paper, the woman naked. He lifted his fist hard between her legs. She bent double, lips parted. He shoved her onto the table, clenching her throat one-handed while he dropped his pants. When she opened for him, he loosened his grip. She gasped, pulled him down. Her nails tore his buttocks. "Cógeme," she teethed. "Sí es lo que tú quieres."

Their muffled grunts. Their sneering grins. Retch finished in a few pelvic thrusts, her heaving breath in his face. Neither of them saw the boy in the doorway. When they looked, only the dog watched.

The torn poblano loosely draped while she swept the broken glass. Retch sat in silence, the liquor large in his head, the brandy smell risen from the floor. He wanted another glass. When she moved to wash the plates, he rose and stood behind her. "Say something, you daughter of fornication. Say something or I'll make your black mouth bleed!" She turned and told him that if that was all he had to give for the night he had better go to bed like a good drunk. A rat's tit gave more milk, she said. A one-balled dog lasted longer.

Retch grabbed her by the hair and pulled her to his room. The torn poblano flung aside. He slammed her onto the bed, the woman spitting in his face as he took her again. "¿Es todo lo que tienes, gringo?" she taunted, holding up a drooped finger. She bit him awake when he dozed. She pinched and scratched. Until the hour of her departure, she mocked him. "Is that all you have, gringo?"

At dawn the driller began to sing.

That morning the bit broke through the granite. "Rubble zone," the driller shouted. He stopped the string and stepped down. "I would have a celebratory drink if you hadn't finished my bottle."

"I didn't finish it," Retch corrected. "I told you. It broke."

"I believe you. Either way, 'tis a good thing brandy ain't handy. Rubble means we can pull the string, throw on the Hughie, and bore the big hole straight to where the six-eyed horny weeps your water."

Retch nodded, head heavy.

"Are you ready for big?"

"Sure."

"Big means more mud. Rubble caves if it's not plastered."

"I can handle it."

The driller grinned. "You reckon?"

"I reckon, Bill."

"A bit of advice, budro."

"What?"

"Don't go drilling elsewheres come dark. Save your energies for this here hole." He laughed. Then he spoke of remedies given to mudmen and others he had dragged from all-night fornication in local brothels. "One was a Chinaman from Sichuan province. Looked like a rice thresher had chewed him. I made him stick his privates in a bowl of bottled lyewater, the kind used to make Jianshui zong. That brought him to life. Straightened his legs like chopsticks. Next hour he was shoveling mud faster than a madchink."

The sun beat on Retch. Her scratches burned. He tipped the thermos. "I'm fine," he said. "Just thirsty."

The driller grinned, a cigarette crooked in his lipcorner. "Aren't we all. Athirst is what we be."

She watched him drink. Water not his salvation, she thought. The opportunity to leave him dead in his bed saved for the next time he touched the boy. Not for him to know the trophy she would cut and feed to the dog. His morsel.

She made breakfast, ignoring the soreness of her throttled neck, the smell of the brandy in the kitchen.

The boy sniffed. "¿A qué huele, mamá?"

"Pigs," she answered. She told him to watch for broken glass.

The boy ate, eyeing the floor. Then he took the dog by the rope.

"Not outside," she said.

"¿Por qué?"

"Because he will bite you."

"¿Mi papi?"

She nodded.

The boy stood in the kitchen. "Like last night?"

"Yes, like last night."

"Was he biting you, mamá?"

She looked at him. "What?"

"Last night on the table. I saw him biting you with no clothes."

She felt the rush of blood to her face. She looked away. "Go to the room."

"But I want to be outside."

"Go!"

The dog followed him. Mud crumbles fell from the rope. Dolores stared at the table. She saw herself naked, legs lifted, their furious coitus. The boy not saved from the sight of what dogs do in the street. Her scar on fire. *El hijo de la chingada.*

She dug the gun from the beanpail, removing the dishcloth before she reburied it under a thin layer of beans. She warmed tortillas, making egg tacos, taking them to where they stood by the machine. She handed them to the driller.

The gringo's thin-eyed gaze on her. "Bring fruit," he said. "On a plate."

In the kitchen she hacked jícamas and mangos with the machete. She dropped the watermelon on the floor. The fruit dumped in a stewpot. At the wellsite she flung the contents from the pot. "¡Ten tu fruta!" she spat.

The fruit sank into the mud.

"The way pigs eat it," she snapped, retreating. She heard the blackman laugh his devil's laugh. From the gringo she heard nothing.

Minutes passed while she waited by the beanpail for him to come. When he didn't appear, she went to the room.

"I call it the Hughie. Fancy pards call it the Hughes tricone."

The bit a blackened head of steel with interlocking spindles and large teeth. Retch reminded of the driller's grin. "Hughes as in Howard?"

"Howard Robard Senior."

Retch nodded. "You knew Howard Hughes?"

"Knew him? Hell, I tested his dual-cone. 'Twas I who put him in the oil business at Spindletop Hill. Me and the one-armed Pattillo Higgins, deputy killer and niggerbaiter, another who bartered away God for grams of his gritty. A man who snubbed me in Corsicana in 1901."

Retch smiled. "That dates you, Bill."

"Didn't I say it was our secret?"

"You did. But that would make you a baby driller when he snubbed you." Retch wanted it to sound funny, but the driller didn't laugh.

"You don't believe me, bud?" He fixed Retch with his skewed gaze.

Retch clung to a smile. "Am I supposed to?"

"If you feel safer not believing, then by all means feel safer."

"Safer?"

"From my craziness." The driller tilted his head.

"I never said you were crazy, Bill. Some crazy stories, maybe."

"But you think I am."

Retch shook his head. "I think a man has to be half crazy to do what you do. And I mean half crazy in a good way."

Suddenly the driller's mouth went wide. His laugh loud like cannonfire. He slapped Retch on the back, the odd sensation returned, a cold hand inside him. "That's my budro. Leave craziness where craziness belongs!"

Retch laughed out of relief. Think water, he told himself. Water.

"I reckoned you wouldn't believe it, but it's still our secret, right?"

"Right," Retch said. *You crazy sonofabitch.*

They pulled the string, removed the rollerbit, and mated a reducer to the tricone. "What the boys on Devil's Island call a horse on the horsefly," the driller joked as he lowered the huge bit into the smaller pilot hole.

The weathered basalt reamed in an hour. The granite devoured by midday. The new hole seemed bigger than the bit itself. Black cuttings darkened the settling pit like the shadow of a submerged creature. The driller dropped his hand into the slurry to test the mud's thickness. Sometimes he shouted for lime. "Can't let the cuttings jam. Can't let the clay clog. Walking the fine line."

Early afternoon when the boy approached. He handed the driller a plate piled with bean tacos. He stared at the hole.

"It will eat you," Retch warned. "Now go."

The boy left. The driller offered the plate. "Fruit, budro?"

Retch ate the beans, the griddleheated corn. Old food washed down with townwater. An hour later he squatted in the latrine. When he returned to the site, the driller had jacked off his boots. His feet dangled in the mudpit. "A'times I get dog cricks." He lifted them from the mud. The feet strangely narrowed and turned inward. Big toes gone, others fused.

Retch stared. "Damn, Bill. What happened?"

"Nature took a nap, that's what. Ainhum and talipes. Dysmelia of the siamang kind. The unlearnt call it the blackfoot malady." He pointed to his boots. "The pointy toes keep 'em straight."

"I've never seen anything like it."

"Never will again. Not in your paltry years. What happens when the son of perdition sleeps with his little sister." He refooted the boots. "You like my rands?" He pointed to the embossed metal caps nailed to the boot tips."

"Sure," Retch lied.

"They came with a gold finish, but it wore off."

"Yeah?"

"Yeah. From sticking it up the butts of mudmen like you." He laughed. Then he got to his feet.

Dusk ran serpentine in a blueblack sky. Mud turned the color of rust in the jaundiced light. Retch stood grimed, arm-sore, his legs burned by lime. The day a year old.

The driller motioned for him to approach, the umbra of his gesture seeming to beckon before the gesture itself. "Need you handy, chico."

"Handy?" Retch waited for what nonsense came next.

"If I holler for mud, you taking to bed ain't handy."

"Okay."

"Bring something to lie on if you're the kind who needs his arse off god's griddle. I'll let you catch some winks when I can."

In the kitchen bean tacos left for dinner. Retch made sandwiches. He filled the thermos with tea. The boy came to the door.

"Papi."

"What?"

"Papi malo."

"Sí, papi malo."

"¿Papi?"

"What?"

The boy pointed outside. "Quiero salir."

"No."

"¿Por qué?"

"Porque el hoyo te mata."

"¿Papi?"

"What?"

"Mamá te mata."

"¿Sí?"

"Con pistola, papi."

He capped the thermos before he fetched the groundpad from his room. When he returned to the kitchen, the boy had bitten a sandwich. Retch smiled. "¿Con pistola?" he asked.

The boy swallowed. "Sí."

Retch took his hand and led him into the woman's room. Dolores lay on the bed. "Don't you ever throw my food away again!" he said from the door.

The woman didn't stir.

"I'm tired of your stinking tacos and badhumor. Do you hear me?"

The woman silent.

"If you think you have nothing to lose, think better."

The boy stood beside him, eating the sandwich.

"Listen, cabrona. You saw what drink does to me, so you better think hard about what you can lose that's precious to you." He patted the boy on the head. "What does the hole do, Epi?

"Mata, papi."

"¿Mata como pistola?"

"Sí, papi."

Retch smiled. "I know you have it," he said before he left.

The boy gave the sandwich remains to the dog.

Days since he had discovered the gun gone, the boxed shells not taken. What a woman would do, their community of villains small. The night in the kitchen he had given her motive to reveal it, but she had thrown beans instead. Biding her time, he concluded. Following a plan. Was it to shoot him without witness, the boy asleep, the driller gone? Bury him without deponent as she had done the old man? A good plan.

He wasn't worried. Only one round chambered in the pistol. Good odds if it came to her pulling the trigger first. He was sure she had never shot a gun.

That night the rubble cuttings rose coarse grained like arroyo sand. Retch made mud. Between batches he napped. When the driller called him, he rose stiff-jointed and dazed. Once he was shaken awake, or so he remembered, the driller whispering with cigarette breath. "Retch, ain't you afraid the Chiricahuas will raid the ranch?"

"What?" he answered.

"The Apaches."

"Apaches?"

"Geronimo's seed. Chased by Lawton into the sierra. They're up there, the renegade bands who scalp ranchers and steal horses."

"I don't have horses."

The driller's face close. "Ain't you considered the possibility?"

"Possibility?"

"That they'll take the woman."

Retch stared. "They haven't come."

"Later, when you have water."

Retch stared. "Take her," he said. Then he was asleep again.

So the night passed, the driller counting Retch's suspirations to some incalculable cipher. So he watched the fretful slumber of men in his employ. So he whispered. So he entered their dreams.

Dolores brought a dishclothed bundle, a bowl of beans. She handed them to the driller.

He unwrapped the cloth. "Holy treat. Flour tortillas."

Retch hadn't bought wheatflour in months. "I'd try one on the dog first," he said for the woman to hear. Then he called her to the hole. "Come, darling, look."

She retreated, silent.

The driller ate the tortillas. "Bit of wisdom for thee," he said. "Be careful of spurning vittles. I knew a man from Cochabamba who paid the price for foul-mouthing his wife's cookery."

Retch shoveled mud.

"He lost love and locution from vain and various imaginings . . ."

Retch shoveled.

"Cut off his tongue and penis with a pair of garden shears."

"What?" Retch grimaced. "She did?"

"No, he did, from the deliriants she put in his vittles. He thought he was pruning roses."

"Damn!"

"Hell's bells in chicken salteñas. A plant worse than poison. Makes you see what's not there."

Retch shook his head. "What became of him?"

"The pruner? Lived the remainder of his days in confabulation. The wife was stood against a wall and shot. I was drilling her father's well at the time. He knew the she-devil that swam from his loins."

Retch shoveled mud.

"So best watch thy vittles talk, you being a fellow with a big tongue."

"Right," Retch said.

Afternoon when the driller asked him to cut wood.

"Wood?"

"Scrubwood."

"For what?"

"A fire."

Retch weighed the words. "Damn, Bill, are you cold?"

The driller's toothy grin with beans. "A'times I like a campfire. Weather don't matter. Drillsteel in any season makes me want to warm my hands. You're the mudman and factotum, budro."

Retch wheeled the barrow into concessionland. "Budro this! Budro that!" he ranted. "What the hell was 'budro' anyway?" At a drywash arroyo he chopped the dead limbs of mesquite and falsemesquite. The smell of tar rose from the cut wood. He rested in the shade, the arroyo sand warm where he lay. Think water, he told himself. Everything else its price. The insane stories. The outlandish claims. That stupid grin. *Goddamn firewood.*

He slept and dreamed of walking on a mudded flat following strange-footed tracks—wide and toeless prints cast deep in the mire. Time unmeasured in his dream, the sun low when he awoke. The barrow axle squeaked as he hurried. At the ranch he saw the woman and boy at the hole. The driller petted the dog.

"Budro, did you take a siesta?"

Retch set the barrow, his gaze fixed on the woman.

The driller grinned. "Before you get the tizzies, 'twas I who invited them."

The string halted, the motor silent. Retch careful with words. "I'm looking like the bad guy, Bill."

"You are the bad guy, Retch, but that doesn't mean you can't win. I was being neighborly. No harm done."

The boy pointed to the hole. His hair gilded in the day's dying light. "Hoyo, papi."

Retch shook his head. "There's your wood."

"Did you bring olneya?"

"What?"

"Irontree. Burns slow. Keeps a nightlong fire."

"I cut what you see." He lifted the thermos and held it out to the woman. "Fill it," he said. "Bring it back."

The woman took the thermos and the boy. The boy took the dog's rope. They retreated to the rooms.

"Grab a bobbejaan, bud. It should feel light now that you're rested."

Retch said nothing.

"Rubble awaits."

An hour later no thermos brought, the woman's defiance complete. The driller drank from his carboy, offering it to Retch. "It's sweet," he said.

In the kitchen Retch found the woman absent, the thermos empty on the table. He swore loudly at her before he filled it and returned to the rig.

A blue moon risen when the driller laid his fire beyond the circle of riglight. The greenwood smoked. Dirty flames lit the darkness. Damn crazy, Retch thought as he shoveled mud. Later he napped in dreamless exhaustion, awaking to see the driller bootstir the embers, his grin bloodred in the reflected glow.

Three days passed. Six joints sunk in the clayplastered rubble. The hole a gulping void cranked by steel. When the mud dawned pale on the fourth morning, the driller shouted, "Limestone! Cavernous limey!"

Retch stared at mudpits turned ashen. In the driller's hand the calcareous cuttings chalkwhite. "We're into seabeds now. What lay beneath Leviathan waters."

"Is this good?" Retch asked.

"Good for you. No more mudmaking."

"I mean is it good for water?"

The driller fixed him with a skewed gaze. "Speaking from my limited experience in the drilling of Panthalassa sediments and what Kober called the Laurasian cratons, I'd answer yes. The wetdream you seek."

"Okay."

"First salty, then saltier, then sweet. Water, women, and life. Write it down, budro."

"Okay."

"No such thing as freshwater anyhow. Just old water running from its past. Like you."

"Right."

The driller eyed the sky before he pointed to the empty drums. "Tomorrow you fetch townwater."

Retch said he could fetch it today.

"Today's no day to travel the desert. Not a foreigner like you."

"Why is that, Bill?"

"Epiphany, budro. The manifestation of the holy semen to night-riding outlanders. You don't want to be on the road in a godforsaken place driving that dromedary of yours. Not today. Herod's seed is out there, most likely headed this way, coming to see what we're up to here, creating visions of our own with a boy closeby, a redheaded one at that. They might waylay a soulless man like you, ask directions. Did you know Jesus was red-haired?"

Retch smiled. "Damn, Bill. You sound more like a preacher every day."

"Once upon eternity I did proselytize in the halls of Pandemonium to the shrunken angels. That's where I got my voice."

"Good to know."

"And shame on you, bud, for not remembering your boy's nameday. Your papi-in-law's too. Two Epifanios."

"I told you. He's not mine."

The driller grinned. "So you did. Still, a failed Christian thee be. A sinner come from disordered desire."

Retch shrugged. "If you say so."

"I do, Retch. I see decency buried in a man before he sees it dead. I see it like I see what's at the bottom of that lightless borehole yonder. I see it by sampling what rises when it's drilled. You sample of lost lamb and the reek of its mother's soured milk. And I ain't but scratched the surface."

"Anyone could guess that," Retch said.

"I knew it before I found you, budro. Why I came to bring you water."

Retch nodded. "At eighty dollars a foot."

"That's the price, not the payment. The payment ain't made yet nor the yield measured."

"Okay."

For the next hours Retch watched the mud rise cindergray, the pits chalked with the ground shells of ancient foraminifera. Midmorning she came with food, the boy in hand, the dog on the rope.

"Ask her if she knows the day, Retch."

"You ask."

When the driller asked, the woman shook her head. "No sais."

Retch laughed. "There's an epiphany for you. Dumb as cement."

She left the food and took the boy's hand, the boy dragging the dog. The driller watched them. "Déjala, Red," he called. The boy released the rope, letting the dog return to the hole.

They ate standing by the rig. The driller took a tortilla and fed it to the dog. "Ever had dog tamales, budro?"

"No."

"Boiled buzzard?"

"No."

"It cures the clap, they say."

Retch said he would keep it in mind.

The driller gave the dog another tortilla.

"So how deep are we?" Retch asked.

The driller chewed. "Deep?"

"Yeah. How many feet?"

The dog licked the driller's fingers. She sat at his feet.

"Not deep enough for either of us, I reckon, but soon to get deeper."

Retch pointed to the joints stacked on the rails. "There's twelve left. That makes thirteen in the hole, right?"

"Sounds right."

They ate.

"So we're at . . . what . . . two hundred and sixty feet?"

"You do the math, bud. I'm counting tortillas. The tally is four to two. Four for me, two for the dog."

Retch drank from the thermos. "That puts us halfway there."

"Halfway to where?"

"To how deep we can drill. The five hundred feet."

The driller looked to the hole as though to measure it. "You do the supposing. Let me do the magic." He took a tortilla and held it over the dog's head, making her sit. Then he ate it. "No time for you to get fat, girl."

The sonofabitch, Retch thought. All nonsense, no answers. The stupid dog more important. "¡Vete!" he said, kicking the dog. She retreated to the rooms, dragging the mudded rope. Retch looked at the driller. "So after the limestone, what?"

The driller grinned. "Sandstone, Retch."

"And after sandstone?"

"Your favorite word, I reckon."

Retch waited. "And what is that, Bill?"

"Agua, budro. Agua."

The sun a rayless capitulum bloodred above the rimland. Retch watched it set from the latrine. *Craziness, yes, but no lost fingers, no cracked skull.* He glanced at his wrist, the pale band of flesh. That morning Digger's watch had fallen down the hole after the metal-link strap was snapped by the Stillson. He had said nothing to the driller. In the latrine he said, "It's yours, Dig."

At dark the driller halted the steel. He brought from the cab a red-labeled bottle Retch recognized. "Let us recount old times, sport."

The whiskey once Retch's preferred brand.

"Another time, Bill."

"Come. A night off. Join us."

"Us?"

"The pup and me. She likes a fire, too."

Retch said he preferred to turn in early so he might depart before sunup to load water.

"Suit yourself, pard."

That night Retch slept through the driller's clamor, the dog's howls. He did not see the roaring fire. Only the woman watched, close by her window. She saw the spectacle of his largeness before the flames. She heard his chants. What drillers did, she supposed. How the land was bled.

Before dawn Retch lifted the Fargo's hood. He read the dipstick with a penlight. He poked his finger into the radiator. When the driller suddenly appeared at his side, he jumped. "Christ, Bill! Make some noise!"

His grin gleamed with a seemingly self-made light. "I'm riding to town to get some particulars and necessaries," he said, whiskey on his breath, woodsmoke clinging to his clothes.

Retch stepped back. "What about drilling?"

"Budro of budros, drilling is my business." His voice a growl. His hulk loomed over Retch. "I'm fire-stoked, chico. Can't you smell the smoke?"

"Yeah." Retch circled the truck, checking the tires.

"Smoke drives off the snakes when they come to tongue-wag in the hole. The dog and me saw some big ones last night."

"Snakes?" A year on the ranch, Retch yet to see a snake.

"Dandies they were." He leered at Retch. "Like I said, I'm riding."

Retch shrugged. "Okay."

They rode onto the dawned rimland, blue bleeding into an eastern sky. Inside the cab a new odor. Moments before Retch placed it. "Bill, you smell of dog."

He grinned. "Snake-tangling fevered the pup. I gave her a bath."

Retch shook his head. *Wetdog, no less.*

The sun rose without splendor. The sky cloudless. At the guamúchil tree the driller told Retch to stop. He pulled a plastic bag from his boot. "I come prepared."

From the truckseat Retch watched with averted eyes as the driller picked fruit from the tree. When he circled the trunk and stopped before the hollow, Retch opened the truckdoor. He stepped into the road to urinate.

"A comfort it is to share the road with a shameless traveler," the driller called out. "I shall join thee directly." He seemed to sniff at the hollow before he reached in and removed the hooked branch. He dropped it to the ground. His hand entered again, arm disappearing to the elbow.

Retch climbed into the cab. The purse beyond reach, he told himself.

The driller's hand reappeared fisted with fruitpods. He held them up. "Paydirt, bud. God's little critters hiding treats in the tree of knowledge." He dropped them into the bag.

Retch lit a cigarette.

The driller returned to the truck with the bag full, his pockets bulging. Chewed guamúchil flesh speckled his grin.

At the mercantile he filled a cart with cigarettes, brandy, and Zote soap. "Citronella," he declared, sniffing the barsoap. "Good for headlice. Calms barking dogs, too."

Retch pulled a brandy bottle from the driller's cart and paid for it. "That's for what I broke."

"You're an honest budro for remembering."

While Retch loaded water, the driller entered the potablizer grounds, ignoring the NO ADMITTANCE sign. At the well he struck a contemplative pose, head tilted, one hand on the discharge pipe. He seemed to be listening.

"Familiar dirt," he said, back at the truck. "The vibrations rise through the same limey we auger."

Retch said the year before he had sounded the well with a dropped stone, calculating from the falltime a depth of four hundred feet.

"Not a bad cipher, but the town sits on higher ground than your spread. Topographically if not morally."

In the plazuela he hailed a shoeshine boy to the wrought-iron bench where he sat. He smoked as the boy dubbed his boots. Retch went to the hotel to check for mail. At the frontdesk the pale clerk clapped his delicate hands before he delivered a message from a driller in Caborca who had answered the newspaper ad. "Raining drillers," Retch said, pocketing the paper with the man's name and number. Back at the plazuela, he found the shineboy spit-polishing the driller's boots with ash dropped from his cigarette. "I want a luster to blind the ladies, budro." After he paid the boy, he said he had a hankering for tripe soup served with clear broth.

They sat among men on stools at a menudo stand in the market. No man looked at the driller, his dogsmell undiminished. He ate four steaming bowls, commending the owner for using tripe from the second stomach. When he said he would refuse to pay for tripe cut from the first, the owner laughed.

At the Pemex station Retch filled drums with diesel before he topped off the Fargo's fuel tank. The driller returned from a corner grocery with a handful of hardcandy. The sun overhead when they left the pavingstone street, the Fargo lifting dust on the silica flat. Retch accelerated past the cemetery, his passenger pointing. "Drill fields yonder. As deep as most get."

In the graveled lot of the town brothel, men descended from pickup trucks, their sombreros daybright. The driller motioned for Retch to stop. "How about a nip and a chat with the pretties?"

Retch slowed the truck. "What about the water?"

"It'll keep." He opened the passenger door and got down with a bottle of brandy. "I believe the sharpie Arenas lurks within." He pointed to a truck loaded with rusted metal. "I can smell the slag on a whorehouse plumber. No perfumed pretties can hide a scrapmerchant."

Retch parked the truck. Bill left alone in a brothel beyond calculable outcomes. When he caught up, he noticed how the driller's newly polished boots shimmered in the noonlight, toe rands catching the sun.

Heads turned, voices hushed. The driller grinned, all teeth in the dark. "Buen día a todos!" he greeted to whores, patrons, the establishment at large. No one answered.

They took a booth, the driller seated large on his side. He laid a fifty-peso bill on the table. He set his bottle on it before he gestured to the barman. "Glasses and ice, sir."

The barman eyed the bottle, the fifty-peso bill.

"We don't drink overpriced, watered-down liquor," the driller explained. "Not for free. Not if you paid us with your life." The barman returned with glasses and ice. The fifty pesos left untouched.

Retch signaled a half a glass. The driller filled it.

"Do you see the varmint Arenas?"

"No."

"Scrapping some prepubescent, no doubt."

Retch drank. "You seem to have a low opinion of him."

"Fat patrónes bedding girlchildren what the Spaniards brought. I don't know the man, only his church."

Retch said Rolando was a sharpie and tailchaser but not a bad man.

"I only want to buy him a drink." He emptied his glass, filled it. A whore squeezed beside him, her red dress shimmering. Retch recognized her as the pimple-faced whore he had pushed from the booth. The driller took in the dress, the face, a small thing measured.

The whore sniffed. She avoided Retch's gaze. When she asked for a drink, the driller pushed his glass before her. "Drink," he said.

She squinted at the bottle, her hand disappearing beneath the table to fondle him. The driller grinned, his skewed gaze unnoticed by the handbusy whore. Then she gave a startled gasp, eyes darting to his face, seeing his teeth, the devouring look. Her hand quickly surfaced. She rose from the booth. "¿Qué traes ahí?" she shrilled, her sallow makeup creased with perplexity. She pointed between his legs. "Eres un pinche monstruo."

The driller drank the brandy. "¿Cuánto?" he asked.

She smirked. "For you, not at any fornication of a price."

He nodded. "A siren song she sings, pard, much to her credit."

Retch said she had once given him a price of fifty pesos. He chinned at the money on the table.

"Did you accept?"

"I didn't have change at the time."

"Y tu, pinche gringo maricón," teethed the whore.

Retch lifted his glass to the insult. "She called me that before."

The driller laughed his deep laugh, patrons turning to look. He waved the whore away, telling her she would make more money screwing blind men in a miner's camp.

"Un monstruo," she spat as she left. "Una bestia. Y apestas a perro."

They drank, the driller beckoning the barman, handing him the fifty pesos. "It's drawing flies, friend." The barman returned with more ice.

From his pantspocket the driller pulled a fistful of guamúchil pods. He dropped them on the table. "Keep you hard in a place like this."

Retch nodded. "No wonder she bolted."

"She's not fond of dogs either."

"No."

"An imaginative girl, nonetheless. Can't blame her confoundment. Damnedest job, whoring."

Retch finished his glass, the brandy smoky, his head clear. He spotted the scrapdealer weaving among the tables. "Rolando!" he hailed.

The dealer stopped to peer at them. "¿Qué pasa?"

"Come have a drink," Retch said.

He didn't move.

"We have a bottle."

"I have commitments. Tomorrow."

"Just one drink. Come. Bill wants to meet you."

"¿Guillermo?"

"Guillermo el perforista."

The driller spoke. "Your friend has offered you a drink. It would be rude to refuse. One drink, Fermín."

Rolando's mouth agape. "How do you know that name?"

"Sit, please, and I will tell you. If you prefer, we can drink outside. Or we can go to your yard. What do you say?"

Rolando approached. "Okay," he said. "One. Then I must go."

"Of course."

He sat beside Retch. He smelled of beer and peanuts. The driller motioned for another glass. He filled it and pushed it toward the dealer.

"Salud," they said, drinking.

"¿Es bueno, no?" the driller asked.

Rolando nodded. "Muy bueno."

The driller offered the guamúchil fruit on the table. Good for an overworked machine, he said.

Rolando declined, emptied his glass.

"¿Otro?"

When Rolando shook his head, the driller refilled the glass. "Por sus favores, Fermín."

The dealer shot a nervous glance at Retch. "¿Mis favores?"

"For the favor of allowing us to use your street to store our casing. For the favor of your company, Fermín."

Rolando said no one but his father had called him that.

"And God," added the driller.

"Of course, God."

"And the yarder from Huásabas. He called you Fermín."

Rolando showed surprise. "That goat fornicator?"

"Yes."

"That son of a stinking violated mother!" The dealer seemed to relax, comforted by his own profanity. He said his father, when drunk, had called him Fermín. Why he hated the name.

"It's but a name," the driller said, pouring himself another drink.

Rolando said he had told the yarder from Huásabas to leave the casing on the street for convenience's sake. So it might be retrieved at any hour. "You saw my dogs?"

"Yes, they are as brave as you," the driller said, watching the dealer drink. "Can we buy you a whore to show our appreciation?"

Rolando thanked them. "I have just come from a whore."

"Word is there are youngsters in the stable. Is this true?"

The dealer said he knew only there were many lies in this place. More lies than whores.

"I will pick one for you," the driller offered.

The scrapmerchant played with his glass. "I'm sorry, but I must go. One drink has become two. I have commitments. Thank you, Bill."

"Call me Negro, brother. Only Retch calls me Bill."

"Bien."

"Say it."

"¿Perdón?"

"Mi nombre. Negro."

"Ah. Negro."

The driller stood. "Un momento," he said.

As soon as the driller departed, Rolando leaned across the table. "Mucho cuidado," he croaked, touching his bottom eyelid, a sign to watch out.

Retch nodded. "You told me."

"Very but very careful." The dealer slid out of the booth.

"You are leaving?"

"Of course. It's him."

"Who?"

"Your driller. He is El Güero!"

"What?"

"He is a black El Güero!"

Retch grimaced. This kind of nonsense came from screwing schoolgirls. "Rolando, do you take me for a fool?"

The dealer looked behind him, shook his head. "No. I'm the fool for not telling you sooner. Now you are mixed up with him, visiting whores."

Retch smiled. "I thought you said El Güero was dead."

"No, he's alive."

"You said he was struck by lightning."

"Yes, but 'dead' I never said. 'Alleged dead,' I said."

"Alleged dead?"

"Yes."

"Was he alleged white?"

"What?"

"I thought El Güero was white."

"He was, but now he is black."

Retch searched the dealer's face for amusement. He saw only alarm. "And how do you explain that?"

"El relámpago, hombre."

"Lightning?"

"Yes. It turned him black. Like a burnt tortilla."

Retch stared.

"Don't laugh!"

"I'm not laughing."

"You're laughing on the inside. I can see it. This is nothing to laugh about. I must go. Your driller is not from our world."

"He's from Texas."

"So he says. But he is El Güero, I'm sure of it. He is big like El Güero and pig filthy like El Güero. He smells . . ."

"That's dog."

"And he is short-fingered. The yarder from Huásabas said he threatened to kill his family. He said your driller is somekind of devil."

"You better get some sleep," Retch said.

"You don't believe me?"

"Of course."

Rolando drew close, whispered. "Careful, my friend. Make no deals."

"Okay."

When the dealer left, Retch tossed back his glass, poured another, relieved to be alone. *Make no deals*. Rare advice coming from the scrapdealer.

The sun risen before Dolores approached the machine. At the hole she peered into the gaping, rock-toothed orifice. Her face close, the dank breath of the hole the same as gravedirt freshly dug. She dropped small stones, listening for splashes, hearing only ricochet chinks. The boy appeared beside her, trying to look. "¿Hoyo mamá?"

"¡Vete!" she scolded. She waited for him to retreat before she took from her dress the bag with toloache and coyotillo seeds, the same used to sicken the man. She weighted the bag with a rock and dropped it into the hole. Something, she thought. No harm too small.

She opened the truckdoor. Inside the cab his sweat stench and tobacco smell. On the seat lay soiled clothes and empty liquor bottles. Jars of bloodcolored dirts stood on the floor. She touched nothing, no money spotted. When she looked under the seat, she recoiled. "¡Híjole!" she blurted. On the driver's side a snouted head peered out through dulled eyes, the animal not one she knew. Beside it lay a coiled snakeskin the color of honey.

"Brujo," she gasped. She remembered the forked stick the blackman had used to find water. She recalled the roaring fires, his songs sung with the devil's voice. Suddenly the mosaic shaped. The bloodred dirts. This head and skin. *The gifted rabbitfoot.*

She closed the door and backed away, sure of it. The big Negro was a witchman. She wiped her hand on her dress. She stared at the cabdoor. She saw his grin and tilted eyes in the scratched paint. Toloache and coyotillo seeds no match for his magic, she told herself. He would find water. He would bleed the land. No task beyond the power of a witchman. Even the unfriendly dog made friendly to him.

She looked for the dog. The silence of the rooms intruded. She listened and then she hurried, circling the rig. At the hole the boy dropped stones.

"El hoyo habla, mamá."

She carried him to the rooms, hearing herself repeat the gringo's warning. "¡Es peligroso!"

"The hole speaks, mama."

"It speaks death. It will swallow you!" She fed and bathed him. Later, while he napped, she took the rabbitfoot from his pocket. Back at the hole, she dropped it by its gilded chain, watching it disappear into the blackness.

The driller returned holding Digger's whore by the hand. "Where's Fermín?"

"Sick," Retch said.

"Sick? A shameful reprieve that is."

Dig's whore tall in glittering silverheels. Her lovely iodine skin. She sat next to the driller and scowled at Retch.

"I brought us a pretty."

"I see."

The driller grinned. "Have you kept company with this lovely?"

Retch said she was the whore of his former partner.

"The prospector? He who preserved his health?"

Retch nodded. The driller guffawed. He poured the whore a drink in the scrapdealer's glass. "Darling, excuse us for conversing in foreign tongues."

She shrugged. She said she cared not what tongue a man spoke—it was all nonsense. She said she preferred to know what a man's tongue could do when not speaking.

"Ah, la lengua del amor." The driller grinned. "Budro, don't you love a pretty who talks dirty?"

Retch poured himself another drink. "She's got dirt alright."

"A linguistic appreciation of men."

She drank. "¿Y el reloj?" she asked, eyeing Retch's wrist.

"Gone," Retch said.

She sneered. "Gone like him?"

"Like him."

The driller refilled his glass. "You lost your fancy watch, Retch?"

He nodded, drank.

"Where?"

"The hole."

"The hole? Hot durn. Well, you'll be tasting it soon enough."

Retch avoided her gaze. She was an astute bitch, sly and edible over endless nights. A trophy harlot unsafe for slumber.

The driller finished his drink. "Shall I ask her which of us she wants?"

"Ask." Retch poured more brandy. He knew the answer but not its eloquence.

She pointed her glass at him. "That redheaded faggot will make me disappear if I go with him. He's a filthy son of a treacherous goat."

Retch nodded. "You win."

The driller's laugh filled the brothel. His considerable blackness seemed to grow in the gloom. "Fair enough."

The liquor large in Retch's head. His glass full. *Faggot? Filthy son of* . . . He flung the brandy, aiming for her eyes.

She gasped, face askew. Then she quickly composed a smile. With practiced flicks her tongue swept the brandy to suckling fingers. Her savoring sounds meant to mock him. Retch threw the glass.

An upholstered ricochet sent it off the back of her head, the glass hitting the floor with a sharp, vitreous clink no one but the barman noticed. Retch saw her hand before he saw the blade, a fingerlength stiletto swiping at his face.

The driller caught her arm, his spatulate grasp swallowing hand and knife. Then he held only the knife. She flailed and swore.

Retch saw the spatter of flung brandy, no blood. The driller dropped the knife into his shirtpocket. "That would be a sight," he said. "You cut. What would the missus say?"

The whore spat in Retch's face. "Vamos," she snapped. She rose, silverheels stepping over broken glass. "You'll pay!" she said. "Dead you are, gringo. I know someone!"

Before Retch could grab the bottle, the driller took it. He slid from the booth. "Don't break another, budro."

"¡Hija de tu reputísama madre!" Retch shouted. He knew he was drunk when he said it twice. He turned to the driller. "You can get your own damn ride! I'm not waiting!"

The driller grinned. "Are you sure, Retch? She'll squeal soon enough."

"Goddamn sure."

He took the whore by the hand. "Don't go killing anyone with the truck."

"Go to hell."

"Pronto, pard."

Retch watched the barman broom the glass. *Wait,* said a voice behind the swirling curtain of liquor. *Wait if you want water.* He pushed the guamúchil fruit off the table for the barman to sweep. "Tequila," he ordered.

The barman came with a glass, the tequila poured.

"¡La botella!" Retch demanded. When the barman returned, Retch seized the bottle, waving the barman away. He drank, staring thin-eyed into the gloom. He searched the powdered whores for a pimpled face. If he saw her, he would have her. Have her but not pay her. Then he would punch her.

He looked at his wrist. Time gone. Dig gone. The driller. *Wait,* said the voice. *Wait for water.* He took the bottle and rose, moving to the door.

"¡Señor, señor!" called the barman. "¡La cuenta, por favor!"

Retch stared. The barman's face a blur. The planet heaved. "Let the black son of a fornication pay," he growled.

Outside, the oppressive luminance flattened him like a shadow. The sunbright gravel a world too stark to stand in. He found the Fargo by circling the lot until he came upon a patch darkened by water—the signature of leaking drums.

The smell of the driller's barsoap strong in the cab. Retch dimly recalled some connection with barking dogs. He sat behind the wheel, closed the door, rolled down the window, opened the door. He tried to start the truck without the keys. The bottle rolled off his lap and fell to the gravel. He watched it drain on the stones.

His hands fumbled in his pockets, a paper found. Retch stared blindly at the name and number left by the driller from Caborca. Then he wadded the paper and threw it out the door.

He reclined on the seat, the mercantile box his pillow, none of him left for the daylit world. He slept with the cab-door open, feet protruded, dreaming strange dreams. In one the scrapdealer chased the pimpled whore. In another the driller stood by the rig without boots, his feet hoofed, his mouth swallowing a woman, her shoes silver.

When Digger's whore hurried past the open-door truck, she saw him on the seat, but she did not stop, not to curse him, not to pick up the tequila bottle and break it on his head. She ran barefooted, holding to her heels, looking back as she ran. She fled as though hobbled, a contorted stride. The gravel hot, her blood dripping on the stones. She hailed a departing patron, climbing into the front seat of his sedan, finally wiping her torn mouth.

Retch slept, and when he awoke, the driller drove the truck, behemoth behind the wheel.

The sun down, the land gray-lit. Retch peered out the window. His pants smelled of tequila. The rutted road bounced in his head. He straightened himself. "I can drive," he said.

"Don't discommode yourself. I haven't steered Canadian made since Failing mounted a corebore on a Hayes Clipper, 1936. The Drumheller field, Alberta badlands."

He drove, the guamúchil tree passing unremarked.

Retch stared at the road, pushing past the tequila. He remembered the barman sweeping glass. "Did you pay?"

"She paid, gave me everything she had—booty and blood, fear and loathing. Paid in full but unpardoned. Barely got away with her fragile soul."

"I mean the barman. What we owed."

The driller grinned. "No charge, he said."

"No charge?"

"I suspect he wants return business."

The truck jounced, the motor revved. Retch wanted to hold his head.

"Budro, are you aware of the erections men get in the face of death?"

Retch closed his eyes. "No, Bill. I'm not."

"Well, the whore knew about it. She performed fellatio on a man about to be executed by a young druglord in town. The druglord had hired her to torture this man—a car-thief, I think—by showing him the pleasures soon to be lost. The poor bugger had an erection when she was brought to him. Imagine that! Hands and feet bound, gun to his head, still rockhard. She sucked until his brains blew clear."

Retch said nothing.

"A whore with a unique perspective on death."

Retch said nothing.

"Which gets me to her man."

"Which among many?"

"Your pard, the prospector. She thinks you killed him."

The Fargo backfired, a single detonation sharp like a gunshot.

"Oh, yeah." Retch yawned. "Well, Rolando thinks you're the devil. So there you go."

The driller laughed his wellbottom laugh. "That's a good one. I'll have to show him my tail."

"He says you're the dead driller they call El Güero."

The grin large. "Dead and resurrected, then?"

"White in a previous life."

The sound of his laughter shook the cab. "So I'm a reincarnated whiteboy and you're an unconvicted manslayer."

"That's the short of it."

They drove, the silence of the road between them, the day fading fast. Retch closed his eyes.

"She says you killed him and kept his watch. That fine timepiece you lost."

Retch spat out the window. "It was his watch all right, but I didn't have to kill him for it."

"She was sweet on him. Sweet on his loving."

"Sweet on his money."

"You think?"

"She's a whore."

The driller laughed. "I'd say you're right, except she didn't charge me. Not a peso or a promise. Not when she saw what I had brought with me. Those monkeypods in my pants."

They rode, Retch's head enlarged by trucknoise, his thirst aggravated by the sound of sloshing water drums.

"You all right?"

"I'm fine." Retch stared at the road.

The driller sucked on a piece of hardcandy. "Mexicans say that to be a man you have to kill one. You think that's so?"

Retch shrugged. "Depends."

They rode.

"On the man?"

"On why he is killed."

"True," the driller said. "The sun would not move otherwise."

They rode.

"It was the watch that riled her, budro. The jewels, I think."

"Forget the watch."

"She said your pard had promised it to her."

Retch said a man promised a lot of things in a whorehouse.

"True. But timekeeping is convenient for a whore."

"Screw her."

The driller's grin candycolored. "I won't say I didn't, but I will say she didn't much like it. Got me a souvenir anyway." He pulled the whore's stiletto from his shirtpocket. "You almost got one, too."

Retch silent. He watched the driller toss the knife out the window.

They rode, dusk unfolding, the thirst of the land large in Retch.

The boy ran to the truck. "¿La perra, papi?"

Retch surveyed the clearing. "No sais."

The driller unloaded his box. "She fought off snakes last night, bud."

"Right."

"¿Papi, la perra?"

Retch shrugged. "She's around."

In the kitchen he drank from the cántaro. "Make food!" he told the woman, words to bludgeon her silence.

That night at the table, the driller watched her serve. He had scented her presence in the truckcab. He had seen their mudprints at the hole.

"Muy rico todo," he complimented. He said his appetite came from an exhausting day in town. He winked at Retch.

The woman silent. She had smelled their tequila and whore scents.

"¿La perra, papi?" the boy asked.

"Stop asking," Retch said. "I don't know."

"She's probably off licking snake bites, but don't mention it."

"I won't," Retch said.

"Could be wrong. Dogs run off, too. Like whores. Like wives."

Later, in the room, when the boy asked for the rabbitfoot, the woman said she had not seen it. When he asked for the dog, she said the same. Later, watching him sleep, she recalled what she had seen under the seat of the witchman's truck. She wondered if the dog would do well to stay away. Something, perhaps, the dog already knew, better than the man.

A booming clap sounded above him. Retch looked up to see mud blasted skyward from the mast.

"Cave-in!" shouted the driller.

The spray arced and fell, a dark rain of drillfluid chilled by well depth. Retch hunkered and covered his eyes. The driller throttled the motor and halted the string. He stood mucked and grinning. "Got us a stopper!"

Retch spat. "Damn, that's rank!"

"It's the limey, chico. Spoilt seacritter soup."

They stared at the hole. "How bad?" Retch asked.

"Could be bad. Could be worse. No such thing as a good cave-in."

Gurgle sounds rose from the bore. The driller rummaged through his toolboxes. "I saw a fellow get blasted plumb through by a rampant mudhose. He was left looking in on himself before he defuncted."

Retch removed his shirt and wiped his face.

"Pent-up mud cuts like a chisel. A pump don't know when a hole caves. It keeps cycling until something gives." He handed Retch a hydraulic hose attached to a gooseneck fitting. "That's the swivel coupling. The hose is shorter than the blown one. I'll raise the kelly so it reaches."

Retch climbed the mast shirtless, pantscuffs tucked in his boots, wrenches in his pocket. Near the top he looped his belt through the trusses to free his hands. He unbolted the ruptured hose, removed the fitting, and attached the swivel coupling. He tossed the blown hose into the clearing before he rebolted the assembly to the quill. The new hose shorter by a foot.

The driller restarted the motor. "Here goes!" he called.

Above Retch the shuttle chains rattled. The winch cable drew down on the crownblock. He watched the braided wire load under the weight of sunken drillpipe. He leaned from the mast, his belt stretched. "Shit!" he teethed. A snapped cable the same as a flying buzzsaw.

"Don't crap!" the driller shouted. "I got mud enough on me."

Retch saw his grin. He saw the woman and boy in the doorway. Then the string lifted, inches, a foot, enough to connect the hose. The cable went slack as the driller engaged the clutch. "Go to it!"

Sonofabitch, Retch said to himself. The god of steel watches. He leaned over the kellybar to couple the hose and mate the flanges, tightening the clamps. He pocketed the wrenches and unlooped his belt. When he heard the shuttle chains rattle, he looked up, a splitsecond glance. He never saw the traveling block ascend. Then it smashed his face.

He took the blow and held on, cold steel mouthed, nose blossomed red, his descent spiraled in profanity. On the ground his bloodspoor a trail of dark mercurial coins oddly minted. In the Fargo's sidemirror he saw a nose newly dimensioned, mouth ballooning. His front teeth wobbled.

The driller stood beside him. "Good grief, budro."

Retch found his shirt and pressed it to his nose.

"Never seen the pawl jump a gear like that. It's the devil messing."

"Boo shee." Retch's snouted words.

"At least you're alive."

Retch shook his head. A consolation as unwelcome as the driller's grin.

"Get thee washed. I'll back out the bit. No need for mud now."

"Uck ud," Retch said.

In the latrine he stuffed toiletpaper plugs into his nostrils. He went to the kitchen where he soaped his face in a washbasin. He wiggled the loose teeth until they fell out.

The boy watched. "¿Sangre, papi?"

Retch nodded.

The boy stared at his mouth. "¡Mira!" he said. "Como mi mamá."

Retch found a clean shirt. The boy right. His mouth like the woman's.

Outside, the roar of the rig motor unusually loud. When Retch returned to the hole, the driller stood over it, looking down. "Bad news, chico. We lost the Hughie."

She watched him dangle. She saw his blood. *Fall, cabron,* she said silently. *Fall.* When the blackman looked at her, she averted her gaze. She wanted to retreat, but the boy held her, seeming to know the man would save himself. After she saw him descend, heard his curses, she pulled the boy inside.

Now she listened to his sounds from the kitchen. Grunts, snuffles. She had seen enough of his face to record the busted nose, the torn grimace. Her only comfort his pain. The clearing rained with mudded water, the coyotillo and toloache flung, nothing gained. Such the power of this black brujo.

In the room the boy whined for the dog.

"De vit?"

"What?"

"De vit amnit!" Retch spat the words.

"The bit? Lost, budro. The collapse peeled her off."

Retch stared at the hole. *What the hell*, he wanted to say. Instead he held up his hands. What the hell, he gestured.

"Nothing left now but to pull the string and rebore. Then I'll drop a sleeve and try to snag her. Called fishing. You like fishing, don't you?"

"What?"

He grinned. "What you've been doing since you came here."

Retch didn't get it. What was so funny? His busted face? His toothless words? Damn Bill and his endless nonsense. Now they had to drill again? Drill to find the drill? Retch held his head.

"Cheer up. Drilling is full of doglegged detours. No straight road to infernal floods. Wretchedness the price, like I told you. Wretchedness for Retch."

His nose bled. A rockchisel hammered in his mouth. The sun too bright. "Go," he uttered, turning away.

The driller watched. "Boil yucca tea for those tooth-holes. Chew clove."

Retch retreated.

"I'll pull the steel and fetch us a fisherpipe," the driller said. "No such thing as good timing, budro, but so you know, by the bye, I'll need another advance for delays and such. No hurry. Just putting in the word. You rest."

In his room Retch opened the brandy. *Yucca? Clove?* He swirled the liquor in his mouth, weathering the fire before he swallowed. He doused his kerchief, holding it to his nose, head back, the hotpoker flush running to his throat. He gagged, recalling a time years before when drunk adversaries had shoved his head into a barroom sink, holding it in the liquor residuum of drained glasses. So the brandy burned.

From the kitchen came cooking sounds but no smell of food. Only the Madera in his nose. He tipped the bottle and drank, washing the ironmetal taste of blood from his mouth. *Goddamn Bill.* The words too painful to utter. He drank again. *Goddamn him!*

He sat on the bed waiting for the brandy to lean on a broken nose. Blood dripped on his boots. *Hell to pay . . . Hell!* He tipped the bottle, listening to the kitchen noise. After another swallow he stretched on the bed. Brandy ran off his chin as he drank.

When he awoke, morning gone from his window, the fusillade of noon peppering his face through the rooftin holes. He sat and probed his crusted lips, the enlarged nose. By the bed the Madera bottle half empty.

In the kitchen the stove cold, the floor swept. No motor sound heard from the clearing. At the wellsite he found the rig shut down, the hole emptied of drillsteel, the mudded joints restacked. No sign of the driller.

He retreated to the dwelling and checked the woman's room. Even the dog absent. Then he remembered the dog not seen since the trip to town. From the doorway he surveyed the rimland before his gaze turned to the clearing. He stared at the corral. The Fargo not there. "Sonofabitch!" He patted his pants. The keys gone from his pocket.

His busted face pulsed as he stood in the sun staring at the fresh wheeltracks. His nose dripped. He kicked the dirt. "That black sonofabitch!"

Back in the kitchen, he scraped slush ice from the freezer, packing it into a ball that he wrapped inside his kerchief and pressed to his nose. He reclined on the table and closed his eyes, seeing them in his truck. He saw the road and he saw the hours unfolding until their arrival, the driller's budro-laced explanation, the woman silent, face dead as dirt. She knew his pockets, which keys.

Take the bitch. But the truck?

A trickle of melted ice soothed the raw-toothed gaps. Water his demon and deliverance. He opened his eyes and sat up, recalling what the driller had said, the last thing wanted. An advance.

He slid off the table and wrung the water from his kerchief. Screwed, that's what he was. A lost bit. A half-drilled hole. A waterless ranch. *Screwed.*

He searched her room, checking the mattress, inverting the bedframe. Under a blanket he found stockpiled beans, rice, powdered milk. Her hedge against hunger or simply the easiest way to steal. From a sack of nixtamal he pulled a jar filled with bills and coins, a neckchain he had seen the woman wear. He reached to the bottom of the sack, feeling for the gun, not finding it.

Afternoon shadows stretched across the clearing when he stood in the doorway surveying the rimland. His gaze fell on the rig, the mudded steel. He thought about it. *You won't have another.*

His nose freshly stoppered with toiletpaper plugs, he climbed onto the platform and began to look. The cabside fitted with toolboxes that held cable, chain, lubricants, a hundred kinds of bolts. Wrapped in a piece of canvas, he found the dogcollar without rope, the cinch unbuckled. Damn neat trick for a dog, he thought. The leather darkly stained. What the odds? he wondered. Odds of a dead dog? He rewrapped the collar, remembering the driller's wet canine stink, his talk of snakes, the bottomless hole of words.

He resumed his search. The toolchests rifled before he descended to open the cabdoor. Bill's prohibition recalled. *Tough luck, Billdro.*

Grimed clothes on the seat, jarred muds on the floor. Empty liquor bottles lay tipped on their sides. No keys in the ignition but the smell of him large in the cab, too much even for Retch's swollen nose. Cigarettes. A musty odor of something old and decayed. Retch peered under the seat. He made out handtools, belts, hoses. Then he spotted what was wanted—the driller's sounding wire.

At the hole he unreeled turns from the wooden spool, the line hashed with footmarkers, its end fixed with a plumb of bullet-shaped lead. Retch slid the spool onto a shovel-handle and centered it over the hole. His hand rode the spoolflange as the wire unwound. He read the marks. Fifty, one hundred. He felt for slackening that signaled obstruction. One fifty, two hundred, two fifty, two seventy-five. He braked the spool at two hundred and ninety feet. *Close.* That morning they had added the fifteenth joint—three hundred feet of drillpipe sunk.

He inched the wire off the reel. Two ninety-five. Three hundred. Three ten. More hole than he expected. Three thirty, the wire taut. At three hundred and sixty feet, Retch tested the tension. The line weighted, the plumb free. He stared into the hole. *Where was the cave-in?*

In the clearing dusk descended. He bent close to the wire, the hashmarks hard to read. He was about to release the spool, allowing the plumb to fall unfettered, when he heard the backfire of his truck.

He pulled the shovel handle to respool the line, winding furiously, the plumb heavy in ascent. When he looked up, he saw headlight penumbra from the rimland.

Three something on the wire, the numbers blurred. Retch gripped by the dead certainty that he should not be found with the sounder. No good would come from the driller seeing his mudman measuring the hole.

Headlamps crested the rimrocks, the dustveiled beams vectoring into the basin, light in search of a restless truth. Retch dropped the spool and hauled in the wire hand over hand, letting it gather behind him, the line slippery.

He heard the motor's rev on the basinslope, an old song in his head. He pictured the driller's grin in the windowglass, the menacing teeth. He pulled faster, his wire-cut hands blood sticky, the uncoiled line bunching at his feet. Too much down the hole, he realized. No time to retrieve it.

He released the line and stepped back, the plumb dropping, the wire coils snaring his boots.

The truck raced, its motor whined. Retch kicked himself free, the line snapping straight, the coils vanishing. The empty spool jumped to the hole and dropped from sight.

Headlighted dust rolled into the clearing before the truck itself. Retch walked purposefully to the doorway, unsure if he was seen.

Moments passed. He stood in the kitchen darkness, hearing the boy's voice. "Mira!" He waited. The wire-cuts hot, his mind retracing his steps. Had he shut the cabdoor? Had he left anything at the hole? He touched his nose. The paperplugs gone.

Dusky illumination reached the kitchen when the rig's floodlamps lit the clearing. The woman appeared with the boy, a balloon tethered to his hand. "Mira!" The woman wore the huipil dress.

"¡Rata!" Retch spat through blood-crusted lips.

She took the lantern and lit it. Silent, stiff-jawed, she led the boy to the room. Nothing she could say not already said by the balloon. So they had once gone with him, a memory without color, faded by endless sunstoked days.

He nearly called her back, demanding whatever came to mind, her sullen silence made to stand before him. Instead he washed his hands.

"Budro!"

The voice felt as much as heard.

"Budro!"

He waited. *Damn his mouth.* What about the truck?

In the clearing the rig's shadow blacker than the night. The driller stood by the hole. Retch raised his voice, anger enunciated. "What'n ell!"

"I got us a fisher, pard." He pointed to a manlength pipe on the ground.

Retch ignored it. "My truck, damn you!"

His grin white in the riglight. "Hell, I couldn't tote this on foot."

The pipe with a slotted flange and threaded collar. "So?"

"So I needed your truck to haul it."

Retch shook his head.

"You lay asnooze with booze, sport. I asked your woman for the keys. It didn't seem right not to invite them. We would have been back before dark if the sharpie hadn't cut himself."

Retch stared. "What?"

"Fermín vermin, lord savior of the lost Hughie. That's his handiwork." He pointed to the pipe. "I went to his yard and found him beer-soaked, whore-stenched, and laid-out in a bucketseat. I said, 'Rise and shine, Fermín. We've got an emergency.' I rattled the sharpie's cage. He had no choice but to open up and sell me pipe. I made him flange and weld it, too. That's when he cut himself, his hands jittery from whoring and drink. I took over and finished the job. When I asked him what was owed, he said he'd settle up with you."

Retch silent.

"I told him, 'Fermín, take care of that cut before it infects. Your yard has tetanus by the hectare.' He said he knew a doctor who could check it. Then I said, 'By the way, I'm no devil or reincarnated white driller, so you can rest your mind about rumors.' He didn't seem convinced. I could have told him he was going straight to hell in a rusty drum for sharping and finagling, but it would have stopped his heart faster than that underage harlot who's got him by the pecker. I loaded the pipe and picked up your woman and boy at the plazuela. Got us a bite to eat before we hit the road."

Retch sucked his teeth, tasting the blood. He thought about the hole, how it had plumbed deeper than the drill-pipe sunk.

"Didn't I say drilling is full of detours? No roadmap to water."

"You shoulda woke me," Retch said, sounding peevish even to himself.

"Shoulda, coulda laid off the hooch." He tossed the truck keys to Retch. "Your nose drips, bud. The stoppers fell." He pointed to the toiletpaper plugs fallen by the hole.

Retch wiped the blood on his sleeve.

The driller lifted the fisher. "Pretty slick, eh? How blind-men bugger."

Retch eyed the pipe. He drank from the thermos. "And the cave-in?"

"We push through it, try our luck."

Retch said that sounded near impossible.

"It does, don't it?"

He waited but the driller said no more. "How deep?"

"The Hughie?"

"The cave-in, Bill."

"Above the Hughie."

The land's silence large in the floodlit clearing. "How many feet?"

The driller grinned. "You tell me, Retch."

"What?"

"You're the mathman."

"Mudman."

"So count the mudded joints yonder." He chinned at the drillpipe pulled from the hole. "Your mud, your depth. Steel in, steel out."

Retch counted nineteen mudded joints. He counted the clean joints, which numbered six.

"How many feet, Retch?"

"Three eighty."

"Give the mathman a cigar—he has a number. Now we know where the Hughie lies but not the plug."

Retch stared at the pipe. More joints than he had seen go in, yet there they lay, mudded from the hole! "I cinched fifteen."

"When you was awake, ye budro of dreams. And when you wasn't?"

Retch silent. Had eighty feet been sunk while he slept? What else would explain why the sounder hadn't bottomed? He pointed to the fisher. "If it misses?"

"The Hughie?"

"Yeah."

"Pray it don't. I lose a bit. You gain a hole."

That night they lowered the rollerbit and added steel. "Cut yourself?" the driller asked, seeing Retch's hands, the wire marks.

Retch nodded, silent. He thought about the lost sounder and what to say if it surfaced. Later, when he went to the truck for cigarettes, he checked under the seat for the gun shells, finding the box where he had wedged it.

She lay in the room, the boy asleep, the balloon tied to his wrist. Her thoughts on the black brujo, how he had talked, how he had made her talk. Part of his magic.

He spoke of places where water ran on the land, places that rained, the noise of it on citystreets, the hurry of women afoot with umbrellas. His threaded words invited her to see herself among them, the lifeloving throng.

She spoke of her mother, of her child days in La Fortuna, the house, its porch, the verbena. Her words strung to a new length. No mention made of the old miner, of the boy's fathering, of how her life came to be cast on the thirsted land. The brujo didn't ask. Instead he asked if she desired water on the ranch. Desired it as the man did.

Her gaze held the road. She said her loathing of the ranch the same with water or without it. The same.

He grinned. "I have agreed to find water," he said. "Money advanced. Such is the contract that binds men to their words."

She shrugged. "So, too, are they bound to their lies," she replied.

He laughed, his deepvoice shaking the truck. "I charge well to keep my word, Dolores. A driller's word is what makes the price of water high."

The road passed. "How much do you charge him?" she asked.

The brujo said he could not quote the price for water found, as it depended on the depth drilled.

She studied the boy. "What of the price for not finding it?" she asked.

He looked at her, his grin larger than before. "A woman must not expect a man to forsake his word for money," he said. "The world would be an absolute disgrace if he did."

"So it is," she agreed. Then she lifted the boy from the seat and she spread her legs, sitting the boy tightly between them. "So it is."

They jounced on the road, nothing more said. In town he left them at the plazuela, giving the boy coins to spend. He handed her a folded bill. "Your man's money," he said. Upon his return he took them to eat. On the trip back the boy slept between them, the wrist-tied balloon bouncing in the cab. At the guamúchil tree the blackman asked, "Shall we stop?" His voice low.

"Later," she said.

"There is time."

"Later. The boy might wake."

He stopped the truck, dimmed the lights, the boy not waking. She remembered the tree as the one where she had rested with the injured boy. "Later," she said.

He got down, his blackness lost in the dark. She waited, the night one color. *If I follow, it's done, nothing left to bargain.* She touched the boy, bumping the balloon. Then she heard branches snap, his steps. When he sat again, he smelled of guamúchil fruit. He said, "You see, he sleeps."

She held the boy, nothing spoken, the truck racing to the ranch. Before they arrived, she said, "He cries for the dog. Have you seen it?"

The blackman's grin white in the dark. "Yes. Tell him not to cry."

Now as she lay awake, hot in the fevered night, she thought how close she'd come to getting down from the truck. The promise given but not the gift. Even a brujo weak between the legs.

"Limey is flesh-eating, budro. It's got a sarcophagic appetite. I had an Indian fellow work for me by the name of Big HeHe. A longboned Comanche who never laughed.

One day he got knocked into a hole by an errant hoisting. Twenty-inch bore. Mudslick walls. Nothing to grab to. He fell slick as fresh frybread, feet first with elbow room to spare. A two-hundred-foot-drop that bottomed in a limestone slurry. The landing should have killed him, but he was a buffalo-hided injun. He hit the limey latte and kicked up. We knew he was alive because he hollered bloodknotted warcries, screeching about fire in the water. We got the wire on him and pulled him out. He winched up fast, weighed almost nothing. When he hit daylight, the bottomhalf of him was gone, limey-dissolved at the tread line. Dissolved and cauterized. Clothes burned off. Fingers worn to bone-nubbins from trying to pull himself clear of the ravenous bath. No HeHe in him before he fell, but he laughed like an imbecile after he came up. He crowed 'til he died. We dug him a short grave and covered it with stones, according to Quohada rites. Then we burned his personals."

The sun up, the white sky cloudless.

"And another mudman bites the dust," Retch said.

"'Tis a thrilling business."

"Seems so."

"That hole was bigger than this one, but watch thy step all the same."

"I will," Retch said, thinking that Bill's talltale of limestone was oddly apropos of what he desired—a dissolved sounding wire, no trace of plumb or spool.

By noon they added the last of the mudded steel, the string rehung at nineteen joints. Minutes later the rig shook with a sudden jolt. The driller reached for the clutch when the rotary siezed. "Hughie rock!" he shouted.

The motor pulled down, stalled.

"That's our bit. Hardest thing down there. Bounce the adamantine prayers off the Grand Penitentiary."

Retch wiped mud from his eyes. See it first, he told himself.

"Grab the bobbejaan spanners. It's time to raise the roller and mount the fisher."

A night and day of steel cinched. Now the unthreading. Soon the rethreading. Retch fetched the wrenches.

When the woman appeared, she held the boy by the hand. She ignored Retch, delivering plated food to the driller.

"Gracias, Dolores."

"De nada," she replied.

Retch watched. "Bring water," he said, pointing to the thermos.

She took the boy but not the thermos.

"Epi, you can stay," Retch said. "Come."

The boy pulled from his mother and ran to the rig.

Retch smiled. "Watch the hole, son," he said loud for her to hear.

She eyed him before she departed with the thermos.

"Bring ice, Retch called. "Ándale."

The driller passed the plate. "Chicken, budro. She's outdoing the old menu."

"Yeah," Retch said. "Her tongue came loose, too."

"I'm gonna miss the homestyle come quitting time. Back to cold vittles and roadstops for me."

Retch surveyed the land. "You're welcome to take the cook," he said. "The cook, the kid. Just leave me water."

The ground shook, or so it seemed to Retch, the driller's laugh as though risen from the hole. "Now there's the offer of a desperate man. Advance or payoff?"

"Neither." Retch looked to the rooms. "A hypothetical."

They ate, the woman not coming with the thermos. The boy played in the mud.

"Speaking of wishful wagering, I knew a granger from the downlands who sold his thirteen-year-old daughter to pay for water drilled on his chalky hillside. Auctioned her in a bar. A rapscallion and drunkard, he was. I'm reminded of Fermín."

Retch looked to the rooms, the woman not coming.

"I took the man's money and drilled his hole. Took the girl's mother, too. I left the rascal thirsting on a drywell, father of his own demise."

"And the girl?"

"Killed the man who won her. Bled him while he slumbered."

Retch nodded, thinking no story too fabulous for this driller.

"Sum of shameless miscreations. Death and dirtydealing. The mother didn't take to the drilling life. She missed the scarpslopes. One day she hoofed it home. Didn't leave a note."

The boy crawled from under the rig, mudded in the sunlight. "¿La perra, papi?"

Retch sent him to fetch his mother.

"Red, you look more the part than your dogtired Daddy."

"¿La perra, papi?"

Retch said, "I told you not to ask. The dog is dead."

The boy's face squinched. "¿Muerto?"

"Sí. Muerto."

He dropped his head, began to cry.

"Now go get your mother."

The boy ran wailing to the kitchen. Retch watched. That should bring her, he thought.

"Damn, budro. Best to lie about such a thing."

"You think, Bill?"

"I do. A boy loves a dog like his mother."

"Right."

"Though it is true. She is dead. I buried her myself."

Retch without surprise. "That so?" At last a story he could believe.

"'Tis so. Remember I told you about the snakes? The big ones?"

"What?"

"The snakes that came to drink, the ones I smoked with my fire? They tangled with your dog. You may have heard her howling. I tried to bleed the venom, but she had too many bites. I didn't want the lad finding her bloated, so I buried her. Kept the collar."

Retch thin-lipped. So much for a story he could believe. "Are you serious?"

"Six foot, spitting serious. Fangs like yarn darners. Their rattling nearly deafened me."

The boy's wail loud from the rooms. Retch said he had yet to see a snake on the place.

"Does thee doubt me? I told you they came to tongue-wag."

Retch knew better than to test that toothy grin. The road to crazy already paved. "I'm saying I haven't seen one."

"Better a snakebit dog than a snakebit boy, don't you reckon?"

Retch looked to the rooms. The woman did not come with the thermos. The boy wailed. "You said you buried her?"

The driller pointed to the hole. "Down there."

Retch's face said he had not expected the deaddog to be so disposed. He stared at the hole. He recalled the foul taste of the mud.

"Don't ask me if I'm serious and don't mortify yourself if you know the answer. The limey took her. I told you it was sarcophagic. No sickness will arise."

Retch shook his head, trying to shake the remembrance of Bill petting the dog. "I'm getting water," he said, leaving before the driller spoke more.

White Clay

THE NOONGAR CALLED HIM Darkdar. White Clay. He was different from the other fair-skinned Nyittiyung settlers who had come to make holes in the land. This stranger told dream stories and he stood upon a digging stick. He spoke Nyungar and ate dingo. He gifted totems to the children. At night he left the white settlement to visit their camps where he sat at the balga fire telling stories of deep underground rivers whose water flew faster than birds. He told of fireheated keipa that shot from earth-holes. He told of places where the dark skies always rained. Stories of water and creation. In the firelight his blue eyes turned silver when he spoke. The elders said his paleface hid another mud, mud of their own kind, mud of the first world. Not a man of ordinary making, they said. Why the name White Clay.

Monster, the settlers of Pilgrim called him. Fiend. Beast. The devil, they called him. But that was later, after the women. In the beginning the stranger was welcomed more than most newcomers to Westrailia's eastern goldfields.

He appeared one morning, dawnbrought, his well-machine hung with a sign that read FOR HIRE. If he had dropped from the sky, his arrival could not have been more fortuitous. The newly gazetted mining town of Pilgrim wanted for water. The Supply Scheme yet commissioned. Railway dams dry. Train tankers came with freshwater to drink, but what the pilgrims of Pilgrim needed was water to mine gold, water to wet claims, to wash the ore. Water to prosper.

No one asked the stranger how he had come to Pilgrim, if east from Port Augusta or west from Perth. None could say whether his rig had arrived by rail or by road. No one knew his name. "Call me Driller," he told his first hire, and so he was called until the day he was hanged.

A lumbering fellow squeezed into narrow boots, his grin too wide for his face, Driller proved friendly and forthcoming, chatty as a cockatoo, full of bullnuggets offered during lateday rum shouts. He claimed to possess the secrets of the first saltdrillers from Zigong in Old China. He boasted of the sinking of the world's only freshwater well through quicksand using a hollowed sycamore trunk, this at Buffalo Lick on the banks of the Kanawha. He recounted the history of a three-hundred-foot hole springpoled into solid Éire bedrock with only a Samson post, a walkingbeam, and manila hemp rope. He professed fluency in multiple mother tongues and the Indianspeak of lost and living tribes. He discoursed expansively upon the hydraulics of alluvial extraction and quartz mining. He claimed to have watered the goldcrazy Dalmatians at Slogget Bay on the Great Island of the Land of Smoke.

His machine was a steampowered cabletool rig with a wooden derrick and a blunt chiselbit strung to a trapdoor bailer. Driller called it a spudder. On his first job in Pilgrim, he hit water at sixty feet. Within the month, five claims washed ore from his boreholes. When word of drilled water spread beyond the settlement, miners came from distant fields to clamor for his hire. Driller kept a tally of their names, asking from each an advance in gold—nuggets, dust, or coins. The more yellowmetal a miner advanced, the higher his name rose on the list. Those who complained about the exorbitant cost of water—pricier than gold, they grumbled—found themselves waiting the longest for their wells to be dug.

So banked upon fortunes advanced before they were found, Driller's tally of the thirsted grew each day. Months passed. The flurry of quickfound water lulled. Wells once completed in days took weeks for Driller to finish. Rumors of dryholes circulated. Those who sought audience with Driller found him drinking in the cathouses instead of drilling in the fields. They observed his newfound friendliness with the local Aboriginals, his late-night visits to their campfires. That he could speak their lingo was no empty boast, his voice the loudest among the wildcries of the brown-skinned tribe.

When the town whores began to disappear—all fresh-faced, pubescent girls newly arrived from Melbourne and Adelaide—no one in Pilgrim thought the world had changed much, certainly not for the worse. Like the trains from Perth, young molls came and left the settlement every week. One girl's disappearance was hardly a sign of trouble.

Then a body was found, but not all of her. Victim of an accident, the finders reported. Not a particular accident, rather one reminiscent of what a train left on the tracks, though the remains were found nowhere near the rails.

Dogs got her, some said. After two more girls were discovered, their heads only, Pilgrim's whoredom hunkered in horror.

It was a miner who narrowed the list of suspects. A sunbright morning when his rifflebox sluiced a delicate hand with painted nails, this risen from a hole Driller had bored but days before. "Hell's own paydirt," the miner would later recount. Not a man to hide any crime but his own, he left the grisly preciosity in his sluice, forthwith hiking to Pilgrim for authority and witness. Within days another wellhole produced a pair of highheeled shoes snugged with feet. The brothels were canvassed, Driller found drunk under a whore. He was roped and dragged into the street. When miners demanded their advances, he replied, "Search the holes, ye diggers. No water too deep." He grinned, eyes turned silver.

Crazy as a cut snake, said those who heard him. Crazy but still a devil, said others.

The land dusked at the hour they strung him from the rig derrick, cablehung with rope tied to the trapdoor bailer, his body left to the night. A few in the mob suggested that Driller be burned with his machine. Others said no fire would combust such a demon. With lanterns they searched the wellrig, finding jarred muds but no gold. "Spent," the searchers said. "Spent on whores and uncorked rum—the 'holes' he spoke of." Then their talk turned to the proprietary rights of waterdrilling and the machine at hand.

At first light Driller's body was discovered gone from the rig, the bailer still cabled to the mast. Early risers had buried him—so said those late to rise. When no one in Pilgrim claimed to know the whereabouts of his grave or the names of those who had buried him, the story started. The mudded Aboriginals had taken him—said the chatter—Driller's campfire friends come in the night, disposing of the body according to their savage rites.

So it was left. A fitting end, most said.

El Hierro y
El Plomo

No LIGHT IN THE STENCILED window. The scrapdealer banged on the door. "Ábreme, cuñado. Ábreme."

He still called the doctor brother-in-law, though the doctor's wife, his sister, had died many years before, a young woman newly married.

Rolando followed him to the back bedroom where he sat on the cot and showed his cut hand. Usually he humored his in-law with some crude story, but not tonight. He felt strange.

The doctor examined the gash, his raccoon eyes close. "How did you cut it?"

The scrapdealer grimaced. "How do you think, Hector? My work."

The doctor cleaned and disinfected the wound. "You need a tetanus shot," he advised.

"I had a tetanus shot. You gave me one me last summer."

"Then you are fine."

Rolando knew the doctor's secondwife had died of tetanus. "Check it again, Hector. I feel something in there."

"I checked. It's clean."

"Maybe you should bleed it."

The doctor reached for gauze to dress the wound.

"No, don't cover it. The bad airs must escape."

The doctor handed over the gauze and tape. "Let it breathe tonight. Tomorrow bandage it."

"Are you giving me any medicine?"

"No."

The dealer pinched the wound. "Do you believe in devils, Hector?"

The doctor said he believed in the angels of modern medicine.

"I know, but I'm talking about evilspirits. One came to the yard today. A Negro. He made me do his work."

"Being a Negro does not make him a devil," the doctor said.

Rolando decided not to say the blackman was once a whiteman now dead. Instead, he said, "But that's how I got cut. He hexed me."

The doctor wiped his hands. "You said you cut yourself."

"Yes. But it was a hex."

The doctor smiled. He was not close to his dead wife's brother. He had never visited the scrapyard, but he knew the dealer ran a profitable business. He knew this from the frequent sightings of Rolando in local eateries, from his patrón paunch, from rumors of his drunken revelry in the town brothel.

"You seem nervous, Rolando. Maybe I should check your pressure."

"Yes, check it. Do you know anything about hexes?"

The doctor shook his head. He cuffed the dealer and pumped the bulb. After he read the manometer he told the dealer his pressure was normal.

Rolando continued to pinch the cut. "It will infect, he said."

"Who?"

"The Negro."

"There is no way to know."

"I think he was talking about what he put in. I can feel it."

"Do you want me to disinfect it again?"

"Yes, yes. Kill it."

When the doctor finished, he told Rolando he should go home and rest.

"But I'm prone to bad dreams if I turn in early."

"Don't think about it," the doctor said. "It's in your head."

The scrapdealer rose from the cot. "That's easy for you to say. You're not hexed." He pointed to the old wallcalendar, the circled date. "You need to get over it, Hector. She's dead."

The doctor followed him to the door. "I will," he said. "In time." When Rolando left, the doctor locked the door before he washed his hands.

"Damn you, woman!"

The kitchen deserted. The thermos empty. Retch drank from the cántaro before he sat in a chair. His hands studied, the cuts and broken nails, the mud and blood, his pale wrist. The history of him.

Outside, the rig motor restarted. "Budro!"

He leaned in the chair thinking, he takes me for a fool, a king-size fool. Snakes? A lime-eaten Indian? Now the dog. *The damn dog!*

"Budro!"

Why down the hole? Dead by his hand or by the dog's doing, still a no-account dog. Retch shook his head, tired of the dirt, the drama.

"Boodro!"

He rose to fetch a shirt. No sound from the woman's room, the door cracked. Spilled beans rolled under his boots as he crossed the kitchen floor. "Move the broom!" he shouted, words punctuated by the sudden splintering of wood near his head, the bullet already through the roof when he heard the pistol discharge sharp like a walnut crack. "Shit!" half mouthed as he ducked, his shadow seeming to cower faster than he. Breath-held instants before the realization came. *She finally did it.*

A startled cry broke the silence. The woman's voice rose in alarm. Retch moved to open the door, the gunfired smell close. In the room the boy held the pistol one-handed. He pointed it at Retch. Retch saw the barrel annulus, the centered umbral depth. He heard the coldmetal click as the woman wrested the gun from the boy's hand.

Her face gray, the scar blanched. She let the gun fall to the floor.

Retch stared. "¿Qué chingado están haciendo con mi pistola?"

She turned on him. "He found it. Leave!"

"You lying daughter of fornication!"

"He found it, I said."

"You stole it!"

"Leave!"

The boy watched them.

"You're lucky he didn't shoot himself, pendeja."

"You're lucky you're not dead."

Retch looked at the boy. "Where did you find the pistol?"

The boy began to cry. He pointed to the bed.

"¡Vete a la chingada!" she shouted.

"Lying, thieving woman. You had your chance. You won't have another!"

"¡Vete!"

He gave a cracked-lip smile. "Do you know where he threw the dog?"

"No m'importa."

"Where I'll throw you if you go behind my back again. Down the hole."

"¡Vete!" she shouted.

"Budro!"

He picked up the gun, opened the cylinder. He emptied the shells into his hand. One dropped to the floor, rolling beneath the bed.

The boy cried. The woman called him a goat, an unmothered whoreson.

In the kitchen he fetched the thermos. He eyed the splintered wood, the roofhole. *My name on it.* He pocketed the gun.

"Budrito!

At the rig the driller rummaged his toolboxes. Retch waited by the mudpits, wondering if the gunshot had sounded above the engine noise. When the driller saw him, he said, "Need a measure, bud. You seen my wire?"

Bring ice, he had said. *Ándale*, he had said, his balls grown large, his words, their menace, still fresh. *Watch the hole*, he had told the boy, his smile hinting at the harm he could do. As though she stood powerless to stop it.

She took the pistol from the beanpail. In the wheel six shells shiny like coins. The thermos she left empty on the table, its unfilling the portent of choices made. She went to the room and waited, gripping the gun, desiring that thirst bring him. Her scar throbbed. Her hands sweat. When she heard the boy's cry, his fastfooted wail, she stuck the gun under the mattress. In the kitchen she clutched him, his mudded length. She heard him say the dog was dead. "No llores," she consoled, recalling what lay under the brujo's truckseat.

She carried him to the room, sat him on the bed. She wiped his tear-streaked face. They listened to the man in the kitchen, his shouts.

"Papi malo," the boy whispered.

She put her finger to her lips before she moved to shut the door. When she turned, she saw the boy's hand beneath the mattress. He pulled the gun, pointed it, his face alight. Then the gun fired, its bullet somehow missing her.

"Wire?"

"My sounding wire, budro."

Retch stared. Sleepless. Shot at.

"You can tell me."

"Tell you?"

"If you saw it."

Retch shook his head, falsehood effortless. "Is it needed?"

"For a precise reckoning, yes."

"Of the bit?"

"Of the battle's outcome, of life's short thread. The bit, too."

Retch said he owned a ball of sisal twine that might be weighted if an exact measurement was required. The driller waved off the idea. "Twine ain't wire, and sisal ain't steel. We'll have to gauge the depth and spare the gnat's ass. I got me a mathematical mudman, right? No magic too simple for him."

Retch said nothing. *He knows.* He busied himself with the wrenches. *He knows the taking but not the place.*

That afternoon they raised the steel. The driller sang ranchera songs of deception and betrayal. His voice vast, bottomless.

> Ya te di mi vida,
> Y tú me tracionaste
> Con puras mentiras

"How's my crowing, pard?"

Retch asked if the serenade was for him.

"Who else?"

The sun down, the rig in shadow when the driller said, "That was some ruckus."

"Ruckus?"

"Your pistol going off."

Retch bent at the hole. The gun still pocketed. "It's nothing."

The driller's gaze took in the daydying land. "Many a sage has said the same. Nothing. Nothing behind most everything."

Retch wiped mud off the wrenches.

"The song of your gun sticks in my head since you shot at me."

Retch said, "Correction. I shot in the air."

"No matter. It was a proper welcome. I would have shot at me, too." He laughed, seeming to mock his own amusement.

Retch sipped from the thermos. The water warm.

"Take care of it, budro."

"What?"

"The gun."

"Okay."

"You wouldn't want the boy to find it. Or your woman. A gunshot belly worse than poison. Best lock away the chances of it." He stared at the dusked rimland. "Don't think much of guns. Too incidental for dispatching the so sacred. Anyone with a finger can do it." He held up his maimed hand. "Even me."

Retch shrugged. "The gun is safe."

The driller's skewed gaze found him. "Glad to hear it, Retch. You should sleep sounder knowing so. I would—if I was the sleeping sort."

"Right."

They pulled the last two joints and raised the rollerbit. Retch watched for the sounding wire. When the bit rose clean, he thought, Damn, some luck finally. Then the driller said, "Lookee there." He jumped down and knelt by the bit, his fingers working between the rollerteeth. He plucked something and held it out for Retch to see. "Got the eagle eye, I do. You know it?"

Retch stared at the shard in the driller's hand. He shook his head.

"Was you who dropped it." He popped the piece into his mouth, spat it back into his hand. He offered it to Retch. "Whitemetal of Helvetian."

Not a wire but a curled metal ribbon. Retch stared, not taking it.

"From that fancy timepiece you lost. The one belonging to your pard."

Retch recognized the shape of a watchspring.

The driller grinned. "The whore's coveting and inculpation. Gone the fanciness but not the malfeasance. You want it?"

"No."

"If I knew I'd see her again," the driller said before he dropped the watchspring into the settlingpit.

Night descended when the hole was cleared. No food brought by the woman. The kitchen lampless.

"It appears the door slammed on vittles," the driller observed.

"Seems so." Retch looked to the darkened rooms.

"I told you to be nice, budro."

"You did."

"Of course, vittles is part of our contractual arrangement, but I can see it's a temporary inconvenience. No penalty applies."

"We have canned sardines if you're hungry."

"Save 'em for breakfast." He reached for the guamúchil pods in the leverwell. "I got me Sweet Ingas."

Retch without appetite or appetence to drag the woman to the stove at this hour. He needed a drink for that. Come morning she would cook or she would hear the boy wail.

He went to the truck for cigarettes, leaving the gun under the seat with the boxed shells. He smoked, watching the driller measure the fisher with a carpenter's rule. Retch struck by his practiced hand. "How many times have you done this, Bill?"

The driller folded the ruler. "If I had a whore's tear for every bit I've fished, I'd have drowned in sorrow."

"Okay."

"We'll blame Fermín should the stars not align."

Retch said the scrapdealer would want his money either way.

"True, but I expect he won't collect." He opened a pail containing a black, pitch-like resin. "Chatterton's compound. Made it from the gutta-percha. Peel the skin off your hide before it shucks a fly."

They stood the fisherpipe and dipped the tapered end into the pail. The driller produced a piece of clothmesh that he wired over the resin. He said the mesh kept the pipe virgin during descent. "I call it the Hughie hymen. Holds off false suitors 'til we reach the chosen one."

The night advanced at the hour they threaded the fisher to the kellybar and lowered it into the bore, steel added behind it.

"Know something, bud? Dogbones help."

"Jesus, Bill!"

The driller said dogbones brought goodluck to a cursed hole if the dog was dropped muzzle first and barking. He said he knew drillers who carried dogs to that end. "Yours was dropped dead, though. Guaranteed."

Retch said he was relieved to hear it.

"I won't call this hole cursed, but the augering of land where dead men lay could be a case where another driller might find a dog useful.

Retch eyed the descending steel. "But not you?"

"The land speaks, budro."

"Does it?"

"Yup. Land misdeeded upon calls out. Burying don't quell the voices. Unburying either. From the salted earth they speak."

"You mean him?" Retch looked to the old man's gravemound.

In the riglight the driller's grin crimson with chewed guamúchil fruit. "Unless you know of another lying elsewhere?" He spat the seeds. "If it's for the dead to keep secrets, then it's for the living to guess 'em. And my guess is you want me to keep my drilling to this here hole and no other. Ain't that so?"

"That's what I'm paying for, Bill."

"So you are. Let deaddogs lay we shall. The march of time dirts us all."

Retch gave a hapless shrug.

"A song, then."

His serenade resumed, his voice deepborne. He sang corridas of thievery and murder. Strung steel disappeared into the hole. Retch silent as he worked. *Unless you know of another lying elsewhere.* As though he knew.

"I sing sweeter on brandy, bud." He sipped from his carboy. "But I ain't about to steer steel while I'm impaired. Nope. Don't want to kill our chances."

Retch silent, unsure if imagination had overtaken sleeplessness. The calling up of his past in Bill's pointed nonsense had to be accidental. The man could no more know about running down a student nurse than he could know the truth about Digger.

When they left the ranch that day, Dig began to moan. Retch stopped the Willys, got down. He fished the pistol from Digger's pants. He removed the jeweled watch and unclipped the billfold. "I'll hold these," he said. With braitrope he bound Digger's hands and feet, tying him to the seat.

"Are you comfortable, Dig? Speak up if you're not."

A plan shaped but not set. Drive. Abandon Digger. Then run. Where not a place but a distance. As far from Dig as he could get. Another world too close to one inhabited by this madman.

He drank the bule water drawn from the cactus still. Stuck in his head the thirsted ranch, the boy's cry. *Had he left them enough?* He knew Dig would have left them nothing, their lives, maybe. Almost nothing.

The sun overhead, the road pitched on arroyo-cut land when he drove again. In the jerrycans sloshed the salted noria water not to be wasted should Dig be left in a shadeless spot. "I'm thinking about it, bud."

On his wrist the jeweled watch glinted sunsignals to the sightless land. He considered what Dig would do with life spared, his maniacal pursuit, where he might look, who he might hurt. His likely return to the ranch.

Then there was the money. Already he had counted the bills in the purse. More than he expected. Enough.

He turned the Willys onto a roughflat and shifted to four-wheel, driving the thornscrub gaps. Dayheat shimmer rose from the land. "I've thought about it, Dig. It's a small chance."

Gray hills rose to the south. He steered the Willys toward them, the gun in his belt. At the black-fossil ruins of a towering ocotillo, he stopped to unhitch the Daxara. He loaded the gorilla bar and a spade into the truck before he resumed his heading, the scrub breaks narrow.

Digger opened his eyes. "Wa da fu," his first words.

"Watch yourself, Dig. Tight going."

Retch ducked. Digger closed his eyes. "Uuuuu! Son a bit!"

His face scratched. His baldness scribbled red. He struggled to free his hands.

"Easy." Retch lifted the lug iron from under the seat. After the scrub opened, he stopped the Willys to sight ahead, the gray hills clear-horizoned.

Digger wriggled, pulling against the rope. Retch tapped him with the iron. "Be still or be stilled."

Digger eyed the bule. "Wata."

"What? You parched?"

"Wata"

"We got plenty. Hold the phone." He descended and filled an empty tequila bottle with saltwater from the jerrycan. He tipped the bottle for Dig to drink. "Go slow."

He gagged, spat, his curses wetted. "You sonofabitch." Retch emptied the salted water on Dig's face. "You're dead!"

"Careful."

"You shit. That's mine."

Retch looked at the watch. "Not now."

"Dead!"

"More water, Dig? It may be a while before your next drink."

"Go to hell."

Retch unknotted the kerchief with the woman's tortillas. The tortillas still warm. He gagged Digger, his bucktoothed defiance. "Smell good, does it?"

"Ckew."

He accelerated toward the gray hills. The scrubland untracked to endless desolation. The white sky without measure. When Digger twisted in the ropes, Retch struck him with the lug iron. "I told you."

The venom large in Dig's eyes. Retch saw there the path taken, how it led to where they drove. An old voice in Dig's muffled snarls. What they had become, the sooner and the later.

"Some hike this would have been, Dig. A shortlegged bastard like you."

He squirmed redfaced, his garbled curses an animal sound.

"I'm not going to kill you, Dig. Relax."

"Rrraaahhh!"

By the time Retch saw the rope travel, Dig had heaved himself into the open door. Handtied, half out, he hung like a sailor hiked on a heeling boat. Then he was gone. The backwheels jumped, the rope cinched, all before Retch could swear.

In the sidemirror he glimpsed the dragged Digger, boots and dust. When he braked, only dust. When he reached the rope's end, only boots. Digger up and staggering in barefoot retreat. Hands tied. Kerchief gone.

"Hold up, Dig!" Retch ran with the gun. After he caught him he kicked him from behind. "I said hold up!"

Feet bloodied, pants shucked, his grimed baldness streaked with sweat. He spat curses into the dirt. Retch stood over him. "Anything broken?"

For an instant he lay still. Then he wheeled and kicked.

Retch stepped back, holding the gun at his side. "I guess not."

Digger's legs scissored the air. "You prick!"

The white-lighted sky large on his twisted face. Lips torn. Teeth bared. When he saw the gun, he spat. "Got the balls?"

"I told you to leave them be. They got nothing."

"No got 'em"

"You think?"

"Never have or you would have." He spat. "Freeloading thief."

"That's it." Retch knew so without the words. He raised the gun.

Digger defiant. "Fu—"

Then Retch shot him twice in the chest. Two holes, one shirtfronted blossoming. No gasp. Eyes open. His face finally surprised.

"Payola, bud, for whatever hell comes next."

Retch surveyed the land, the weathered soulless self without. No better spot, he decided, returning to the Willys for the bar and shovel.

Rimland dawned, the night bled when they coupled the nineteenth joint to the fisherpipe. The driller unfolded his ruler and stood it against the drive. A stick of dirty chalk appeared in his hand. "How much are we long? Four feet? Five?"

Retch suggested four and a half.

"This ain't whore dickering, chico. It's soft landing a puckered bunghole on a two-penny nail. If I had my wire, there'd be no guessing."

"Four, then."

The driller climbed onto the platform and girdled the kellybar with the chalk. "Four, says he." He refolded the ruler and resumed his perch, the chalk hung in his lips. He powered the drawworks.

The nineteenth joint inched into the hole. The driller's hand lightly rode the winchlever, his eyes fixed on the chalkmark. Half the measured length passed below the table before he engaged the rotary, adding a barely perceptible rotation to the string. "Screwing with our eyes closed, Retch. Dipping in the dark. No slambang. Back to virgins we be."

Retch fought fatigue. Blind luck, he decided. That's what lay at the bottom of this hole. Blind luck. A drillbit.

The chalkmark dropped below the table. With each rotation the white girdle made a kaleidoscopic shift. When the mark disappeared into the hole, the driller slowed the descent. He began to hum. Then he whistled.

Damn breezy, Retch thought. Would he whistle in an hour? To fish the bit on the first try a stroke of good fortune unknown to this hole, to the land, to his tenure on it. The tricone could tilt. The fisher could angle. Nothing lined up so in life, not fates, not bullets. He expected Bill to advance and reverse the string in attempted retrievals. He expected complications.

Then the whistling stopped. Silence before the driller spoke. "Got it."

His short-fingered hand gripped the kellybar, its rotation stilled. His other hand finessed the winchlever with a jeweler's touch. The chalkmark rose from the hole. "Yup. She's caught."

The surprise on Retch's face more than his words expressed. "How do you know?"

"Finger stumps, chico. The pull of taut steel calls to my broken carpals. Sensibility of the limbless. The winch feels it, too."

Retch stared, denying himself disbelief. "Damn. That's some trick."

The driller grinned. "You thinking it impossible, ye budro of no faith."

"Near impossible, I said."

"Not with dogbones in the hole. I told you they got pardoning power. Even the bones of a dead one."

Retch said nothing.

The desert daylit. To the east, the rimland etched blackly above the heaving day. The jagged cordillera hem cut from a pale sky. Near the rig, first shadows shaped, that of the driller's stretched beyond the clearing, a shadow like himself in largeness but not in flesh. A shade only he could see.

In the gray light the rooms stood older than built, the bricks without pattern, the tinroof of a piece with the sky. Retch drank from the thermos, washing from his mouth the bitterness of nightlong cigarettes. He looked to the doorway. An hour, he decided. She had an hour to come with food.

The driller winched the kellybar above the jointcollar. He sleeved the slips and locked the rotary. He stepped from his perch. "Before I pull the Hughie, budrito, I'm going to need that advance—the one I mentioned back when you smashed your pucker. Remember yonder?"

"Advance?"

"Yup. I need it to advance. Why they call it that."

"Today?"

"Today it is wanted."

Retch frowned. "How much?"

The driller gave his number. He grinned. The amount so exceeded Retch's expectation that he was sure he had misheard. "How much?"

He repeated the number, his grin large. "A new reckoning."

Retch stared. "That's not an advance, Bill."

"An adjustment, then. For delays, inconveniences, and such."

Retch stared. "What inconveniences?"

"To start, the inconvenience of my lost sounding wire. Second, no vittles. Then there's the inconvenience of a mudman who drinks and bears arms."

"What?" Retch almost laughed. "The gun is my business. And if I drank, when I drank, it was on my time or at your insistence."

"Ah, budro. You should know a mudman's time is not his own. Unless he's dead. Then all time to himself."

Retch said he did not speak as a mudman but as the owner of the job. "What of our contractual arrangement, as you called it?"

"I told you a hole in the ground becomes a hole in the pocket. I told you about collapses, bits stuck, bits lost. Full disclosure and fineprint spoken."

Retch's tight smile of tolerance. He pointed to the chalkmark. "How do I know you have it?"

"The Hughie?"

"The bit."

"You doubt me, budro?"

He wanted to say *don't call me that stupid name.* He wanted to say *I doubt you as much as I dislike you.* He wanted to ask what guarantee had he that the bit would be raised after the money was paid. *Extortion!* he wanted to counter, but he voiced only the cold truth. "You've got me over a barrel, Bill."

His grin at its widest. "The barrel is under both of us, Retch. Who stands to lose a Hughie if you don't advance the cause? I'm saving you from a dryhole. You ought to be grateful."

"Right." He took the thermos. Gone the cash, he thought, if I do this.

"Tell you what, Retch. Go to your cowboy bank. Bring the money. In the meanwhile I'll strip steel and raise the Hughie. Honest Apache—"

Retch turned to leave.

"—and when you come back we'll powwow. I'm willing to negotiate, good faith in hand."

"Negotiate?"

"Dicker us a new deal. Ain't all about the money."

"Yeah."

"And since you're going that way, bring me more monkeypods, as a favor, not wearing your mudman hat. I'm plum out and still got the hanker."

Retch nodded. "Sure," he lied.

The land heaved sunward when he drove off the ranch. The woman yet to bring food.

She had not slept. The room hot, the machine loud, the nighthours passing in fitful restlessness. She tossed on the sweatsoaked bed as though stretched on a wire. Her neck stiff, her spine bonetight. The clampjawed grinding loud in her head. She felt strange.

The bullet recalled, the near miss of what had spared their lives or doomed them. She wondered if death dreamt could be undreamt. She thought about the black brujo, his lie about the dog. She thought of his promise, her own. The window daylit at the hour she heard the truck depart, its motor gunshots echoing off the rimland. She rose brokenbodied, leaving the boy asleep, his mudded face streaked with tears wept for the dog. In the kitchen she swept the spilled beans. She was cooking tortillas when he began to sing. A deepvoiced tune risen in the morning quiet.

> Tengo una maldita suerte
> Paloma Negra
> Que me llevarás a la muerte

She listened, the song last sung by the old man before his skullfront stoved with a flathead sledge. He knows, she thought. Nothing hidden from a brujo. He knows the words, the deed. He knows the red-blossomed music of death deserved.

His low croon near the kitchen, the song resung. Then he stood there. "Buenos días, Dolores."

"Buen día," she said, unturned from the stove.

"Una mañana hermosa."

The morning's beauty unknown to her.

"Your man is gone," he said. "Gone but not for good."

"The man is not my man," she corrected.

"Gone to the devil, then."

She cooked tortillas, feeling his eyes.

"Gone to fetch money. Left me without breakfast."

"Sit," she said.

She served him plated eggs, a stack of tortillas. She stood by the stove.

"Did my singing wake you?"

"I was awake," she replied.

He grinned. "*Paloma Negra* is a favorite of mine, a song that speaks to what we live for. Luck and death."

Dolores silent. The plate cleaned, the tortillas gone. "¿Más?" she asked.

He held to the plate, not letting go when she took it, his voice close. "Yes, give me more," he said.

She cooked fresh tortillas, fried more eggs. The plate served again.

"And you?" he asked.

She said she had no appetite. She would wait for the boy, who slept.

He ate watching her. "Dolores, you hunger for a place other than this. That is your appetite and your thirst."

She looked to the boy's room. "I told you so," she said softly. "The water means nothing, this ranch, nothing. As for what I want, I want it for my son, what every mother wants."

He wiped his plate with the last tortilla. "¿Y tu marido sabe?"

Dolores said it mattered not what the man knew since he was not her man, as she had said. "He can stay or go." She left the stove and stood at the table, her weaved huipil brushing his back. "We talked in the truck," she said. "About payment."

He turned where he sat, his unwashed hand reaching beneath her dress. She felt his full-fingered grasp. She saw his eyes slide away, that queer stare.

"Will you take me?" she asked.

His teeth with unchewed food, his breath not of cookery but of dirt. His maimed hand clasped her from behind.

"Take you?"

"The boy and I."

"To places unseen?"

"Anyplace. There you may leave us." Between her buttocks his missing fingers as though grown. A brujo trick, she thought. His mouth on her dress, the largeness alive in his pants. She whispered. "So?"

"Claro," he croaked.

"¿Cuándo?" she asked, listening for sounds from the boy.

His hands seemed to meet within her. His sharp and darting tongue snaked through the huipil weave, finding her skin.

She asked again. "¿Cuándo?"

"Luego," he blurted.

She felt the yielding urge, but his answer empty. *Soon?* Soon a promise without measure. Soon what life promised death.

"Not here," she said.

Suddenly her feet in the air, legs spread. He lifted her onto him.

"No," she protested, eyes turned to where the boy slept. "Después."

She heard him growl. She heard the boy stir.

"No!" His writhing enormity felt. She smelled the mudhole on him.

The boy called out. "Mamá."

"Voy," she answered.

He held her, his hands clamped on her waist. She reached for his head, the wiry hair too short to grasp. She spat in his face. "¡Aquí no!"

The man in him sightless, the brujo looking, his grey-metal gaze how the old miner had stared from his grave.

"Después," she promised, a hurried plea.

His teeth close, his dirt breath. He tilted his head like a bird. "You will scream," he said, releasing her.

She rose, her legs as though rejoined, the fire wet between them.

"I know."

"Cry and bleed," he said.

She straightened her huipil, moved away. "Take us first."

His grin his face, the rest devoured. "Is that your price?"

"My price. Your word."

"Quid pro quo?"

"¿Qué?"

"A deal, darling." He looked beyond her. "Red!" he called.

The naked boy stood in the doorway watching them, his hand tightfisted. "Mira," he said, showing the spent shell from the gun.

When his mother moved to take it, the boy hid the shell behind his back. "¿Y la pistola?" he asked.

Retch pressed the gaspedal to the floor. The Fargo climbed at a crawl, trailed by blue smoke. New sounds rose from the motor—a bearing knock, the tick of broken piston rings. He stopped on the flat and raised the hood to check the dipstick. The oil black and gummy, the measure down two quarts. Retch kicked the dirt. "Sonofabitch!"

He waited, letting pass the desire to slam the hood. He lit a cigarette, recalling how the driller had raced the Fargo down the bajada. He stared at the land.

The motor restarted, he drove advertent to the dashboard gauges. The thermos water saved should the engine overheat. When he passed the guamúchil tree, he didn't stop.

Blind to the daybrightness, he saw beyond the land's advance. His thoughts on the driller, his outrageous demand. *Negotiate*, he had said. *Powwow.* They would powwow when he got back. The cost of a motor repair part of any deal. And what had he meant: *Ain't all about the money?*

Before him new possibilities unfolded. From an old past one certainty apparent: surprises not a lunatic's monopoly but shared by desperate men, too. The driller ignorant of *his* road traveled, the journey to this money, what he would do to keep it.

His hand searched beneath the seat, feeling for the gun, the boxed shells. *Don't pay the bastard! The rig sits there.*

He recalled the driller who had called from Caborca. Retch tried to remember where he had put the paper with the man's name and number.

He stopped to empty the thermos into the radiator. Under the hood the burnt rodbearing thumped like a metallic heart. When he reached the town brothel, the buildings shuttered, no trucks in the lot. He drove past the cemetery, the oil-pressure gauge reading zero. At the first house he sighted with a car, he killed the engine. The house with a locked gate and a gardenhose coiled in the frontyard. The car latemodel, recently washed.

Retch's busted face and thirsted look met with open wariness by the young woman who answered his greeting from behind the gate. A wellfigured girl with coiffured hair, no storebought complexion. Retch reminded of Digger's whore without the wear. When he asked for the owner of the car, she said he was not present. When he said he would pay a driver to take him to the parts store to buy oil for his truck, she said there was no driver. Her eyes watched the road.

He walked with the thermos, the pavingstone street reached before he caught a ride. At the parts store he refilled the jug from a garrafón dispenser. He bought pailed motor oil and a plastic funnel with a flexible spout. The sun high at the hour he returned to the Fargo in a hiredcar.

"Are you the one who lives on the Anguamea ranch?" the driver asked.

"I am," Retch said.

The driver nodded. "They say you are perforating out there."

"I am."

"A black driller, they say."

"Black he is."

The driver asked nothing about Retch's busted face. "I knew the old miner, Don Epifanio," he said. "A good man."

"Then you know he is dead," Retch replied.

"Of course. Everyone knows." The driver shot nervous glances at the gatedhouse, the washed car. In a confiding voice he said the woman who lived in the house was the preferred mistress of a local Mafioso. "That car belongs to him. He has many."

"Many cars or many mistresses?" Retch asked. He said nothing about having seen the woman, her guarded manner.

"Los dos."

The driver an old face in La Fortuna. A tall man hunched from a life behind the wheel of his hiredcar. Rumor his right of way and road.

"This spot," he continued, "is not a good spot for a breakdown, not if the young Mafioso happens to visit. He might ask our business."

"He will see our business," Retch said.

"Even so," the driver replied, "he comes with guards and many cars."

Retch nodded. He knew about the guards, the cars.

"I think we should hurry," the driver said.

He held the funnel in the fillerpipe while Retch poured oil from the pail. Half the pail emptied before the dipstick marked full.

The motor lurched but did not turn when Retch hit the starter. From beneath the truck he tried to hand crank the pulley. He remembered the toolbox left at the ranch. When he asked the driver if he carried a socketset, the man shook his head. "I will take you to a mechanic," he said. "Let's go."

Retch thought of the scrapdealer. He had tools. "Llévame con el chatarrero Arenas," he said.

The driver showed surprise. "Rolando Arenas?"

"Sí."

"I can take you to his yard," the driver said. "Or I can take you to him."

Retch said wherever the scrapdealer could be found.

"Did you know him?"

"I know him," Retch said, ear hooked.

The driver pointed out of town. "That's where you'll find him."

Retch turned. "Where?"

"In the cemetery."

He looked at the driver. "In the cemetery. Working?"

"No, sir. In his tomb."

"¿Qué?"

"He was buried yesterday."

Retch saw how the man's eyes marveled at his ignorance. He seemed pleased to be at the wheel of fresh news. "¿Está muerto Rolando Arenas?"

"Of course, dead," the driver said. "He would not be buried otherwise."

Retch stared out of town. The driver offered a ride to the gravesite.

"Drive me to the parts store and back," Retch said. "Then you may go."

As they drove, the driver observed, "True the saying, dirt spares no man."

Retch silent.

"I heard his grave is marked with a cross of his own making."

Retch recalled the painted cross offered to the woman. When he asked how the dealer had died, the driver grabbed the shirtfront above his heart. "Too much drink," he replied. "Too much fornication. He did too well for shady dealings. He strawmatted himself in the cathouse under a whore. Scrapped his own metal."

They passed a school-age girl hanging laundry on a barbedwire fence.

"They sent for the doctor," the driver said. "His own brother-in-law."

"When was this?"

"The night before last. The doctor called it strange. So they say."

All life strange, Retch thought. A heart attack in a whorehouse. A doctor's wife dead from tetanus. Two days ago the dealer had sold Bill the fisherpipe. Speaking of strange.

"He is a good doctor," continued the driver, "but not so good as to revive an overfornicated man. The whore was arrested, as she deserved to be."

The driver turned off the road and zigzagged the streets, stopping before the scrapyard gate. Retch unsure if the detour was taken for his benefit or to satisfy the driver's own curiosity.

"There it is, never the same," the driver remarked.

The yard the same, Retch observed. Rusted metal. Chaotic cumulation. The dogs barked at the fence, death unnoticed. "Are there children?" he asked.

"Many, but no wife. They'll fight over this. There is money here."

Drums, Retch thought. Many drums bought here.

"Que en paz descanse," the driver said, crossing himself.

Retch nodded out of respect, not because he agreed. No rest for Rolando if whores went to hell. No peace if they went to heaven. He would always want a deal.

Levelland

The farm, which lay nearer to Sundown than to Levelland, kept the farmer in his truck from dawn to dusk. Cotton fielded in the east. Cattle ranched where the hidden Mescalero sands sucked water from the western rangescrub. Four thousand acres of Estacado plain inherited from his father, who had inherited it from his, who had settled it when the tableland belonged to the comancheria, who had come on ponies descended from the horses lost by Coronado when crossing the same steppe. A caliche-panned llano dotted with dry playa lakes, the indurated entirety leveled across the Ogallala formation. Land so flat the sky seen between a walking man's legs.

The farmer turned off the Entrada asphalt and drove west on Nightrider and then north on Wildcat Road. Unlike his forbears, he resided not on the land but in town. The ancestral homestead he rented to his foreman. The horses he kept for show. Raised by men who shot coyotes and spaded a garden, the farmer carried neither shovel nor rifle in his truck. But he came to the land, driving the daylighted hours upon its acres, stopping to count whitefaced herds, to survey crops—a routine that filled a life, his tether to a distancing past.

On this day his foreman off shooting turkeys in the hillcountry. The farmer glad for the chance to visit the far end of the upland ranch to purge a windpump on a newly sunk waterwell. The pump with towered cisterns that needed draining before a hardfreeze.

The sun up. West Texas daybroke and infinite. The sky larger than the land, its cerulean unwrinkled, depthless, the only sight the farmer couldn't claim to own. A good early, he thought as he drove. The morning cold enough for coffee and cabheat.

The last time he had visited this field, the cotton stretched in a whitewashed carpet laid to the land's edge. Today the field stubbled and snowdusted, another white. Enough powder fallen to imprint fresh tiretracks. He saw where the drillrig had abandoned the field and taken to the road.

Grackles lifted en masse ahead of the truck, a winged negritude of birds, their shadows unhelled upon the immense whiteness. He had never tasted grackle, but he knew his hiredhands ate it. Mexicans mostly. Mexicans ate anything.

He parked by the tanks and sipped his coffee, savoring beyond its taste the flavor of good fortune and God's bounty—this land, what it gave him. Then he saw blood on the snow. A bloodtrail.

Damn driller cut himself, he thought, trying to recall the man's name. Peterson. Bob Peterson. Or was it Bill? A name in the checkbook. He had never met the fellow or spoken to him. The foreman had hired him on referral from the Hockley County Extension Service after Red Wilson drowned while boating on the Brazos. Red had been a friend of the farmer's father. He had sunk the llano's western waterwells, more than twenty, and the farmer still thought it worse than terrible for Red to die that way. A welldriller *drowned?* It wasn't right.

The farmer followed the bloodspoor from the snowless footprint left by the rig to the newly sunk well—a trail of drips and spatters as bright as the morning itself. Hours fresh, his guess. At the casing he found the sealcap with blood. Damn fool, he thought.

He opened the discharge valves on the cisterns, watching the water run clear. Not another man did he see upon the llano, though nearby he observed footprints enough for ten drillers.

After the tanks drained, the farmer returned to the well where he released the tailvane stay on the windpump. He looked up, shading his eyes. When the torque spring stretched, he engaged the rod and turned the purge lever. Three hundred feet of sunken wellpipe began to flush at his feet, first with rust, then with a color the farmer had seen run on a slaughterhouse floor. The water too red for clay deposits. At his feet the snow turned pink.

He stood by, waiting for the water to clear. No tools in his truck to remove the sealcap. When something shiny shot from the purge pipe, he braked the rotor and locked the tailvane On the ground lay a pantszipper clung to frayed denim. The zipper pumptorn. The denim bloodblack.

"How in the Sam Hill . . ." said the farmer, his first words uttered to the Estacado silence. He left the zipper where it lay and got in his truck, driving to Levelland where he called the police from his homephone.

El Fin y El Inicio

AT THE PARTS STORE Retch purchased a socketset, screwdrivers, and a can of startup ether. Back at the Fargo, the hired driver shot a furtive glance at the gatedhouse. "Should he come," he advised, speaking of the young Mafioso. "Try not to act suspicious. You look too gringo for a local fool."

Retch paid him, the motor cooled before he climbed into the engine compartment and removed the sparkplugs. With a folded cigarettebox he funneled a driblet of oil into the cylinder plugholes. He crawled beneath the motor and unscrewed the clutch inspection plate, levering the ringgear until the flywheel rotated. As he worked, he observed the young woman watching from the doorway. When he crawled from under the truck, she stood at the gate. "Go!" she said.

Retch said, "I'm trying." He pointed to the gardenhose in the yard. "Can I fill my radiator?"

"Go, please!" she said, disappearing.

He climbed into the cab. Pretty, he thought. Pretty and scared. Why she was kept. Why he should leave.

He cranked the engine and then he got down to spray the canned ether into the oilbath cleaner. On the second try the engine sputtered, almost caught. He got down again. Here of all places, he thought. Surely the young buyer of the Willys would remember him.

On the next attempt the engine backfired in a fusillade of ether-fueled explosions that shook the truck and sprung the glovebox. A sound too much like gunfire, Retch feared. He pumped the accelerator, cranking the motor until it started. An eruption of blue smoke engulfed the truck and filled the deserted street. He geared the shiftlever, let out the clutch, the motor backfiring as the Fargo advanced. He eyed the oil gauge, its needle risen with cold pressure. When he checked the sidemirror, the gatedhouse lost in a smoky haze.

At the Pemex station he fueled and filled the radiator before he pulled the dipstick. The oil clean, the crankcase full. He topped the thermos from the station's waterhose. Then he drove to the plazuela where he bought iced beer. He ordered a plate lunch at a sit-down fonda, the same eatery where he had brought the woman and the boy on their first trip to town. Retch ate, drinking the beer, remembering the trip, the ride in the dealer's truck, the visit to the town pump where Rolando had recounted the story of El Güero. So came the idea of a drilled well. A year passed, the events of its making and where he sat.

He opened another beer, recalling their last encounter, Rolando's hurried departure from the brothel. Bill the new El Güero, he had claimed.

Retch shook his head. One outrageous story had possessed the dealer and now he was dead. Dead in a whorehouse! He drank, not finishing the plate lunch. Fucked the death of us all, he reflected. If not by woman, then by man. If not by man, then by greed. If not greed, then what greed brought.

The last beer opened, the can studied. Bad luck for the whore, he decided. Arrested for a heartattack. One of the unfortunate of La Fortuna, Rolando would have called her. Retch wondered if the dealer's brother-in-law, the raccoon-eyed doctor, would set it right.

He paid the bill. A resolution made to stop at the cemetery and find the newdug grave stuck with the metal cross. He would leave Rolando a beer.

Outside, he stood in the ceiba shade, watching an ambulant balloon vendor pass, his colored globes tied to strings. Retch walked to the mercantile where he purchased a spool of galvanized wire and a rollup tape measurer. A plan made. Bill's reckoning and replacement.

He crossed the street to the hotel. At the frontdesk the pale clerk tilted his head with interest as Retch explained the message from Caborca taken days back with the name and the number of a welldriller. When Retch asked if a copy was kept, the clerk looked apologetic. Unfortunately, he replied, messages delivered were just that: delivered. Then his face brightened. "But," he said, turning to the cubicles behind him. "I think . . ." His delicate fingers searched the recesses. "I think you have another. Yes. Here it is." He held out a postcard.

Opposite a smudged postmark Retch read the return address of Tex Hinton. On the back the words written large, almost run together. BILL PETERSON NOT COMING. CALL ME.

A deal, he had said. *A deal, darling.* Then he had called it something else. Witchman words.

The sun high, the man not returned. *Gone but not for good*, the blackman had said, as though departure a door soon closed. *Gone to get money.* Money for what, she had not asked.

His roughhands still felt. The flick of his tongue. His measure beyond manhood. *You will cry*, he had said. *Bleed.*

As though such forfeit new to her. She had bled. The machete hung in the kitchen her witness.

She stood by the window watching him work. His behemoth shape bent at the hole. How much longer, she wondered. *Soon* his word, but soon not a time. Not before soon would she give him what he wanted. First the stinking ranch left behind. Then her promise kept. No truth true except its doing.

In the room the boy played with the shell. No longer did he ask for the dog. "¿Y la pistola, mamá?"

"Stop asking," she said. "The gun is gone!"

"¿Dónde?"

"Gone!"

She had told the brujo the same.

"Where is the gun?" he had asked when the boy stood in the kitchen with the shell.

"Gone," she had said. "The man has it."

He had examined the shell. "Does he have more?"

When she had answered yes, a box full, the brujo had grinned.

Now as she lay on the bed, she was glad she had not lied. She watched the boy play on the floor. This child my only life, she thought. No other to save, none but he to save me.

The rooftin hot at the hour she rose to feed him. She stood stiff-boned at the stove, her neck crooked from bedrest. While she cooked, she listened for the man's approach, the truck backfires. Soon his time. The thirsted ranch his to keep. Water his misery.

Already she had readied them for travel. Their clothes bundled. The money jar emptied. Her mother's chain on her neck. He would know.

"¿Por qué ríes, mamá?" the boy asked as he ate.

"I'm not smiling," she answered.

"Yes you are. Look!"

She touched her face, the strange sensation felt, lips stretched into a twisted grin. She cupped her mouth, turned from him. No mirror to see herself, she went to the room and kneaded her lips until they relaxed. Nerves, she guessed.

Back in the kitchen, she relit the stove and cooked tortillas, making tacos to feed the brujo's two-man appetite. The machine silent, the blackman absent when she left the dishclothed bundle for him to find. She held tightly to the boy's hand as she retreated. She saw the hole without pipes, black-mouthed and gaping.

"Dead? But how the . . ." Retch tried to keep the beer out of his voice.

"I don't know. West of Lubbock. Suspicious circumstances. That's what the papers said." Tex had answered the phone on the first ring, food in his mouth. "The mail must be slow down there. It's been a month since I wrote."

"It can't be, Tex."

"You have Western Union?"

"It can't be Bill Peterson. I left him at the hole this morning."

Gone the sound of Tex chewing.

"He's been here since Christmas. We're down four hundred feet."

"Well, that must be another Peterson because the one who took the job is dead. Obituary in the paper. Picture, too. That's dead."

Retch stared at the wallphone. "Was he black?"

"Black?"

"The man in the obituary. Was he a Negro?"

"Hell, no. White as creamed corn. I don't know of any black drillers off hand. Though now that you mention it . . ."

"This one is black."

"I suppose there could be."

"Got to go, Tex."

"So you say his name is Peterson, same as the man I sent. That's some coincidence."

"It's probably not his name."

"How did he find you?"

"He found me." Retch thought back to the driller's arrival. *Damn blind.*

"Sounds like you got lucky. Did he give you a good price?"

"No."

Tex spoke away from the phone. "Honey, turn off the hose. It's Retch."

"Got to go, Tex."

"Rose says hi."

"Hi back."

"She says she wants to come visit. No idea, this woman. But that doesn't mean I won't come. Four hundred feet, you say."

"Yeah."

"Any water?"

"Only trouble."

Tex laughed. "Well, you're into it now. That's drilling. Trouble, then more of it, then water."

Retch thought Tex sounded like Bill. Not Bill. The man he called Bill.

"Call me if you need a read on your cuttings. Or send a wire. They must have telegrams in Old Mexico."

Retch said, "Got to go." Then he said, "Are you serious? About coming?"

Tex silent.

"If things don't work out with this fellow, I could use your help. I'm thinking I might buy his rig."

Tex offered a tentative "I suppose." He chewed again. "What's the rig?"

"Old."

He chuckled. "An old rig turns a man to drink. Is your guy sober?"

"He's got one foot in the bottle."

"It sounds like you've had a few yourself."

"I have, but seriously. Think about it."

"Okay."

"Come save my ass, Professor."

"Your driller is willing to sellout, you say?"

"He might. I'll let you know."

Retch hung up. The street sunbright, the beer large in his head when he stood outside. "That lying sonofabitch," he said, loud for passersby to hear. "Who in hell?"

An old woman, ragged and shoeless, stopped before him. She held out a shriveled hand. "Some help, sir."

Retch looked down. "Go, he said. "I've given."

The woman observed his busted face, his grimed clothes. "Que Dios lo bendiga," she said from a toothless mouth before she moved on.

In the truck the beer warm. He opened a can. Tex's question still unanswered. *How did he find you?*

The early morning hour recalled, the dog's first bark, those big teeth seen before the rest of him. Everything wrong in memory. The dog knew, though later she was tricked. That grin, the oldboy familiarity, his coming to a ranch in need of water. *How did he find you?* Because he was wanted. Because he was expected. "Because I'm a damn fool!"

He started the truck. The oil gauge ignored. Water, he told himself. Water what mattered now. Finding it. Not how this lunatic found you.

The can emptied, another opened. He backed into the street. A fool, yes, he thought, but not the only one. Bill soon to find himself by the shorthairs. A hole bored but not paid. A rig stuck in hell's backyard. Ain't all about the money, Bill. But he wasn't Bill. He was some black bastard.

The plazuela circled before he sped off the pavingstones and down the street past the gatedhouse house where he had stopped the Fargo. On the street a yellow Willys parked. Armed men milled nearby. They observed his approach, followed his passing. When Retch pressed the accelerator, the motor backfires made the men jump. Some clutched their weapons before they were swallowed in a overtake of roaddust.

The truck raced by the cemetery. Later, Retch thought. Later that beer for Rolando. The dealer's words remembered. Mucho, mucho cuidado. *He is not who he says he is.*

Retch tipped a warm can. What would Rolando say if he knew the truth? A driller called El Güero no more fantastic than one called Bill Peterson.

He drove, finishing the beer. *Make no deals*, the dealer had said. His last words. Retch opened another can and drank, not tasting it. The piston slap loud. Blue smoke his new sky. A deep metallic clang rose from the rodbearing as he slowed the Fargo at the guamúchil tree.

The hooked branch lay on the ground. In the dirt shoe prints with pointed toes. He knew the purse was gone, but he fetched the wire from the cab. He shined his penlight into the hole as he fished, making certain the hollow was empty before he returned to the truck.

He drove deaf to the motor misfires, to the burnt steel knocks, his foot pressed to the accelerator. "Sonofabitch! That sonofabitch!" In an arroyo climb-out three kilometers from the rimland, the overheated motor threw the bearing. Retch swore again before he took what he needed from the cab and set out on foot for the ranch.

A shrill whirring woke her. She rose bedsweated, the boy not in the room.

The sunbrightness hurt her eyes as she crossed the clearing to where they stood by the hole. "I do not want him here," she said. The shrill sound a knife inside her head.

The brujo touched something on his machine, the noise silenced.

"Mamá, the dog lives."

She saw wires run on the ground. The boy held a gardenhose.

"Dolores, you are dressed for town," he said, regarding her neckchain.

"I said I do not want him here."

"The dog lives in the hole, mamá."

"No she doesn't." She held out her hand for the boy to take. "Come."

The brujo grinned.

"Speak no more of the dog," she said. "The boy should not be here."

"He came while you slept, Dolores."

"I did not sleep."

"He said you slept."

"Wait is what I do." Her hand outstretched. "Come," she said to the boy. When he dropped the hose and ran behind the machine, she stood with legs too stiff to chase him. "Epi, you will not eat," she warned.

The brujo watched her. "Dolores, will I eat?"

"Bring him and you will eat," she answered, retreating to the rooms.

On the kitchen table she found the dishclothed bundle of tacos left at the machine hours before. She unwrapped the towel, finding inside a leather purse etched with engravings of gallos, the zipperslide pulled to reveal a pocket yawning with bills. The purse smelled of guamúchil fruit.

"Fruto prohibido," the blackman said.

She looked up. He stood by the table, holding the boy.

"From the tree of knowledge where woman defied man." He set the boy on a chair.

Her face said what words wouldn't: life's fortune also its misfortune. "He won't give it up."

"He has given it up, Dolores."

"Mooni," cried the boy.

The blackman laughed. "You remembered, Red."

"Mooni."

"Ye shall inherit the earth, lad, if it doesn't claim you first."

She wrapped the purse in the dishcloth. "¿Qué hago con ésto?"

"Keep it," he replied. "I need it not where I go. You need it not where you go. Keep it for the boy."

She stared. More witchman riddles. "¡Qué fregados!" she said. "Háblame claro."

He grinned. "Dolores, this is the purse you desired, the one that kept him alive because you could not find it."

Her gaze averted. No secret safe, she knew. "For this money he will follow us."

"You do not want it?"

"What I want is to leave. I do not want him to follow."

His grin undiminished. "Is that your desire now? That he not follow?"

She stared. "I asked you to be clear, but your words have holes. Is your promise a hole, too?"

"The promise is given, like your own, like this money. Now you must keep it. Keep it and wait."

She stared. "He will know."

"He knows already."

"He has the gun."

"I know."

When he stepped from behind the table, she saw his bootless feet, their narrow and twisted shape. His floor tracks mudstreaked.

He saw her looking. "So I am made," he said. "The clarity you seek!"

She met his gaze. At last the witchman seen. "Nothing changes," she answered. "Take us and you shall have what you want."

"I have what I want, Dolores. Your desire."

"You have but a taste. You must wait, too."

"I wait for him and for you. Both."

They looked at each other, the boy and purse between them, as close to truth as they stood.

"And when he comes?" she asked.

"He will not follow, Dolores. You will see it so."

She said nothing and then she said, "Bien."

After the brujo left the kitchen, she shut the boy in the room before she took the dishclothed purse off the table and buried it in the pailed beans. That afternoon the truck backfires sounded from beyond the rimland, but the truck did not come. From the doorway she saw him on foot. The sun set, the clearing dayshadowed when he arrived holding the waterjug.

The driller grinned. "You lied, budro." He pointed to the Hughes tricone lifted from the hole.

Retch saw the sounding wire wrapped on the bit. "We're even, then."

"I have another for you."

"You're not Bill Peterson."

"No. I had your woman."

Retch set the thermos on the ground. The boxed bullets emptied into his pantspocket. The gun tucked in his shirtback. "Oh, yeah," he said.

"You know the rule, amigo. Shoot the woman first. As for my sounding wire, I'm charging for its unauthorized use."

"I'm charging for the truckmotor you ruined."

The driller nodded. "Didn't I say we can dicker us a new deal?" He pointed to the bulge in Retch's pocket. "Are those my monkeypods?"

Retch stared. "Who the hell are you?"

"I told you."

"You lied."

"No. 'Twas a falsehood of your own fabrication."

"Who are you? I asked."

"Call me Negro."

"Your name, dammit?"

"Nigger, then."

Retch stared, defiance measured. "What happened to Peterson?"

The driller shrugged. "Not where you reckoned him, I guess."

"How did you find us?"

"News of your thirst traveled far. The world of drillers is marble size."

"Bullshit!"

"Seriously."

"You lying sonofabitch. You stole my money!"

"Be nice, budro."

"Don't 'budro' me. Where's my money?"

A look of surprise came to the driller's face. "Your money?"

"Yeah."

"You mean my advance, budro."

"I told you. Don't call me."

"And I told you, it ain't all about the money. Listen close. I kept my word. I raised the Hughie. Now yours is kept. The money is given."

"Given?"

"Your woman has it. I gave it to her."

Retch spat. "Don't bring her into this."

"A new reckoning, bud. Didn't I say it was so?"

"To hell it is. Where's the money, goddamn it?"

"I told you. It's kept. Until we finish our reckoning."

"You're a goddamn lunatic."

The blackman grinned. "And you're a one-trick pony." He pointed to the garden hose. "In a tizzy about money while water flows at your feet."

Retch saw the hose sunk in the hole, the electric wires run on the ground. When the driller stepped to the rig and hit a switch, Retch heard the highpitched whirr of a pump. He saw water run from the hose.

To the east, the sky daybled, the land turned gray.

"For you, the uninformed, this water comes from a permeable sand aquifer that's been in-ter-cep-ted."

Retch silent.

"Good Lord, cast off the works of darkness and put upon the speechless the armor of light." The driller laughed. "In case you're awonder, that pump runs on twenty-four volt galvanic current. It splits the flow to an eductor-jet hung on the deep end. One of a kind and you the sole beneficiary. Water rises like Christ resurrected."

Retch stared at the hose.

"Drink, man, drink! No salt. No town taste!"

"You put the dog in there," Retch said.

"The aquifer is too deep for defilement. Drink and believe!"

"You drink!"

The driller lifted the hose, his large teeth chopping at the stream. Retch eyed the hose and the wires. He saw no piped return, no hydraulic trick. What the driller drank rose from the well.

"It's sweet, budro. Sweet and cold as madre backbone water. You'll remember the taste from your prospecting days."

Retch said he wasn't thirsty.

"Not thirsty?" The driller dropped the hose. "Well, there's a recent development. Hard to hear from a dirtdried and quenchless wretch like Retch, he who is drought of prosperity but not perfidy."

"I told you!"

"That you're afeared?"

"I'm not thirsty!"

"Don't fret about the dog. No taste of her lingers. Trust me."

Retch said he would trust a cut snake before he trusted a liar and a thief such as he.

The driller laughed, his bottomed voice seeming to shake the ground. "So you would. It's familiar terrain we belly upon, you and I. Snakes shed from the same skin."

"That's the last thing we are," Retch retorted.

"You think? That sharpie Arenas told you that I was once a paleface, same as you. White driller reincarnate."

Retch said nothing.

"And how fares Fermín the vermin? Did you two visit this trip?"

The hose water pooled at the driller's feet. Retch silent.

"I'd feel slighted if you two whored without me, though I suppose one shouldn't overindulge."

Retch spat. "You sick sonofabitch. Rolando is dead."

The driller's teeth flashed. "Fermín dead? But I just saw him. We worked the fisherpipe side by side. I told him to take care of that hand."

"Cut the crap. It wasn't his hand."

"A whore, then? Your pard's hussy? Desperate to get even, was she?"

Retch stared. *Digger's whore?* "What? No! It was some other. His girl."

The driller grinned. "I'm supposing too, bud. Motives and the dirty particulars reckoned. Didn't she say she knew someone?"

"She has nothing to do with this. Where's the goddamn money?"

"May the sharpie rest in peace."

"Stop pretending!"

"False appearances the world's greatest truth, chico. You know it's so." He turned off the pump and pointed to the puddled water. "But enough of whores and their treacheries. Does ye squat to pee, budro?"

"Screw you."

"I heard you do, and from more than one, but no matter. Once a mudman, always a mudman, never a driller. Don't overfool yourself into thinking otherwise. The hard part cometh."

Retch rested his hands on his hips. "Give me the money. Then we'll talk the hard part."

"Unpredictable waters flow beneath thee. You'll need my manpipe for the dicking. Does thee know how to use a surgeblock?"

"The money."

"The stolen money?"

"That's right."

"Which time?"

"Which time what?"

"Which time stolen?"

Retch scoffed. "Spoken like a thief."

"Deadmen speak. So, too, their money."

"Oh, yeah."

"I know, budro."

"You know what?"

"Secrets are but holes to be drilled."

"You know shit, you crazy bastard."

"I know you won't go into a hole. That's what I know, budro."

"Stop calling me that, goddamn it. I want the money." He pulled the pistol from his shirtback and pointed it at the driller. "Hand it over!"

The blackman feigned surprise. "Retch. Not again." His grin all teeth. "I know you're cash-strapped and overly preoccupied by the situation, but—"

"Shut up!" The gun felt strangely small in his hand.

The driller reached to the sky in mock surrender. "Search me. Search the rig. Search the hole. No place too deep for thee." He guffawed.

"You won't be laughing if you don't give me the money. I swear."

"I told you, your woman has it."

"Bullshit. She'd be gone and you'd be dead, your throat cut. I'd be cleaning up the mess."

The driller nodded. "She would be gone but not by her lonesome. She wanted to elope, sport."

Retch knew not to shift the gun. He kept it loosely gripped. "Take her. Take the kid. Take them and turn tail out of here. Now's your chance."

The blackman's grin white in the twilight. "Is that your best reckoning, Retch?"

They stood beside the hole in the descending dusk, their shadows cast to grayness. In the clearing the adobe rooms a dark construct of seamed earthwork devoid of life or sound. Retch glanced at the empty doorway. He kept the driller before him.

"You're the one who wants to deal, so here's the deal. I get the money and the rig. You get to walk out of here. You take them, too."

The driller's grin undiminished. "Now there's an offer."

"The money and the rig for the woman and the boy. A fair trade. You had her. Now take her."

"I'd call that drinking another man's poison."

"A new dickering, nigger. Otherwise you're dead and I keep the rig."

"And your wife and boychild," amended the driller. "Keep them, too, you will."

"Don't bait me, goddamnit."

"You're baiting yourself. I'm just reminding."

Retch deadfaced. "I'll find the money."

"You think? I've told you where."

"I know, *Bill*, whoever you are, a nigger who steals names like he steals money."

The driller's grin bright in the ebbing light. He stood large by the rig, his arms folded. "Ain't stealing if it's taken from a deadman, Retch. You know that. I'm but a witness to its truth."

Retch nodded. "All the more reason to shoot you." He stepped back from the hole.

"But will you find water or blood, budro? That's the question."

He towered above Retch, his presence looming like an enlarged shadow of himself.

"Enough. You heard the terms. Take 'm or lose 'm!" He raised the gun.

"From the hole, budro? Will you drink water or drink blood?"

"Last chance, nigger. Hand it over."

Retch perceived a target of increasing size. The driller seemed to move toward him even as he stood by the hole. "Stop your black ass right there!"

His crazed grin a half moon. "Blood, I think." When he unfolded his arms, he seemed to take another shape—a twisted hulk of grotesque proportions. Suddenly he had Retch by the shirt.

Retch saw the driller's teeth near his face, the mouth wide enough to devour him. Dragged to the hole, Retch saw its black yawning beneath his feet, an orifice seemingly larger than the hole itself. He straightened his arm and pushed the gun into the hulked shape.

"Drink," croaked the driller, his grin unhinged.

"To hell," Retch said, unloading the pistol into the driller's chest.

She listened near the window. The machine silent, the man's voice loud above the brujo's rumbling laugh. That insect whirr again. More talk and more. The boy asleep on the floor.

When the gunshots sounded, she knelt to cover him. The sharp cracks quickly volleyed then swallowed by the land. She waited, the boy not awakened, the silence loud. "Al fin," she whispered. When she looked from the window, the clearing dusked. The brujo lay motionless on the ground, a beaten shroud in the crepuscular gloom. She saw the man standing over him, a stark figure cut of whiteflesh.

"No . . ."

She dropped to the bed, her breath sucked, the world collapsed, the room a nameless place. She gazed numbly at the sleeping boy.

With rope cut from the shoehoist Retch noosed the ankles before he pulled the boots from the driller's misshapen feet. He shook each boot and patted the shirtfront, the pants. Unable to kickroll the body, he turned it over two-handed, checking the backside, finding no money.

He unfolded the knife blade and split the shirt from yoke to hem, its cloth bloodrun. The deadman's back without exit holes. "That's lead, Billy."

Retch cut the waistband. He shucked the denim over the driller's buttocks. "But wait. You're not Bill. You're a no-name thief." He rolled the body again, the pubic mass skied, an enormous penis flattened on his belly.

"Damn! No wonder."

Dusk benighted the silent land, no sound from the rooms. Knife in hand, Retch stood over the driller, taking his measure. *I had your woman*, he had boasted, then called it a lie. Retch fingered the knife's edge, a blade last whetted by Digger, another roped and left bootless, shot and straddled. So he stood with the knife. So he considered the truth cruelly gifted to the woman, what she had known hers to keep. He looked to the rooms before he folded the blade and pocketed the knife.

His gaze took in the clearing, the gravemound, the covered noria. If not for the damn truck, he thought. Then he spoke to the driller. "Didn't you say so? From one hole to another."

He tied the rope to the shovelhandle and dragged the driller across the clearing. At the noria he disinterred the revetment stones and shoveled off the dirt. Night descended before the cover half cleared, the tinsheets lifted. Darkness immeasurably lucent to Retch, the land cut large from the sky. He pried loose the mesquite posts laid across the hole, and he retook the rope and circled the noria, pulling the body into the opening. When it didn't fall, he levered the torso with the shovel and he chopped at the arms and legs. The driller fell folded, buttocks first, his splash loud. Retch stepped back, the saltwater tasted. He spat. "Your last hole, bud." Then he tossed the driller's boots into the well.

With the riglamps powered, he searched the platform. He emptied the storewells and toolboxes. He dug through piles of hoses and belts, no money found. Inside the cab the red-labeled whiskey lay on the seat. Retch opened the bottle and drank, the driller's clothes heaved out the door, guamúchil fruit shook from a bag. He ransacked the soil cores and jarred muds. He extracted the dog's cinchstrap from beneath the seat. The cab without rooflining, doorpanels, or glovebox. The seatback fixed to the body. Under the dashboard his fingers groped the wires and gauge housings. He lifted the hood and checked the motor. Beneath the rig he found the driller's carboy hung with its cup, the jug almost empty.

The whiskey half gone by the time he gave up the search. He sat on a pail and stared at the rig. His gaze fell on the hose, the wires. He rose and threw the switch, listening to the whirr. When no water ran, he picked up the hose and pulled, the hose as though rooted in the hole. He turned off the pump and sat again, tipping the bottle. He stared at the mud.

No matter. Mine. All mine. Mine to finish. But the damn money?

He looked to the rooms, his gaze narrowed on the unlit kitchen. His slow headwork. The words recalled. *Your woman has it.* Seeming truer now than before the whiskey. He reloaded the gun and he took the bottle and switched off the riglights. In the kitchen he lit the lantern and searched the wallpantry before he called out to her.

She lay bone-stiff and aplano on the bed. Outside, the chink of shoveled rock. His digging as though inside her head. The room dark when the boy spoke. "¿Mi papi?"

"Out."

"Can I go?"

"No."

From the clearing came metallic scraping, muffled thumps.

"And the other?"

"Gone," she said.

"Where?"

"Quiet," she said.

When he asked for water, she rose leg-knotted to fill the bule from the cántaro, no thirst of her own, her lips wirestrung. She found tortillas. She unhooked the machete from the mesquite pole. In the room she gave the boy the bule to drink. The machete she slid beneath the bed before she shut the door and made the boy lie with her.

"I dreamed the dog," he said.

"Sleep."

"I'm not sleepy."

"Quiet, then."

"The dog lives, mamá."

She said nothing.

"I saw it."

"A dream lies."

"But I saw."

"Sleep. It is gone."

"In the hole?"

"Yes."

"Can I see it?"

"Sleep and you will see."

She waited, the hours what hung next in the night. His nakedness cool to her fevered touch. His dirtsmell the land's gift and nothing else. The boy asleep when she heard the shrill whirr. Later his footfalls sounded in the kitchen. Chairs dragged. A ceramic clatter. "¿Dónde está?" he shouted.

She listened for the beanpail spill.

"Where is it, you daughter of fornication?"

She sat, the boy unstirred.

"I know you can hear me. I want the purse!"

His liquored voice and lanternlit shadow near the door.

"He's dead, eh. No more rides to town, cabrona. No ride for you. I know you screwed him!"

She laid the machete on her lap and waited. The gun imagined.

"Don't make me come in there, pendeja."

Fool another, she thought. She rose from the bed, sickness shrugged.

"I'll shoot you, woman!"

She moved in the darkness to stand beside the door.

"As for the boy, I might take him, I might not."

The door without latch. She readied the blade.

"I know you have it. He told me."

She waited. How he knew mattered not. Lie or truth, he knew.

"Give it over and I'll make sure the boy gets to a church."

Silence.

"He paid you, whore. My money for a screw. Give it over!"

"I did not let him," she replied.

"¡Mentira!" he shouted. "Dáme el dinero, chingado!"

Glass shattered. The man swore. She listened, the boy not waking. A liquor smell rose in the room. She spoke to the door. "Take us," she said. "Take us to La Fortuna. Leave us. Then I will tell you where it is."

His laugh. "Take you?"

"Yes."

"On my head I'll take you. There's no truck, you fool."

His weight against the door.

"Keep the ranch," she said.

He laughed again. "¿Negociando, eh?"

She said nothing, the machete tightly gripped.

"Walk if you want," he said. "But first the money."

"No."

"I'll find it!"

"Find it," she said.

His retreating steps ground on broken glass. She heard the wallpantry searched, pots dropped. She waited.

"Mamá?"

She put the blade behind her, her voice sucked. "Sshh. No te muevas."

"Mamá. ¿Qué es?"

Her hand on his mouth. "No hables," she whispered.

The idea come as quickly as newfound strength. She lifted him and moved to the window. The machete she poked through the screen and slid along the frame, the wiremesh opened like flesh. "Run!" she said in his ear. "To the latrine. Hide. I will come."

"But—"

"Ssh. Coyotes. Run!"

In the kitchen the man broke dishes.

"Quick!"

She lowered him out the window, his nakedness gone, the sound of his running.

At the door the crunch of glass again, his voice. "You whoremother of a stinking fornication! Where is it?" Words slurred. His breathing heavy. His doorcrack shadow moved from side to side. "I want it. You hear me. Or the boy pays."

She lifted the machete. "The boy won't," she answered. "You will."

His shadow stilled. No sound of glass.

"Give me the money, chingado. I'll hurt him!"

"Come then," she dared. The blade trembled in her hand. The door didn't open.

"Pinche puta. Hija de la chingada."

"It is buried," she said. "You will know where after I take the boy."

"Goddamn you. You stupid, thieving woman. You sorry-ass lying . . ."

She waited. His foreign curses a bark to other dogs. "Vete," she said.

"Go to hell!"

"Vete a dormir."

"Go to hell, whore!"

"In the morning."

He grunted, heeled on the glass, his door shadow gone.

"I will kill you both, do you hear? Him first!"

"Yours the ranch," she said, her voice neutral, not daring his retreat. "The money tomorrow."

From the kitchen his clatter resumed. The refrigerator opened, its door slammed. Rage now, not search. She heard the beanpail kicked, its full-bucket thud, the chitinous chink. She listened for the spill, but his foot swung elsewhere. He moved outside.

The machete heavy in her hand. Bone tiredness fought. She listened by the window. The clearing in view but not the latrine. Drunk, she thought. Brimmed with urine. He will piss.

She waited, eared to the boy's voice. *Go! No matter the end.* She heard the man's steps, his grunts muttered by the window. The cut screen near where he stood.

His animal splatter loud in the paused night. Then the sound of him stumbling into his room, his curses. She waited, breath held. Soon, she thought. Her heartbeats tolled before she heard his bedsunk snore.

In the kitchen the beanpail stood by the stove. Nothing else as it was. She found the boy seated in the latrine. "¿Los coyotes?" he asked.

"Ssh," she said, taking his hand in silent hurry. When they edged the clearing, she saw the noria, its black hole. So the witchman buried, she realized. The salted well for him.

The boy's eyes grew large when he saw the kitchen havoc. "¡Mira!"

"Ssh," she said, taking the lamp.

In the room he drank from the bule. His nakedness ripe with the stench of shat lives. Outside, the coyote jabber begun, their basinland chorus sung to the yearning night.

"Do they come, mamá?"

"Sleep," she said. "They have come."

She lay with him on the bed, no thought but him. After he slept, she waited, listening to his child breath, to the man's snorts. What they become.

The cadence kept, the hours passing, no life in her opened eyes, blood congealing to resolve.

Before dawn she took the machete from beneath the bed and she advanced into his room without lamplight, closing the door behind her. His liquored smell. His silhouette hemmed in blackness. Her first blow meant to halve him, the others struck blindly to fraction his malignity. The warm spray of him, the clean thunk. She swung until he sang empty, his death fleshed, her life depleted.

The door closed, her hands washed, the water splashed in darkness. Back in the bed, she lay listening to the dog howls, their calling. When she slept, no dreams came, only voices from the void.

Retch Barter glared at the lamplit kitchen, blind to where the machete had hung. *All of it mine.* His pants wet with urine. His fury contracted. The whiskied madness night screamed from an old past. Later he slept, goddamn her his last thought and desire. Wakened by the first cut, its sudden violent hush. The blades that followed not felt in any world.

He pointed to her bloodstained dress. "Sangre, mamá."

The window daylighted. The screen mesh curled. She lay on the bed, remembering the witchman's words. *You will bleed.*

"Coyote," she said.

The boy's eyes wide. "¿Sangre de coyote?"

"Sí."

"¿Y mi papi?"

"Sick."

"Where?"

"The room. Don't go."

"Did it bite?"

"Yes."

"Where?"

"The room."

"Did it bite you?"

"No."

He stared at the red-bladed machete. "Is it dead?"

"Yes. Keep away."

"But . . ."

"Promise."

He looked to the door.

"Prometes."

"Prometo," he promised.

"Nunca."

"Nunca."

When the boy said he was hungry, she lifted the tortillas brought from the kitchen.

Later, she thought. Before the flies, before the stink. Later she would barrow his pieces, burn the bed, his clothes. Later.

The sun high, the room hot, the window too bright for her eyes. She lay marrow shrunk, no strength to stand. Her arms stiffjointed, face gone mad. Sometimes she grinned.

When the boy asked why she smiled, her answer a drymouthed word. "Nada." Her throat tight.

So she lay. The noria imagined, his black body afloat, its bloated largeness enlarged. She wanted to see it. Then what she did not know.

She beckoned the boy. "Pail," she whispered.

"¿Cubeta?"

"Frijol."

She heard the spill, his shout. He returned with the wadded bills held out for her to see. "¡Mira!" Her rockhard fingers unable to grasp them. So its worth, she thought, the witchman's riddle solved.

He played with the money, her grin returned. *Good for that*, it seemed to say. Later the boy drank water from the bule.

. . .

Dusk darkened the window. Fresh spasms entwined her. Her back arched above the bed in the curve of bridges not built. She felt her heart beating behind her. Not seeing the boy she saw what lay near. Holes. Blood. Thirst.

"Ven," she croaked, lips upturned.

"¡Mamá, tu cara!"

The reason not remembered why he smelled of latrine. "Stay," she said.

"Stay?"

"Stay."

His breath felt, what he was to her.

"Wait."

"Mamá?"

"Someone."

"¿Quién?" he asked.

"Someone. Wait."

"¿Aquí?"

"Sí."

"Mamá."

Her silence.

"Mamá, tengo hambre."

Then his voice adrift.

Hours later her skeletal glass stretched then contracted, an annealing fever her forge. Night set in the room. Set, too, her lockjawed look at nothing, darkness immersed. The drowning silence broken by the sound of water. His drinking the last thing she heard.

So she lay, tetanized on the bed, unknown to her how poisoned bones had begotten the tonic posture. No connection made to the old miner disinterred, her punctured heel his last gift. So she left the world not knowing, a dumb witness to the mystery, to the land's full circle, to life's noxious symmetry.

"Mamá?"

She lay as though to look behind her. Eyes open, mouth twisted in a dark-toothed grin. She stared but did not answer. On her dress the blood dried black.

"¿Agua, mamá?"

Gone the familiar feel when he touched her. Gone warmth. Gone him from her eyes.

A night passed, the coyote howls making him shudder. Now the room grown hot. His mother with a smell he didn't like. A fly walked on her lips.

"¿Agua?"

The bed wet where he had left the bule, its plug loose, the water drained. In the kitchen he stepped over broken glass, shattered plates, an unshelved world. The thermos lay empty on the floor. He righted a chair, climbing to reach the cántaro in its hanger. When the claypot tilted too far, the water drenched him. "Mamá!" he cried, his glistened nakedness freshcut from brown flesh. He licked his hands, his arms.

At the refrigerator he tugged the jamseam until the door swung open. Inside, no water. He stared at the man's room, his promise remembered, the coyote, its blood. His voice small as he called out. "¿Papi?" Behind the door a drone. The floorcrack black with flies

Outside, the land a silent surmise swept of shape and shadow. The sky white. No coyotes seen from the doorway. He walked to the noria where he peered over its edge. The water black, its surface unbroken. He stared at his mirrored reflection, the thin shape of him. His first self-seen look of entirety, his feet upon blackness, the sky his halo.

He lifted two-handed a revetment stone, letting it drop. Then another. The darkwater dared until finally a splash wet him, the water tasted. He spat. "Mal."

At the cistern he raised himself on its galvanized rim to view the empty tank. A length of hose lifted, but no trickle ran from it. The steel drums lay on their sides.

The goats watched with shrunken gazes, following his steps to the trough. When he raised the feedbucket, they came as one, their herded conviction voiced in feeble bleats. They sniffed the waterless trough. After the boy dropped the bucket, they retreated, gathering again in the shade.

Beneath the machine the carboy found bottomed with liquid, the neck hung with a tin cup. He set the cup on the ground and filled it, the pouring roiled with suncolored bubbles, the liquid with a smell he had nosed before, its memory a hotbreath on his face. He sipped, the first taste bitter, the second less. Two cups swallowed before he left the carboy on its side.

Rig shade where he sat, the drink warm inside him. His lips tingled. He gazed at the rooms, no reckoning come. The land his own, the marvel and mystery. The planet's heave no end. His mother had told him to wait, and so he waited. Someone to come.

His face felt funny. When he stood, the world spun without him. He sat and curled on the ground. After he awoke, his head hurt. "Mal," he croaked. He stood and peed, thirsted again.

The dayshadows long at the hour he climbed onto the cab footboard. Unable to push the door's latchbutton, he pressed his face to the window, peering through the pane.

On the seat lay the dog's cinchstrap. He jumped down and ran to the back of the machine. "!Perra¡" he called.

At the hole he sighted over its edge. "¿Perra?" The orifice with wires, a hose. He pulled the hose with both hands, his feet sinking into the mud. He leaned and tugged. When he heard a distant whine, he paused to listen. "¿Perra?" The hose quivered. Suddenly it yanked. Then the rimcrust broke at his feet.

He grabbed the wires as he fell, the hole closing around him. He hung, light above, dark below, the motor whine what he heard as the yellow Willys neared the ranch, aimed at rooftin, bristled with armed men. The young Mafioso come to visit the red-haired gringo who had shot at him in the street two days before.

Aquiferous Cavities

JAIPUR, JAN 16 (REUTERS)—
Authorities remain baffled by the disappearance of a three-
year-old boy who fell into a borewell in the Dausa district.
The body of Amit Pranami of Harla was not found Sunday
when a recovery team reached the bottom of the three-
hundred-foot well.

Ninety hours of anxiety turned to despair and confu-
sion when Police Inspector Usman Singh Ali announced
that the boy's remains had not been recovered.

According to eyewitnesses, Amit, the son of a migrant
worker from Rajasthan, fell into the borewell Wednesday
evening. The well had been covered earlier that day, but
neighbours claim a delivery driver set in motion the unfortunate events after the tyre on his truck caught on the cover.
In a bid to maneuvre the vehicle, the cover was removed
and never put back in place.

Soldiers began digging a parallel tunnel Thursday
morning. Friday, the army took help from a group of civilians
adept in digging borewells. The effort intensified after Delhi

Metro brought in their specialized equipment. A senior army officer admitted that the operation was slowed by the rocky terrain. "We could not dig as fast as we wanted," Brigadier SP Joshi told reporters. The chief minister of Rajasthan state, Kinjal Man Singh Chauhan, joined the family at the scene. He said firefighters from Jaipur had been called to add their expertise.

Over one hundred officials from the army, fire, police, health, and revenue departments were present as thousands of onlookers gathered, wishing luck to the team. Vikram Singh Verma, the sarpanch of Harla, said the army and the National Security Guard came promptly but fought publicly on who should do the job. Sanjit Nayak, owner of a private hospital in Mahwa who supplied oxygen for the diggers, accused local police of not responding soon enough.

Meanwhile, the whereabouts of the boy's body remain a mystery. Sudipto Hore, a hydrologist at Mody Institute, said a fall of three hundred feet likely fractured the child's body allowing a hydraulic pressure differential to thrust the remains into aquiferous cavities.

The search for the boy has been suspended.

"Who will give us back our son?" asked the boy's distraught father, Neeraj Pranami.

Last year, the Central Ground Water Authority banned the digging of borewells without a permit. Despite this, local landlords and the "tanker mafia" continue to dig borewells illegally and abandon them without closing.

Saturday, the Dausa police arrested Rajat Kumar, owner of the plot. He had been on the run since the incident took place. The whereabouts of the well driller, described as a dusky Bangalorean, is unknown.